THE OTHER COUPLE

ALSO BY CLAIRE McGOWAN

Crime fiction

The Fall

What You Did

The Other Wife

The Push

I Know You

Are You Awake?

Let Me In

Truth Truth Lie

The First Girl

Other work

This Could Be Us

Non-fiction

The Vanishing Triangle

Paula Maguire series

The Lost

The Dead Ground

The Silent Dead

A Savage Hunger

Blood Tide

The Killing House

Writing as Eva Woods

The Thirty List

The Ex Factor

How To Be Happy

The Lives We Touch

The Man I Can't Forget

The Heartbreak Club

You Are Here

THE OTHER COUPLE

CLAIRE McGOWAN

This is a work of fiction. Names, characters, organizations, places, events, and incidents are either products of the author's imagination or are used fictitiously. Any resemblance to actual persons, living or dead, or actual events is purely coincidental.

Published by Thomas & Mercer, Seattle

www.apub.com

EU Product Safety Contact:
Amazon Media EU S.à r.l.
38, avenue John F. Kennedy, L-1855 Luxembourg
amazonpublishing-gpsr@amazon.com

ISBN-13: 9781662530760
eISBN: 9781662530777

Cover design by The Brewster Project
Cover image: © Joseph Shields / Arcangel Images; © NayaDadara
© Roman Samborskyi © Prostock-studio © mbond77
© Vaclav Volrab / Shutterstock

Printed in the United States of America

THE OTHER COUPLE

Prologue

The body drifted gently in the surf. It was almost peaceful, the slow drag and return of the waves, the morning sun red on the glassy surface. The woman's dress was red too, long and flowing out around her like the tentacles of some twisting sea creature. Her hair was also long, tangled in the folds of her dress, wrapped around her fingers. Her arms and legs weightless in the water. There wasn't even any blood. Her toenails, painted gold, flashed here and there with the turn of the waves. Who knew death could be so quiet? She could have just been floating, if not for the position of her head, drooping down beneath the waterline. The waves brought her closer to shore each time. In, out. In, out. Her drifting feet began to catch on the sand.

The calm was broken when someone spotted her. A child from a nearby hotel – one that didn't ban under-eighteens – was building a castle in the damp, packed sand. He didn't know what it was, which was a blessing. Something curious, maybe a big mannequin or a rogue flotation device.

'Mummy? Look, Mummy.'

His mother, exhausted from being woken at five even on holiday, furious with the child's father, who was still asleep and snoring in their room, looked up from her phone, where she was numbly scrolling Instagram reels about improving your marriage. She blinked. Was that – it couldn't be – oh God. She ran and picked up the child under his arms, making him cry as his sandcastle crumbled.

'Don't look, baby! It's OK!' She pressed his face against her as she waved down an employee in a clean white polo shirt who was setting up the sun loungers for the day. In that hotel – adults-only, not the one she was staying at – the guests did not surface this early. 'Please, look! There's – there's someone . . .'

She let herself understand what she knew. It was a body. Someone was dead. A woman was dead, and washing up on the tourist beach. She could not still be alive, with her head under the water like that.

But wait, someone was in the sea with the body, she could see now. A man, splashing through the waves, as if trying to drag her out. His arms under the woman's, pulling the dead weight of her. Across the still morning air, the sound of weeping reached the mother's ears, and she looked hesitantly at the hotel employee, who was just a kid, not much more than eighteen she guessed, and possibly didn't speak a lot of English. He seemed frozen in shock.

'Should we help?'

You saw on TV that people sometimes did CPR and revived drowning victims. People who seemed dead coughed up water and came back to life. But surely it was too late for that.

The mother and the child and the teenage boy stood paralysed for a moment, at the beginning of a day that had promised at first to be like all the others in this place, cloudless, hot, filled with banging dance music and watered-down cocktails. Then he took out his phone to call the police.

Alison – then

Holidays were fun. That was the general belief, wasn't it? Relaxing, enjoyable, a chance to re-connect with loved ones and escape the pressures of daily life.

God, Alison missed the pressures of daily life. Her hand kept twitching to her phone to check on the progress of her current cases – a stabbing moving its way through CPS, a suspicious death that needed ruling out, and a house fire she needed forensics on to prove was arson. But every time she would reach for it, she'd remember she'd left it in the hotel room in order to 'really unplug and unwind'.

Alison hated unplugging and unwinding.

'OK?' Tom shot her a look over the top of his thick biography.

'Fine! Just relaxing.'

He sighed. 'Look, I know it's hard to break phone addiction . . .'

'I'm not addicted! It's just work. People need my help.'

'They need mine too, but I'm managing.'

It was hard to complain about your job when your partner had the same one. And he'd managed to forget all about his heavy caseload in the surveillance team, somehow. She told herself what he did – watching hours of street CCTV to try and spot wanted suspects on the run – was not life and death, or maybe she just cared more than him? But she knew that wasn't true because she also wanted her phone to scroll true-crime videos on TikTok and to check her horoscope and do today's Wordle. So yes, maybe she was addicted.

Alison lay back on the sun lounger with a sigh. She should have known that a relaxing resort holiday would not be relaxing when she couldn't drink. These places were only fun when you could lie like one of the human characters in *WALL-E* and pour intoxicating liquids right into your mouth, ideally without ever leaving the pool. Her belly was so rounded in front of her she could barely prop a book on it. Two more months of this, plus a year (OK, six months) of breastfeeding before she could neck a single Chardonnay. And she couldn't even complain because it had been such a long road to get here, so many tests and disappointments and peeing on sticks in the ancient station loos with zero privacy, then the round of IVF that they'd been lucky to even get funded on the NHS, making it under the line of her turning forty with only weeks to spare. This holiday was being paid for with the money they'd saved for another go, in case the first hadn't worked. And it had. It was a miracle.

She eyed her stomach. How strange that they'd taken their baby with them on the holiday, and yet they had never met. Like a mystery package she had to cart around for nine months. Waiting to find out what kind of person they were going to be. They hadn't wanted to know the gender, or at least Tom hadn't. She was finding it hard to picture the baby at all without knowing even that.

'You want anything?' Tom, always kind and attentive, was like a golden retriever since she got pregnant.

'I can't have anything,' she grouched. Booze was of course off-limits, as well as too much sugar, even juice.

'Snacks. Water. Suncream.' He eyed her. 'Shoulders are looking a bit red.'

'Of course they are. I have Irish skin that frazzles the second I even step in the sun.'

And yet they were in Tenerife during a heatwave and it was due to hit forty degrees later that day. She was only comfortable if standing directly in the pool, and that was full of young people with taut bodies and weird eyebrows drinking cocktails and listening to loud music on their phones. Alison wished she had powers of arrest for people who did that. She might be addicted to hers but at least she didn't bother anyone else with it.

Bored and too hot and not interested in her stupid book (having to actually pay attention to something and not scroll onwards every three seconds? In this economy?), she let her eyes roam over the guests gathered around the pool. It was nice here, she had to admit. Waterfall features and trailing shrubs. No children either, thank God; it was an adults-only hotel, their last hurrah before they had to find one with a kids' club and 5 p.m. dinners. Alison was not ready to enter the world of parents, not just yet. And sunglasses were a good cover for her natural nosiness. What a crowd! So many tattoos, and muscles she hadn't even known existed. Lip fillers and fake breasts abounded. Both men and women were so stacked in the chest she wondered they didn't topple over like Barbies.

Her eye was caught by someone more her speed – a woman of around her age (forty, if pushed to reveal it), normal-sized, and unlike everyone else round the pool, looking absolutely miserable. With a gaze trained by years of working on cases of unimaginable grimness, Alison checked her over for bruises. Nothing. Sensible one-piece swimsuit, not unlike Alison's own, Birkenstocks, a big shady hat and a jumbo bottle of suncream on her lounger. She was reading the Philippa Perry book with the green cover which Alison had bought for three different friends, and drinking a fruity, creamy-looking cocktail with an umbrella in it that Alison coveted instantly. But something was not right all the same. Something in the hunch of her reddened shoulders, the puffiness of her jaw.

As Alison watched from behind her own sunglasses, the woman took hers off to reveal swollen eyes. What could cause weeping in such a luxury resort? You only had to turn your head and a waiter would appear with a drinks list or to tilt your umbrella around with the sun. The pool was huge and clean, there was an amazing spa for anyone not currently incubating another human, and the beach was just a few steps away, also with loungers and umbrellas and waiters to bring you cocktails after you lolled in the gently swishing waves, the water warm but still refreshing. And yet this woman was alone and crying by the pool.

What's up with you? Alison continued to watch her counterpart across the water, finding the intrigue her book could not supply. Forget fictional thrillers and cops with inner demons. There was nothing that cheered her up more than having a real-life mystery to solve.

Beth – now

Beth could hardly see where they were through the rain pounding against the window of the Uber. She had called one at Heathrow despite Vince's insistence that the Tube was quicker, and he'd been right, the drive had taken forever, and now he wasn't talking to her. But then, he had barely spoken to her for the entire holiday, and even before that. It seemed they were finally home, at least, as the familiar dingy sign of the local Nisa came into view.

'On the left, please, mate, by the Chinese restaurant.' A phrase she had heard Vince say to every driver in every cab they'd taken together since they bought the flat, coming home from nights out, from dinners at friends' houses, from holidays. These were the little moments that made up a life, the struts that held you together, knowing what your partner was going to say in a particular situation, or what story they were going to tell anytime you met new people. You might even roll your eyes or interrupt them, *That's not how it was, darling,* but secretly it was comforting to be able to predict them. But she knew now these things were not the constants they had always appeared to be. They could vanish overnight. People could change, appear like strangers in your bed. Tell different stories, or none at all. Do things you never could have imagined.

Vince was taking their cases out of the boot. There'd been a time when he would open car doors for her, maybe even hold an umbrella over her head against the rain. When had that stopped? Beth opened her door, blinking as the drops hit her in the face. London was grey, and cold, leached of colour and of hope. A world away from the crushing heat of Tenerife. She said thanks to the driver and watched him speed off, no doubt wondering about the weird tension between the couple who had not spoken the whole way from Heathrow. And had the wife been crying as they passed through Shepherd's Bush? Not his problem, anyway.

Vince was already unlocking the door of their flat and going inside, not waiting for her. She noticed he did not take his shoes off, as she'd trained him to do years ago. Had he been waiting eight years for the chance to do that, walk mud on to the beige carpet? She wouldn't say anything. If she did, if she nagged or criticised at all, she would have lost the stand-off. Become a nag, been insecure, been anxious. The weight of everything she hadn't said for weeks – months – was so heavy inside her she could hardly draw breath sometimes.

'Are you OK?' she risked.

He said nothing. Stared out the window at the rain for a moment and heaved a deep sigh. He moved to lift his suitcase, but she stopped him.

'May as well get the washing out first.'

She always did a wash first thing on getting in from a holiday. Vince was an unpack-later type, but usually let her have her way, knowing she couldn't settle until she'd sorted and tidied up. This time, he released the case handle with a roll of his eyes and an audible tut. She ignored that too.

'What shall we do for dinner? Deliveroo?' Her voice was as brittle as sugar glaze.

'Made of money now, are we? You want to spend it all exploiting the gig economy? Honestly, I've told you these companies aren't ethical, Uber, Deliveroo.'

She bit her tongue. 'Well, you could go down the chippy and get us something? That would be cheaper.'

'I'm not hungry.'

He banged into the living room and sat down on the sofa. Soon she heard the beeps of his computer game starting up. His case remained sitting where it was in the middle of the kitchen floor. She went through the motions of things being normal – unzipped her own bag, loaded up the washing machine, took the rest of her things to the bedroom and neatly stored them away, washed her hands and took off her make-up. It was only when she met her own eyes in the mirror that she began to cry.

How had they ended up here? Where did it all go so wrong?

She knew the answer to that. On the bloody holiday, that was when. But also, long, long before that. The holiday was supposed to save them from everything that was wrong, the festering sinkhole that had somehow opened up in the space that was their relationship, and instead had made it so much worse.

Beth did her best to stifle her sobs and clean up her face in the bathroom. She went back into the bedroom, smoothed the duvet cover, closed the curtains, and then she noticed a scrap of paper on the bedroom carpet, fallen from her case, and stooped to pick it up. *Policia*. An instant sinking stone in her stomach at the word, despite knowing they were free and safe here in London. Images she was trying to blot out, of sodden red fabric, trailing feet with gold-painted toenails. Vince's face ashen under fluorescent lights. The paper had a list of phone numbers, and stated a requirement to stay at the same address until officially released from suspicion, to be contactable and keep in touch.

In other words, they had been allowed to come home, but that didn't mean they were innocent.

Alison – then

God, she was bored. Won't it be lovely, everyone said – her terrifying boss, Colette, who spent three weeks in the Caribbean every Christmas, her mother, her sister with the four kids who was clearly looking forward to watching Alison struggle with motherhood. *Just relax. Because you won't get to sit down again for eighteen years, ha ha!*

The trouble was, Alison had no idea how to relax. It was years since she'd sat down and read a book, and it turned out she no longer had the concentration for it. Despite what Tom said and the articles he sent her all the time about phone dependency, she did find it soothing to scroll through hundreds of videos of women cleaning parts of their houses you would not have even believed existed.

Urgh. Look at Tom, engrossed in his giant biography of Alexander Hamilton. He hadn't even seen the musical. She didn't remember when they'd last been out into town, what with their conflicting shift patterns and not drinking much for the years it had taken to conceive. Anyway, there was too much to do to just . . . relax. Apart from all their work back home (at this her fingers twitched reflexively to her phantom phone, the need to check her emails was so visceral), they had to get ready for the baby. It seemed crazy you were allowed to just *have* one, without taking a course or reading a lot of books (Tom was reading them; Alison had bought them, then not actually read a word). They had to get a cot, put it up, renovate their boxy spare room, which was currently filled with a half-broken sofa bed and the exercise bike Alison's mother had foisted on her, also never used. She wasn't ready. Why was she lying here in a puddle of her own sweat? She hoisted herself up.

Tom looked up from the page. 'What do you need?'

'I just have to – a walk or something.'

'I'll come with you.'

'No – no . . .' She flapped her hands at him. 'Sorry. I love you, you know that. I just already have another person with me all the time. I need some space.'

Tom bore it well. 'Alright. Let me know if you want anything.'

It took her longer than usual to stand up, her centre of gravity all off. She slid her feet into her sensible sandals, which reminded her of her spiritual sister, the crying woman across the pool. Alison looked for her, but she was gone. She'd left behind a tote bag and her book, so she was probably coming back. Perhaps a meeting could be engineered.

Alison shuffled off towards the beach. It was pretty, she conceded, the sunlight sparkling on the water, the gentle shsss of the waves, like that, what did they call it – ASMR. If only there could be no other people about, shrieking and splashing, or having top-volume video calls while strutting up and down in tiny Speedos and flexing muscles. She felt like the only real person in a Barbie and Ken world, her pregnant belly parting crowds before her like a leper.

Well, here we are. It's the beach. It's nice. But the murmur of the waves reminded her of the whirr of a new recording at the start of a suspect interview, one of her favourite sounds in the world. The look on their faces as it began – smugness, or terror, or naked guilt. Underestimating her with her boring trouser suits and messy hair. The solicitor trying to be inscrutable, but most of them Alison knew so well she could judge the guilt of the client by the twitch of their brief's eyebrows. The game of it all, but the realness too, putting dangerous people behind bars. Fighting back a bit against the tide of scumbags and perverts. And she was supposed to give that all up to rest, and then sing nursery rhymes and change nappies?

There she was! The crying Philippa Perry-reading woman. She was staring out to sea like a sailor's wife watching for a shipwrecked husband, an empty cocktail glass dangling from her hand. Alison sidled over, as well as one could sidle when the size of a beached manatee.

'Lovely day.' That seemed a redundant remark in the Canaries, but whatever.

The woman started, wiping at her cheeks under the sunglasses. Her voice was choked. 'Um – yeah.'

'Shame about all the racket.' Alison inclined her head towards the stereo system blaring club anthems into the beach bar over the heads of the oblivious patrons, who lay sprawled and oiled on loungers while listening to their own music and videos, also at top volume.

'I know, it is very loud.'

'No kids, at least!' Alison said this merrily, and saw the woman looked confused as her eyes travelled down to her belly. 'Oh, I'm planning to stay away from the little buggers as long as I can.'

'Your first then?'

'Yep.' Alison didn't ask if the woman had children. That could be the reason for her red eyes. Alison herself had sobbed in many a work loo and on trains, and once in the toilets of a service station off the M25. 'You're British too?'

'Yes. London.'

'Ooh, me too, what part?'

'South. Thornton Heath.'

'No way! We're just outside Beckenham.' So this woman lived on her turf, in fact. That made it more acceptable to interrogate her, Alison felt. 'Here with someone?'

'Um, yes. My husband. Vince.'

That was the source of the issue. Alison could tell from the flat way she said his name. Married a while. Not a honeymoon. Not exactly no love there, but a weight all the same, a pain.

'Well, I'm here with my other half too. Let us know if you fancy a drink one night – gets boring, just the two of you, doesn't it?'

The other woman frowned. 'Oh, maybe. Bit tired today though.'

On holiday in so-called paradise and crying? 'Of course. I'm Alison, by the way. Nice to meet you.'

The other woman hesitated for a second. 'Beth. Hi.'

Beth and Vince. If only she had a surname, she could have looked them up on—

Jesus Christ, Alison! She caught herself contemplating a casual breaking of the law, looking people up on the police database with no reason. Maybe Tom was right and she really was addicted, not just to her phone, but to her job. To seeing crime everywhere and dead bodies behind every bush. Likely this was just a standard couples quarrel, an argument over the luggage or getting a cab from the airport, or their dog had recently died or something like that. *No crimes here, Alison. Get a hold of yourself.* Philippa Perry would no doubt have some choice yet wise words to say about it.

Beth – now

The post-holiday glow had well and truly gone, Beth thought, as she waited in line in Sainsbury's to pay for her coriander and crème fraîche. She'd asked Vince what he wanted for dinner that morning and he hadn't even looked up from the game he was playing on his phone. Grunted, barely. Back at work, she'd found almost six hundred emails in her inbox and a mouldy half-drunk cup of coffee someone else had set down on her desk then just left there. She'd hardly had time for lunch, and now the rain had soaked into the hem of her trousers and she felt a cold coming on. So much for summer. Outside it was gloomy, autumnal despite being only early September. And as for Vince . . .

The familiar panic started up somewhere under her ribcage, the racing thoughts that made her lose her breath. What was she going to do? How could they exorcise this ghost that had risen up between them?

The word *ghost* was a poor choice. All at once she pictured it again – the billowing red in the water, the flash of gold from the toenails. It was traumatic, having seen a dead body in real life like that. Being one of the first to find it – *her* – and all the questioning after, those terrifying days when she wasn't allowed to talk to Vince, and thought she might never see him again. She had to put it behind her now. It was no one she knew, and not her tragedy to be engulfed in. She had her own problems to worry about. She would go home and make a Thai curry, Vince's favourite, and maybe he would be nice to her today. Maybe the old Vince would come back.

Her eye was caught by a display of discounted wine, but she knew what he'd say about that, even if it might help them both relax a little. She grabbed a bottle of red anyway, just in case. She swiped her groceries, obeying the disembodied voice of the automated till. Life felt bleak. The Canaries – sun on the water, the lap of waves around her feet, sand in her toes – felt seasons and worlds away. Not that she had been happy there either. But at least it was warm. Now there was nothing ahead of her but the slow death of the year, then Christmas, which would be a total disaster if things carried on like this. Maybe they wouldn't even make it that far. The thought made her chest heavy, and a lump came to her throat. She had to stop this somehow, CPR their failing marriage. But how? She had tried everything she could think of. The holiday was supposed to be their last-ditch saviour.

She'd forgotten her tote bag, and wouldn't pay for a plastic one lest it set Vince off about recycling and the environment, so she stuffed the groceries into her big handbag and trudged out into the rain. It was only September – was it meant to feel so dark and wintery already?

She had just stepped into the street when she saw the woman. Someone who did not belong to this South London world of rain and yellow-sticker discounts and nights drawing in. A slender figure with tawny hair bundled up above her head, no umbrella, and a long swishy skirt and sandals – yes, sandals, in all this rain! – and lots of silver jewellery. It was her.

Beth's body had a visceral fight-or-flight response. For a moment, she thought about pretending she hadn't seen her, and ducking off the other way. Running for the hills, never looking back. But it was too late.

The woman came towards her, big smile on her face, arms out. 'Beth! Oh my God, it is you! Beth!'

A scent enveloped Beth as she let herself be hugged. Sandalwood and musk – the same smell that brought back sun on her shoulders, the red glow of sun behind her eyes, blisters between her toes from unaccustomed flip-flops. Coconut, like the drinks round the pool. A knot of terror at her solar plexus. The holiday.

She turned and smiled weakly, the rain dripping off her hair and down her face. 'Yes, it's me. Hi, Corinna.'

◆ ◆ ◆

Beth let the door shut behind her too hard, hands full of groceries, and it slammed. She winced, knowing what would happen, and five seconds later Vince stuck his head out from the living room, face cross. He looked like he hadn't slept in days – she'd heard him get up around three, the floorboards creaking, and then seen the glow of the TV under the door and heard the beeps of his games. Jet lag – or a guilty conscience?

'I've told you—'

'I know, I'm sorry, it slipped. Can you help me?'

He sighed, but stooped to pick up the avocado that had rolled from her bag down the hall. 'These are air-freighted, you know. And out of season.'

Beth let that one go, because she had bigger news. 'You'll never guess who I just ran into.' He didn't take the bait, just carried an armful of groceries into the kitchen and began putting them away. She followed him, like a faithful dog tugging at his hem. 'Corinna. It was Corinna! Outside Sainsbury's!'

Vince flinched, dropped the carton of yoghurt he was holding. Beth lunged forward, but it was too late, and it broke open on the tiles and spattered everywhere.

'GOD!' she shouted. Vince flinched at that too. 'It's OK,' she found herself soothing. 'Just a spill.' Then they were both running around for cloths and kitchen roll and it took a minute or two to wipe it off the cupboards and chair legs.

'Corinna,' Vince said, rinsing the cloth into the sink. His voice was flat. 'What was she doing there?'

'She said they've moved to the area.'

'What? I thought they were out of town somewhere.'

'Something about dry rot in their flat so they're borrowing a friend's place, I don't know. She seemed fine, anyway. Weirdly cheerful.'

'At least someone is.'

Beth hesitated with her final piece of news. 'She suggested getting together. To talk it all through. Process it, she said.' She braced herself for the explosion, but strangely, it didn't come. Vince turned off the tap and hung up the cloth.

'Hmm. I suppose that's a good idea.'

'You think?'

'Well, it was pretty messed up, Beth! All that happened, then they just sent us home? No follow-up? And we never even got to talk to Joel and Corinna. That's weird, don't you think? The way they just left?'

'I know. So – I should set something up? She gave me her number.'

In fact, Corinna had wrestled Beth's phone from her hand, typed in the number, drops of rain collecting on the screen. It was odd. Why would such a vibrant young couple want to hang out with miserable, basic Beth and Vince?

Doubts wormed their way into her mind, as they had back in Tenerife. Could it be – was it maybe – no, no. It was all in her head.

Vince walked past her and left the room without answering, a new tactic he had started employing. Beth tried to calm her breathing so as not to scream after him, terrible things like *What the hell is wrong with you? Why do you blame me? I didn't do anything. Why won't you talk to me?* Screaming would not help. He'd been through a lot, and she just had to give him some space. But it was hard. As she turned her gaze upwards, she saw that there were spatters of yoghurt on the ceiling, just beginning to drip down.

Alison – then

'. . . and she was just staring out to sea, and she'd definitely been crying, so I made some excuse to talk to her. I didn't see any bruises, but of course it can all be psychological these days . . . What?'

Having worked with Tom for many years, and been in a relationship with him for several more, she knew his every facial expression, and this one was conveying mild irritation and concern. 'We're on holiday, Ali. We're meant to be relaxing.'

'I'm not *not* relaxing.'

'You're finding cases even on the beach. You don't know why she was crying – maybe her mum's ill, or she lost her job. Or had a miscarriage. Or maybe it's just allergies.'

'But—'

'Ali! Do we not have enough cases back home without finding more here? Where we don't even have jurisdiction?'

Alison humphed into her hummus. Tom was eating a delicious-looking plate of garlicky grilled prawns, which she of course could not have. His glass of chilled rosé, beads of condensation inching down the outside, also looked delicious. They were eating dinner in the hotel's waterside restaurant, the light soft and violet, the waves lapping beneath the deck they sat on.

'Come on, babe,' he said gently. 'I know you haven't relaxed in, like, ten years, but give it a go? For the ba—'

'For the baby, for the baby,' she grumbled. 'Everything I do is for the baby. I'm still me, aren't I? It's just – a temporary lodger.' She touched her belly, struck by superstitious worry. 'I mean, a very welcome one. I just can't switch off my entire personality.'

'Your personality is finding phantom crimes everywhere? Hmm, I suppose it is, actually. But unless this woman asks for help, or you see something more worrying, you have to let it go, OK?' He nudged her hand playfully. 'What would Philippa Perry say?'

She'd say Alison was perhaps struggling to accept the loss of self and career that might accompany becoming a mother. That catching bad people was at the core of her identity. That she was a chronic busybody who'd rather nose into other people's lives than read a book (as if, Philippa would never be so mean, though Alison's sister would say this and indeed had a few times). She sighed. 'I can at least order dessert, can I? Some sugar's still allowed?'

'I'm not the boss of you,' Tom said mildly. She couldn't even find anything to be annoyed at him for. Alison's vetting instincts for partners were off the charts, having seen every shade of bad relationship behaviour in her time, from coercive control to rape to murder. And Tom had passed it all. Not that she didn't watch him like a hawk. She had never yet gone through his phone, knowing that was a step too far, but he always told her she was welcome to. She knew she'd just find page after page of speculation about the chances of Tottenham in the FA Cup this year, until she slipped into a coma from sheer boredom.

What were you supposed to do on holiday? Just sit around each night chatting to the same person you saw every day anyway, not even drinking wine or eating seafood or soft cheese, then go to bed in a less-nice space than your home? Tom had picked up a brochure from reception about massages, including one for 'mamas to be', urgh. Alison could not understand why people enjoyed massages. You were so vulnerable, naked except for some pants made of mesh, and at the mercy of the total stranger you were paying to put too much pressure on your neck. Not to mention all that oil took forever to wash out of your hair, and as for the way it seeped into your bum crack . . . no.

She tried, 'You'll never guess what Colette said about my latest case . . .' but he just shook his head at her.

'No work chat. No Colette!'

'But we met at work, Tom! What else do we talk about?'

'I don't know. TV. Family, friends. Our baby.'

She softened at that. 'Our baby will be the best baby.'

'It's actually going to suck for all the other babies, not being as good as ours.'

'I know.'

'So what do you want to do here all day?' he asked, through a mouthful of prawn. 'Sightsee? It's a bit hot for you to be on your feet, maybe.'

'And the spa's out, thanks to the lodger. You could go.'

He shuddered. 'It's boiling outside. Why would I go into an even hotter room that smells of feet?'

'Well, I also can't do wine tasting, or walk very far, or any adventurous activities . . .'

'So, relaxing then.'

'Relaxing.' Alison sighed again.

She had just sunk a spoon into her tiramisu – Tom had questioned the baffled waiter about the caffeine content – when she saw them.

'Look!' she hissed. 'That's her. Crying Woman. That must be the husband with her.'

He didn't look evil. Gently balding, wearing one of those floral shirts she quite liked but which Tom wouldn't countenance. Trendy glasses. He looked nice, in fact, though she'd seen plenty of evil bastards who did too.

'Stop staring,' Tom whispered. But Alison had already caught the eye of Crying Woman – no longer crying, actually quite glamorous now in a white linen dress, her make-up nicely done – and waved. The woman – Beth, that was her name – looked a bit embarrassed and gave a tiny wave back, but didn't come over. Never mind. Alison had no shame in these matters, much like her mother, who had once climbed over the neighbours' fence to have a nosey at their new conservatory and then claimed to be 'looking for the cat'; she did not have a cat.

She beckoned them to the table, waving like a kids' TV presenter on drugs. She saw Beth hesitate, as if thinking about pretending she hadn't noticed, but then British politeness won out, and she changed course over to Alison and Tom's table, the husband in tow with a sour expression on his face.

'Hi! Here for dinner too?' chirped Alison. Tom shot her a look. Of course they were here for dinner. It was a restaurant.

'Yes – is it nice?'

'Tom had the prawns, which looked good, but I had the mezze as there's about a thousand things I can't eat right now. This is Tom, my baby-daddy.'

Tom said that phrase was classist, but she found it amusing to bring out when doctors and midwives insisted on calling him 'Dad' or else 'your husband'. Neither of them could seem to get up the enthusiasm for an actual wedding.

Beth said, 'Hi. This is Vince, my husband.'

Vince gave a rictus grin. 'Hi.'

'We met at the beach earlier,' said Alison to Vince. 'Having a nice time?'

He shrugged. 'I don't know. We only arrived yesterday.'

'We arrived today, but it's a lovely hotel, isn't it, Tom?'

She and Beth were like parents introducing recalcitrant toddlers in the park. Tom had also gone taciturn now. 'Not bad, yeah.'

An awkward silence fell. Beth said, 'Well, we'd better go get our table.'

'Sure, sure. Enjoy!'

They walked off and sat down at a table a few metres away. Alison drank some fizzy water and looked out over the sea. It was nice. The violet light as the sun went down, distant gold still touching the sea, the gentle lap of waves against the wooden jetty the restaurant was on, still warm after 8 p.m. Nice nice nice. What was wrong with her that she'd rather be looking at a corpse in the morgue?

But now Tom was frowning into the distance. 'What's up?'

'Um – nothing.' He looked down at his prawns, spearing one on a fork but not eating it.

'Come on. You're the world's worst liar – what is it?'

'It's just – the husband.'

'Go on,' said Alison, with what she realised too late was unseemly interest.

'I think I've seen him before somewhere.'

'Oh! Down the nick?'

'I don't know.' Tom was a super-recogniser, meaning he never forgot a face, but he couldn't always place one right away. It was the reason he'd been recruited to his current team.

'You mean you arrested him? He did something?'

He shook his head as if to clear it. 'It's not coming to me. I'm sure it's nothing. Eat your dessert before it collapses.'

Alison dug into the mound of cream and coffee, already soggy and too sweet. She was sure it wasn't nothing. The wife had been crying, avoiding conversation, and Tom, a police officer, recognised the husband from somewhere? She'd been right, not just bored and inventing crimes. There really was something dodgy here.

◆ ◆ ◆

Back in the room, Tom locked himself in the bathroom for what she could tell was going to be another marathon session, since the man was incapable of admitting spicy food did not agree with him (despite his Asian heritage). Restless, she slid open the glass door to the balcony and went out into the warm night air. Immediately she heard the buzz of a mosquito, and slapped at it with irritation. Say what you liked about a hiking trip in the Lake District, there weren't any mozzies, and a much lower chance of being stuck to the toilet the whole time. Plus you weren't very likely to get heatstroke or third-degree sunburn. She couldn't even use the good insect repellent because of the baby.

Bored and still not able to settle into her book, which featured an entirely unrealistic crime investigation that was just annoying her, she sat back in an uncomfortable wicker chair and looked out over the resort. In the distance, the opal glow of the pool, and the murmur of the waves reaching her even here, palm trees swaying in a light breeze. She shut her eyes for a moment, willing herself to be able to relax.

'. . . going to stop!' Below her, a voice rose sharply.

Alison was on her feet right away. She loved eavesdropping on arguments; it was one of her toxic traits. A couple were huddled several storeys below, in a well of darkness between the lights that illuminated the path from the restaurant to the rooms. He seemed to have hold of her wrist, and what he was saying was inaudible, but the vicious tone was unmistakable.

The woman jerked away, and Alison caught the shimmer of her gold-woven pashmina in the spotlight. The sound of flip-flops running on the stone path, a sob caught in a throat. Beth. It was Beth, the crying woman, crying again. Arguing with her husband, whose hand had been clasped tight around her arm.

Beth – now

'That's the view from the balcony. And that's the pool, the big one. There were three, I think. And the spa, of course. I had a great massage one day.'

'Oh, lovely.' Janice, her 'work bestie', leaning dutifully in to look at Beth's 157 snaps of vaguely blue water. 'And no kids at all? God, I'd love that. I'd leave my lot with wolves if it meant I could lie by a pool with no one asking me for snacks or splashing me in the face.'

'Wolves!'

'Or a big dog, you know like in *Peter Pan*.'

'I think they'd call social services nowadays on the Darling family.' Beth put her phone away. They were in the Pret two streets away from their office, as opposed to the Pret right opposite it, which was always full of their colleagues buying tuna baguettes, and therefore not safe to gossip in.

Janice gathered up her braids, which were in danger of dipping into her latte, and sat back in her chair. 'So you had a nice time? The two of you?' She must have noticed there was not a single picture of Beth and Vince together in the whole collection. Most of the time he'd stayed in the hotel room, or if she ever coaxed him out he'd stayed hunched on a sun lounger scrolling through his phone, unwilling to go in the pool or sea, moaning that he didn't want to get burnt. It had been like having a solo holiday, except that might have been nicer, because she could at least have read a book at dinner rather than trying to make conversation with someone who answered every question in monosyllables or grunts, or raised his eyebrows every time she ordered a glass of wine. Desperate, she had started making little lists in her head of things they could talk about. Boats. What colour to paint the bedroom. The choice of forks in the restaurant. One night he hadn't even come to dinner at all, saying his stomach was upset, and Beth had eaten on her own, the staff constantly asking if someone else was joining her. When she'd returned, having drunk five glasses of wine and stumbling slightly in her mules, he had been asleep, earplugs in and eye mask on, back turned to her. Then there was that night he'd lost his temper with her. And the last night, of course. But she could hardly bear to think about that.

Now she said, 'Um. To be honest, it wasn't what I hoped for. He was so withdrawn the whole time, like I could hardly get him to look at me, and . . .' A sudden lump came to her throat, silencing her. She took a gulp of flat white to cover it. 'Also, something awful happened. Not to us, but we got mixed up in it. A woman was found dead, on the beach.'

Janice's hands flew to her mouth. 'No! What, like a migrant washing up, that kind of thing? A drowning?'

'We thought so at first. But no, she was a local, and she'd been – murdered, it turned out.'

Strangled. Someone's hands around her slender neck, choking the life from her.

'Oh, how awful. It didn't make the news over here. But how did you get involved?'

'Well, Vince – and me – we found the body.'

She remembered the awful way he had stooped to pull the woman out of the water, how he'd bawled and sobbed. What was that about?

Janice gaped at her, and she wished she'd never brought it up. 'Oh my goodness, Bethy, how awful. Did you get questioned by the police?'

She nodded. 'They kept Vince in. For, like – two days. I didn't understand it. I think maybe it's because he's . . .'

'. . . black?' supplied Janice, gently.

'Yeah.' Vince had a black mum and white dad, not that Beth had ever met either of them.

'That can happen. Mark's always being pulled aside for "extra screening" when we go on holiday. Spain can be bad for that kind of thing.'

'It was so horrible. I didn't know where he was, and I can't speak Spanish, obviously, and they wouldn't tell me anything anyway. I was frantic, really.'

'But they let him go?'

'Once we got the alibi sorted. This other couple we met, kind of made friends with on holiday, they said he was with them all night, signed a statement and everything.'

'He wasn't with you?' Janice's gaze was steady.

Beth paused, trying to remember which story she had ended up on. 'I'd gone to bed. Too much sangria.'

'Oh.' Her expression shifted. 'But you found the body together?'

'Yeah, we— Vince was coming back along the beach in the early hours, I was walking to find him and – well. We saw her.'

She'd told the police she had gone to bed, leaving Vince with the other couple. She'd never admitted to the several hours of the night that she just didn't remember, including how she'd got back to their room. But that was OK, wasn't it, because Joel and Corinna had been with him the whole time, they said, until he'd stumbled back along the shore, the sand already touched with the red light of dawn, and seen the woman floating in the waves. Even though it didn't really make sense to go from Joel and Corinna's room to Beth and Vince's via the beach, since their building was right opposite. And if she hadn't exactly been with him when he found the body, well, what difference did a few minutes make?

Janice stirred her coffee, a frown appearing between her eyebrows. 'And these other people, did you keep in touch with them? They were British, English?'

'Yeah – well, he is, I'm not sure what she is, but they live here. In fact, I ran into her the other day. Outside Sainsbury's.'

'That's very weird.'

It was, wasn't it? How often did you simply run into people in London, especially the very person you were trying to avoid? And yet there Corinna had been, barely two days after the end of the holiday.

'Nah, I think they just live in the area too. Coincidence.'

Janice was fiddling with her coffee cup. 'Did it come up with the police about – you know?'

'What?'

She knew. And wished she was not so open, that she hadn't shared secrets about her husband with friends and family. Once you admitted to those things, and saw the look on someone's face, the judgement, it was pretty hard to go back.

'That thing a while back. At the wedding.'

Beth dipped her head. She had been avoiding thinking about that, praying the Spanish police would not get wind of it, because it wasn't relevant to this case, it was just a mistake. Wasn't it?

'We told them everything,' she lied, draining her own coffee. 'Anyway, they released him as soon as they got the full story. He was with those people the whole time, it was just – a miscommunication. Just some local matter. I think they were being racist, to be honest, not looking for the real – culprit. Really sad, but nothing to do with us. Come on, we'd better get back.'

She hurried to put on her coat and throw away her cup, trying not to see the worry in her friend's eyes. Trying not to think about black spots in her memory, and heavy, white limbs hanging down from a stretcher.

Alison – then

Vincent Castries, that was the husband's full name. She'd peeked over the desk when they left dinner last night and seen it on the reservations computer. Now, back at the pool the next morning, with every inch of her shaded and creamed, she settled in for a nice soothing Google-stalk. It was an unusual name, and she found him quickly, though annoyingly he had very little online presence. Nothing Alison liked more than a dodgy person who spread their whole life over Instagram and Facebook. For Vince she only found a sponsorship link to a triathlon for MS research, a LinkedIn profile. She didn't click on that as it told the person you had looked, but it said he worked at a company that made solar panels, as a senior research manager. In the picture he looked professional and smiling.

The wife had a different surname, her googling revealed – Beth Jones. Too common, too hard to work out which one to look at of the hundreds online. It took Alison ten minutes to find the right Instagram account, and soon she knew Beth's birthday and age (thirty-seven), where they lived, and where she worked (the local council). In contrast to her husband, Beth loved an arty shot of margs with the ladies, or her 'outfit of the day' in a mirror, or her own hand holding up glasses of wine. There was a recent shot from Heathrow, a selfie of Beth in front of the departures board, which helpfully told Alison which flight they had taken. Then a shot of Beth's legs by the pool with the caption '*Not a bad place to spend the week*'. Various other images of drinks, the spa, the beach. No sign of Vince.

Alison studied Beth's face in the airport picture. Was there sadness in the smile, or was she just imagining it because she'd seen that incident last night, the shouting, the grab of the wrist? She scrolled back down, looking for any shots showing bruises, or posts about 'clumsy accidents', a common technique she'd seen used to explain DV, and before she knew it she was up to Christmas. They'd spent it with Beth's family. Mother, father, sister and sister's husband and kids. Did that mean that—?

'You've been doing that for over an hour,' said Tom, from the neighbouring sunbed.

'I'm on holiday. Let me enjoy my hobbies.'

'Careful you don't accidentally like a post from last year, you stalker.' Tom always said Alison had only joined the police because it paid her to be nosey. He wasn't totally wrong.

She sighed and put the phone down, stretching out a cramp in her right hand. 'I didn't find anything, anyway. He's hardly online.'

'Well, that's not evidence of criminal activity.' Tom was not a fan of social media, having briefly worked in a department that dealt with hate crime. He felt it brought out the worst in people. Certainly it made Alison want to kill her own sister if she posted up any more Strava run times, but it was undeniably useful for investigations.

'Wish I could do a cheeky HOLMES search.'

Tom lowered his book and looked at her sternly.

'I won't! I'm just saying I wish I could.' Just then she saw the couple, Vince and Beth, appear at the other side of the pool, carrying tote bags and towels. 'Look! There they are.'

She'd spent so much time stalking their profiles it was almost like seeing celebrities. She put on her sunglasses to better observe them. They were having some discussion about sun loungers, which could be hard to come by at this time. Alison took a dim view of people who left them reserved for hours while they went off to do other things. Beth was standing by a single lounger in the shade, her shoulders hunched, stance timid as she pointed at another in the full sun. Perhaps she was saying it could be moved.

Vince was answering now, waving his arms. His body seemed rigid, full of rage. What could be making him so cross? Alison watched as he stomped away and sat down on another lounger, far from Beth. He put in headphones and took out his phone. His whole posture indicated unhappiness, fury, a general desire to be far away. Totally shut off from his wife, who sat down slowly on her own lounger and put on sunglasses. Her hand went up now and again to wipe tears away. Alison's heart ached for her. To have come all this way and be having a miserable time was the worst. The pressure to have fun and spend time with your loved ones could tip unhappy people over the edge. As a DC and DS she had attended many a festive- or birthday-related murder.

But that wasn't going to happen here. Right? Why was she so obsessed with one unhappy couple having rows on their holiday? Maybe she was deflecting, trying to control something random when the rest of her life felt like it was slipping from her grasp. In two months a baby would be tearing its way out of her, and no matter how many books she read or birth plans she made, it would come when and how it wanted.

Still, her eye was drawn to the couple opposite, sitting metres apart, marooned in their own worlds of misery. Nothing online that might incriminate him, but that didn't mean there wasn't a trail of broken women behind him.

After a while of gawking, Alison felt a familiar twinge in her bladder. Once she had been proud to go an entire day without peeing – maybe not healthy, but disciplined. Now she could barely last an hour.

'Going to the loo,' she said, hauling herself up. Tom nodded, watching her lumber off. At least he wouldn't follow her there, and a selfish part of her was grateful to have five minutes' respite from his loving surveillance. It was nice he cared, but she no longer felt like her body was entirely her own. Inside, the lobby was blessedly cool and air-conditioned. In the mirror of the ladies, she could see her face was flushed red as a tomato. Her hair was frizzing up, and despite her best efforts with the suncream, her shoulders and chest were indeed pink. She sighed.

She went to the loo and did her best to cool down with water splashed on her face. On her way out, her attention was caught by singing in the lobby. One of her favourite songs, though she'd never have admitted it even under oath – Ed Sheeran's '*Perfect*'. It was coming from the lobby bar, a dark, windowless space done up to resemble a Tudor pub, a few long-suffering holiday husbands sitting with pints, as if they were at a Wetherspoons in Leeds instead of a luxury resort in Tenerife. Alison walked a few steps closer, curious, and saw that the singer, standing beside an upright piano, was a young woman who the heat had clearly not affected. Tan, slender, in a spangly blue dress that wasn't quite the thing for 1 p.m., she sang with her eyes shut, sweet and melodic, an older man in a black suit accompanying her on the piano. Her Spanish accent sounded on some of the words as she belted out the song.

Alison felt a brief pang for her own age, her advanced state of pregnancy, her general dishevelment. But then she got a grip on herself. She'd never been the type of woman who men gazed at, like this slim, sparkly singer, and so much the better. It meant she could watch them instead, and figure out what they were up to.

When she got back, Tom was watching for her. 'Here's something for you.'

'What?'

'If you're going to get obsessed with a couple, some new candidates just arrived. Very "look at me".'

A different man and woman were lowering themselves into the pool near the swim-up bar, talking in loud voices. They were tanned already, glossy, with the presence of minor celebrities or royalty. Early thirties, perhaps, or late twenties, the man with tattoos covering his chest and arms, the woman slight, with no visible plastic surgery or fillers.

As she looked them over, she caught a glimpse of Vince Castries. He had taken off his sunglasses and was staring, white-faced, into the pool. Right at the new couple.

Beth – now

'Sure about this?'

She combed through her hair with her hands in the hall mirror. She'd been going for artfully tousled, like Corinna always pulled off, but it just looked like she hadn't brushed it for days. The green cord jumpsuit she'd liked so much online gave off strong mechanic vibes, and not in a sexy, Charlene-from-*Neighbours* way; more like a Bob the Builder way.

Vince was already standing at the door wearing his coat, holding a bottle of mid-priced red wine. 'We're not going to cancel at the last minute. That would be very rude.' Why did he sound so angry every time he spoke to her now?

'No, but – you know. It might be upsetting for you.'

He said nothing.

She tried again. 'You know, it could bring back memories.'

'You think I've forgotten it?' His tone was nasty. The old Vince never spoke to her like that.

'No. Of course not.'

'Well, then. I think it might be helpful. There's a lot of things I still don't understand about that week. Don't you want to know what happened?'

'Of course. OK.' She hated the humble, soothing tone of her voice. Placating, accepting such treatment.

'We're going to be late.'

'Sorry. Let's go. Do you think that's enough wine?'

He'd picked up the bottle she'd bought in the supermarket the other day, which she knew would not impress their hosts.

Another eye roll. 'For God's sake, Beth, it's a weekday night, how much are we planning to drink?'

'Sorry. Yes, OK.'

They went out and she waited for him to double-lock the door and set the alarm, not that they had anything worth stealing, and then started walking down the road to the bus stop. It was drizzling again, and Beth had forgotten an umbrella, so she felt droplets settling in her hair, making it look even more bedraggled. Vince didn't hold her hand, and didn't say a word as they waited. The bus splashed water up her legs as it came around the corner, but that was just par for the course. On the bus, he scrolled endlessly on his phone, while she sat mute, waiting for him to say something, look at her. He didn't.

The address Corinna had given was in a new-build block of flats near Crystal Palace, with flashy lifts and fake bookshelves in the lobby, a security guard at a desk scrolling on his phone also. In the lift she saw the flat number had PH after it – penthouse, that must mean.

'I wonder if it opens right into their flat,' she said. 'You know, like in films. That would be cool.'

He said nothing. As they went up, she watched their reflections in the steel interior. Hollow-eyed, frazzled, as if they had never been on holiday at all.

The lift did open right into their flat – jazz playing, candles burning, Corinna in a cashmere jumper and jeans, barefoot to show her red-painted toenails. It was odd to see her in clothes. On holiday she had never not been exposing acres of tanned golden skin, and yes, even here her hair looked salt-kissed and perfect.

Joel was in the kitchen, doing something with a sous vide machine. He was wearing shorts and was also barefoot, an open-necked linen shirt on top that showed his tattoos. No concession to the dreary September weather outside.

'My guys! Team Tenerife all back together!'

He came over to hug Beth, and she braced herself for the hard-packed pressure of his body. He gave Vince a handshake and clap on the shoulder. Corinna reached up on tiptoes to kiss Vince on the cheek. He wasn't even tall; she was just a tiny fairy of a woman.

'So!' Beth exclaimed, covering the awkwardness with hearty cheer. 'This isn't your usual place, is it?'

It was a nice flat, with a wrap-round balcony and glass windows looking over the park. It had the anonymous feel of an upmarket Airbnb, with mustard throws and rugs and knobbly candles in wonky holders. No personal pictures and no clutter. As if they were standing in a film set.

Corinna looked over her shoulder as she opened a bottle of champagne. Actual champagne, not Prosecco. The wine they'd brought had been set to one side.

'Oh, no. Our place has dry rot, can you believe it? Nightmare.'

'Ten grand to fix,' said Joel, doing a convincing impression of someone who believed this was a lot of money. 'This place belongs to friends who are overseas.'

'Strange it's so near us,' said Beth. All that time, she'd been wondering if they'd ever see them again, ever hear their memories of that night, and now here they were.

'I know! Must be fate. Anyway, I hope you like *kleftiko*.'

Beth had no idea what that was.

'Lamb,' explained Corinna, with a little smile. 'We took a cooking course in Greece last year; Joel's been making it for dinner parties ever since.'

Meanwhile, Vince hardly ever cooked, and had been known to eat mince from a tin on nights when Beth was out. A sense of unfairness surged through her, like ink percolating through water. Or blood.

God, she needed a drink.

Following her gaze, Corinna eased out the cork with her thumbs, displaying none of the anxiety Beth always felt when opening fizzy wine. She passed out the flutes – not normal ones; they were artfully askew in some way that made Beth worry she was going to drop one – and clinked them.

'Here's to holiday friends.'

Joel came over for his, draping his arm around Corinna and swigging champagne. 'Team Tenerife!'

Beth set her glass down. 'I mean, it wasn't the best ending to it all.'

Joel knit his brows. 'Of course, of course. So weird, wasn't it? In fact, I think we should talk it through. After all, no one else really understands what it was like out there.'

'That's the thing!' Beth blinked in surprise at Vince's vehemence. 'No one does understand. How awful it was. Seeing her. And then . . .'

Corinna rubbed his shoulder in a way that made Beth blink again. 'I know, I know. For you it was a nightmare.'

Joel was nodding sympathetically at Vince. 'You hear any more from the police out there?'

'No. I had to give them all my details to be able to leave the country. Get the consul involved, even.'

'Awful. You know, I think you might have a case against them. I can talk to some lawyer mates if you like.'

Vince thumbed his eyes. 'I don't know. I can hardly make sense of it. One minute I'm by the pool drinking cocktails, then the next I'm in a cell and they're asking, "Who is she? Who is she?", and I don't even know who they're talking about. They didn't even tell me for ages that it was – her.'

Ana Garcia de Vasquez. A regal name, Beth always thought. Though she was just a normal girl. A local. A singer. And she was dead. They had found her body floating in the sea, her red dress sodden with water.

And Beth's husband had been right there beside her.

Alison – then

Zzzzzzrrrggrr.

Alison sighed loudly enough to wake the people in the next room, but Tom did not stir. She tried prodding him on to his side, and the snoring did cease for a moment. But now she was wide awake. Sleeping in general seemed to be so much harder in this hotel room than at home. She'd never understood why whoever was responsible for designing them made sure the curtains were paper-thin, and filled the room with various small LEDs. Above her head, the smoke alarm had a flashing light that pulsed out in green every few seconds. And she could hear noise from outside, laughter and shouting.

Now into the second day of the holiday, her brain was slowly unwinding itself. She'd seen Beth and Vince about the place a few times, but not noticed any other concerning behaviour; and she'd also seen the new couple, who seemed to be doing posed photos or videos everywhere they went. The woman, a tiny slip of a thing with a perfect tan, was especially annoying, always kicking up a foot or putting her hands beneath her chin, like a whimsical child. They were so glamorous, so full of life. She bet neither of them ever ate petrol-station sandwiches for lunch in the car park of the South London Murder Team offices.

As for the look of horror she thought she'd seen on Vince Castries's face when the new people showed up, Alison had witnessed no interaction between the two couples and was wondering if she'd been mistaken. Or if, like her, he just hated people who felt entitled to record loud videos in public.

Zzzzzgrrrffl. For God's sake. Alison threw off the covers. The room, which had been arctic when they returned from dinner after the cleaner set the aircon to 16, was now suffocatingly hot. She shuffled to the window, irritated with herself and with life in general. A large part of her wished she was back in South London, with the creeping black mould over the radiator in the hallway. They'd have to get that sorted before the baby. She rested her hands on her stomach, tapping it lightly like a drum.

'Hello in there,' she murmured.

They could hear your voice, apparently. Here was a person who was going to call her Mum. Crazy.

Who was making all that racket? She could hear music and laughter, carrying on the still night. She opened the balcony door and stepped out into the air, which still felt heavy and stifling at – what was the time? The bedside clock, another needless illumination, said it was 2.37 a.m. She traced the sound to a balcony on the opposite building, craning out to see it. It was that couple, the glamorous ones. They had a mini-speaker and were blaring out techno, never mind that other people might be sleeping. Alison watched as the woman leaned out over the balcony, perching right on the edge. Was she crazy? That was so dangerous. She itched to shout something over, but she was trying to curb her busybody tendencies. And it might startle the woman and backfire. But it did make Alison fume to see people being so reckless.

She was just going back to try and sleep beside her snoring, boiling-hot partner, when she heard it. A scream, piercing the night air. Alison froze, her police instincts kicking in. She listened hard for a follow-up. One scream, that could just be high spirits, someone getting playfully pushed in the pool, or tripping over drunk. Nothing more. It had sounded like a woman, though. She looked at the clock out of habit, noting the time – 2.38 a.m. now.

Should she call down to reception and flag it, and maybe complain about the music at the same time? It would wake Tom if she used the phone now. And there was no follow-up commotion, no shouts or sirens in the night. The laughter and techno from the far-off balcony did not stop. Maybe she should listen to Tom for once and actually mind her own business. Huffing and grouchy, Alison went inside, and shut the doors behind her.

Beth – now

'. . . really, you can't go wrong with crypto, what with all the extra regulation hedging lability in the market.'

Beth had long since stopped listening to what Joel was saying. Surely this whole dinner wasn't a pitch to get them to invest in his supposed ethical crypto business? They didn't have any money. No matter how many tiny salary increases she got at the council, every month it seemed to go less far and their credit card debts seemed to increase. Beth didn't understand where the money went. The holiday had been expensive, true, but she'd felt like they needed something nice to pull them out of their tailspin (that had certainly backfired). A few times she'd tried to sit down with Vince and look for unnecessary expenses – subscriptions, gym memberships, takeaways – but he'd always get frustrated and storm out of the room. They still had their own accounts, so she had no idea what he actually earned or what he spent it on. With the cost-of-living rises, she'd said a few times they needed to up their payments into the joint account they used for bills, but she was maxed out as it was and he had so far refused to engage. Was there anything more annoying than stonewalling? The word was apt because it felt like slamming yourself into one, over and over.

She toyed with her wine glass, feeling fuzzy and unstable. She'd had too much to drink for a school night, but who could blame her with such tension in the air? They had hardly even discussed what had happened, the woman who died or the way Joel and Corinna had just left.

Vince seemed engaged in what Joel was saying, however, nodding along. 'So you reckon it's worth putting some into?'

'Oh, definitely, mate.' Joel reached over and topped up their glasses with more red.

Beth was aware that she was drunk, and that something was evading her. Some undercurrent she had not understood, just like in Los Colibris on that night they spent together. Like she was the only one not in on a joke.

Corinna had been listening with one hand under her cheek, elbow on the table and bare brown foot twitching in time to the gentle jazz they were playing. On the table was the remnants of dessert, some kind of honey cake drizzled with edible flowers and yoghurt, looking straight out of a cookbook and free from refined sugar, as Corinna had explained. Apparently she was a nutritionist as well as a life coach. It struck Beth that this was an odd job title. Someone who was so good at life, every aspect of it, that they could coach other people on how to do it. Whereas here was Beth, overweight, pushing forty, childless, in a dead-end public-sector job where a fifty-quid pay increase was cause for celebration, and her marriage clearly on the rocks.

Corinna shook herself now, as if in a daze. 'Anyone for a digestif? Coffee?'

Beth would never sleep again if she had coffee, and usually Vince had an Ovaltine after dinner or nothing, so she was surprised to see him agree to an espresso. Since when did he drink those? With a hollow feeling in her stomach, she remembered the article she'd read. Ten signs of an affair. New habits or tastes in food, music, or culture. Where would Vince even have met someone to have an affair with?

Her stomach lurched down another floor as she watched Corinna lean on his shoulder when she passed him the espresso in a little Le Creuset cup, the set in bold primary colours causing Beth great covetousness. Corinna was just tactile, though, wasn't she? With her ballerina's body and exotic scent and long, tangled hair. Now she was dancing in the kitchen, swaying to the music, cleaning up a few plates.

'Can I help?' asked Beth, half-heartedly.

'Oh, no, thank you. You just relax. I'm sorry the holiday wasn't very restorative in the end.'

'You can say that,' said Vince ruefully. 'Not even covered by travel insurance.'

Joel took a swig of coffee. 'So what happened in the end? Was the case closed?'

Beth had looked it all up. 'I don't think it's closed, but I got the impression they'd hit a bit of a brick wall.' She thought of the slip of paper they'd had to sign, promising to return if there were any further developments. She'd been so afraid at the airport, waiting for the plane to board, expecting any moment to be seized and Vince sent back to a Spanish prison, never to get out. The moment the wheels lifted she had let out all the air in her body. Then had a few seconds of relief, before she started to worry again about what was going on with her husband. Why he seemed to hate her all of a sudden. What had happened on the beach that morning, and if it might mean something, after all.

She heard herself say, 'I guess it was just lucky you two were able to alibi Vince.' All three of them looked startled for a moment.

'It was,' said Joel, who was now rolling a joint with practised fingers. She hoped he wasn't going to spark it up in here.

'We never actually heard what it was you told the police. It was all so confused.'

There was a brief pause. Corinna said, 'Well, we just told them the truth. That Vince was with us.'

'But when was that? What time was it you all went to bed?' In other words, when had Vince been alone? When did their alibi run out?

Joel licked the paper to stick it. 'Ooh, no idea, but the sun was coming up, wasn't it, Vince, mate?'

Vince said nothing. He was looking into the empty cup of coffee. Beth had never heard him say what had actually happened that night, and knew better than to ask. She tried, 'Corinna? Do you remember?'

'Well, we drank in the bar till they kicked us out, then I guess we went to our room because we had some tequila. Sat on the balcony. We just drank there until it was light, then I suppose Vince left. You remember you'd gone off to bed earlier, Beth.'

Slightly pointed, and it was true Beth had essentially passed out, but not before embarrassing herself horribly. One of the reasons she wanted to know was that she didn't remember large parts of the night herself. It was just there in her head, a blank space, and every time she thought of it she felt an overwhelming sense of dread.

Of course, the food had been amazing. The lamb falling off the bone, fragrant with garlic and rosemary, fluffy home-made flatbread, thick, minty yoghurt. All the wine had been interesting and well chosen (the one they'd brought had never been opened). But Beth had felt a tick of panic all night long, at the base of her spine, on the back of her neck, in the pit of her stomach. Why did these people, so glamorous and beautiful, even want to talk to her and Vince? It hadn't made sense in Tenerife, and it didn't make sense now.

It was getting late when she excused herself from the table, littered with joint ends and crumbs from the home-made bread. Joel had opened the doors to the balcony while smoking, but it was still going to be in Beth's lungs and hair and clothes. She'd been surprised Vince not only tolerated the weed, he even took a small drag. She'd never known him to do drugs of any kind. But then, did she know him at all?

When she got up to go to the loo, no one really noticed, they were both so focused on Vince and extracting every detail of his ordeal. Vince had needed it, she could tell, getting relief from recounting it, from their unquestioning belief in the injustice he'd been through. The arrest, the days in a cell, the questioning, then the final release. What Beth really wanted to ask, but didn't dare, was – why had Joel and Corinna left in such a hurry, the morning the body was found? Up until God knows what time, then clearing out before the police got round to interviewing any guests? They'd said they were staying for longer, Beth was sure. It niggled at her.

The bathroom was aggressively modern in a style Beth hated, no bath, just a rainfall shower, angular sink and loo, chrome taps, grey tiles. Spotlessly clean, not a hair or smear or toothpaste to be seen. She snooped through the bathroom cabinets and found a box of pills with a long name. She snapped a picture of the name, feeling grubby. When she finished and washed her hands, she hovered in the hallway.

Corinna was saying, 'Of course they seized on you as the person who found her, just so unfortunate, really . . .'

No one would notice her gone, so Beth slipped into the bedroom. It had the feel of a bachelor pad, grey sheets and carpet and built-in wardrobes. Clean, but very anonymous. She opened a few drawers – socks, men's T-shirts neatly folded. Where was

Corinna's stuff? She had to use tons of beauty products to look like that, surely (the alternative was unthinkable). The drawers of the bedside table on one side were empty, which seemed weird. In the other were condoms – she looked away, reddening – a few documents and loose photos, presumably of Corinna's family – and something she recognised. The brochure from the resort they had stayed at, with a map showing where everything was. Los Colibris. The hummingbirds, it meant, and Corinna had reminded her of one – small, beautiful, darting. It was dog-eared, and there was something scribbled on one corner of it. A number. She snapped a picture of that too, feeling very foolish, then jumped as she heard footsteps in the hallway. Vince was standing there with his hand on the bathroom door.

'What were you doing?' he hissed.

'Oh, I walked into the wrong room – stupid!'

He stared at her. She was a terrible liar, always had been. She waited for him to ask why she'd been in Corinna and Joel's bedroom, their strange, empty, show-home bedroom, snooping about. He didn't. He just turned around and went into the bathroom. Beth tried to reset her face and returned to the living room.

'Such a nice flat. The views are incredible.'

Joel topped up her wine glass and started talking about leaseholds and freeholds, but Beth caught a direct glance from Corinna across the table. It was only for a second, but it turned her stomach upside down. Something wasn't right here. She just didn't know what.

Him

Holidays were always difficult. At home it was easier. He'd leave in the morning before she even woke up, then could usually plead working late, or train delays, or client entertaining, and arrive back after she'd gone to sleep, several days a week. She complained of course, but she liked the money too much to really kick up a fuss. He'd make sure to be home at least two nights, and when he sensed she was getting fed up he'd even get home before her and cook. Or rather, decant overpriced food from the deli near the office, but she didn't know that. He took care to bury the containers deep inside next door's bin, and when she asked what was in the dish he'd just make up ingredients. Then they would watch TV or a long film until it was time to sleep, and taken that way, they could go for entire months without looking into each other's eyes or talking about anything that mattered. She was a champion natterer-on-er. Everything from trimming the hedge to where they might go on holiday to the ins and outs of her office politics. Look at her now, stirring a pot at the stove, cooking something she thought he loved but which he actually couldn't stand. Going on and on about some issue at work. She was flushed, her hair sticking to her forehead with sweat, and he pushed down his repulsion. He knew how to pretend to listen, nod along, make interested noises and sometimes ask a pertinent but all-purpose question like *Well, if you feel so strongly, maybe it's time to do something?* Or *Honestly, what's up with people nowadays?* That could get him surprisingly far.

It was easy to please women. He had no idea why some men complained about not getting female attention when it was so very easy. You didn't even have to be good-looking. Just stay in reasonable shape, dress OK (no pet hairs, no bobbled tracksuit bottoms, pull up your trousers instead of displaying your pants to the world), shower, use a nice aftershave, get trendy glasses and make sure your hair was cut and nails trimmed. Ask them questions. It was astonishing how few men ever thought to do that. Sometimes buy flowers or chocolates, write down a few pertinent facts after each conversation and bring them up again in future. He kept a document on his phone for this purpose.

And the thing that made it easiest of all was that women actually wanted to be duped. They didn't want to know the truth of a man's inner life, the grind of corporate work, the worry about the mortgage and bills and how to pay for all the expensive holidays she kept dropping links to into his WhatsApp. As long as you were nice to them and bought them things, they didn't care what else you did. They didn't want to know what was actually happening on those nights you 'worked late', or why you insisted on washing your own clothes sometimes, or why you were so protective over your phone. None so blind as those who don't want to see.

But lately, the system had been slipping. Things had happened that even she couldn't shut her eyes to, and his mask had been harder and harder to don. He had snapped at her a few times, and seen the surprise on her face, followed by the hardening of anger. He didn't want her angry. Angry women did inconvenient things. Such as look at your phone, or your bank account. Such as divorce you and take half your things. Such as ask questions. Or remember incidents, small details from the past that maybe you would prefer they not think about too closely. He knew he needed to step it up with her, use a kinder tone of voice, ask about her day, buy flowers or even something more expensive. Make love to her, though the idea was revolting now. He kept a meticulous note of anniversaries and birthdays, but none were coming up. Would a surprise piece of jewellery look too suspicious? Maybe a meal out or a weekend away, except they'd just had a holiday, and that had made things much worse, because on holiday you were with someone all the time, and it became harder and more exhausting by the minute to keep up the act. To wear the human-being disguise that you climbed into every day, more and more resentfully each time.

He was starting to feel alarmed, if he were honest. He had dipped too far into his account with her, and he didn't have the energy or resources to top it up. And she knew things. Things that could get him into a lot of trouble if she blabbed. So he had to turn it around with her, and fast, but he had no idea how to do it, because all he could feel towards her was absolute hate, hate and contempt. Hate that she saw too much of him. Contempt that she did and yet still did not leave.

Alison – then

Day three of the holiday, and they already had a rhythm, setting an alarm to make the 10 a.m. breakfast cut-off time and then hitting snooze several times so they had a mad scramble anyway, only to get caught in the queue for the omelette station. Alison was eating about ten times as much as she would for breakfast back home (a banana in the car if she was lucky). Fruit. Yoghurt. Pancakes. Sausages, beans, bacon. Little flaky pastries. Since she couldn't have coffee, she drank gallons of pink smoothies in little glass jars, then had to pee all day. Tom brought her a stream of water and juices by the pool, and she scrolled through silly online videos and sometimes even read her book. Was this relaxing, this feeling that your mind had shrunk to a pinprick and all you had to decide was whether to put on more suncream or to swim in the pool or the sea? If so, maybe it wasn't that bad.

But today something was off. Today, as they shuffled along the continental buffet, filling up their plates, she noticed a change in the energy. People were talking with heads down, eyes darting about. The staff wore glazed smiles, and she saw that the usual omelette chef was absent from his post.

'Something's happened,' she said. She had a sudden flashback to the night before last, the altercation she'd seen from the balcony.

Then last night, that scream she had done her best to ignore. Oh God. Had he hurt her, Beth? Was she alright?

Tom had felt the shift in energy too, with instincts born from years in the job. His hand rested on her lower back, protective. 'Here, you go and sit and I'll find out what's going on.'

But Alison already knew, deep in her bones, on the edge of her conscience. Come to think of it, hadn't there been a police car parked outside reception as they hurried through to fill up on fresh orange juice and hand-iced mini doughnuts? Her subconscious had taken it in even as her conscious mind was thinking about bacon. Now, she turned to look towards the beach and caught sight of a huddle of people, police uniforms, the flash of a blue light. A scene that was unmistakable in any language.

'Someone's dead,' she said, with the accidental portentousness of a character in a Russian play.

◆ ◆ ◆

'*Perdone, perdone* – excuse me, can I just – I'm a police officer, thank you.'

She squeezed through the rubbernecking crowds on the beach, using her belly as a battering ram to part them, glaring at those with their phones held up. She would make it a criminal offence to record a crime scene or even anyone having a bad time, a public meltdown or a seizure. People had no manners anymore.

She tried to assess the scene. There was a police cordon, and some Spanish officers were standing about in what seemed to her a desultory manner. She'd have had words with her PCs if they hadn't secured the scene better than this – the cordon didn't even stretch down to the waterline, and various tourists and gawkers had already gathered. But what had happened?

Then she saw it.

Dead bodies have a weight to them that no one alive displays. The mind rebels against the horror of it, especially when it's a young person, because Alison saw now this was a woman, who was perhaps in her late twenties. Not Beth. Dark hair tangled about her like seaweed. A red dress heavy with water, hiding any bloodstains that might have been on it. Eyes blank and staring. Face that terrible ashen hue that all corpses have.

It was all she could do not to charge forward and start bossing everyone around, lecture them about dignity in death, close the entire beach and have a stretcher and body bag ready. A hotel employee was in the sea up to his waist, lifting the body with his bare hands, for God's sake. A police officer stood up in it to his knees, arguing with the employee.

Not your jurisdiction, Alison reminded herself. And where was Tom? She'd lost him in the crowd in her irrepressible urge to run towards murder and mayhem. She stepped back. She was here not as a police officer, but as a tourist. A bystander too, and a pregnant one at that, who should take her baby far away from this monstrous act.

And that was when she saw them – the couple from the restaurant, the crying woman and her husband. They were standing a few metres away, on the inside of the cordon. The woman – Beth – had her arms folded tight across her stomach and her face was white and pinched. The husband – Vince – had his hands slapped to his face in horror. They were both fully clothed, in linen trousers, him in a patterned shirt, her in a loose cotton one and a wide-brimmed hat, as if they'd been up for hours.

Alison scanned the crowd for Tom, located him towards the back with an anxious look on his face, and waddled over.

'Can you not just run off like that?' he said.

'Sorry. I know, I know, not our business. God, what a thing to happen. That poor woman. Do you think she fell off a cruise ship, or maybe a migrant boat?'

You saw that sometimes on the news, bodies washing up on tourist beaches. Alison's mind was busy processing what she'd seen. No, that couldn't be the case, could it, because the woman was wearing an evening dress of some kind; also she was white which made it unlikely she was a migrant. Was it an accident – a drowning, a boat propeller? No, there would be blood in that case, and she couldn't see any. If only she could talk to the pathologist, maybe observe the post-mortem . . . 'But no, that's mad. Isn't it?' She often did this, spoke only part of her thoughts out loud, but Tom could usually follow her anyway. 'They're not going to let me near it. Or do you think they have some kind of, I don't know, exchange scheme for police?'

But this time he didn't answer. He was looking at Beth and Vince too, the same line between his brows as the night before at dinner.

'What?' She knew that look. 'Do you think they found her or something? That couple?'

That would explain why they were waiting beyond the cordon there, to give their statements. Maybe she should offer to help them, since they were British, and perhaps that could be her way in. Was it suspicious? In Alison's experience it was not unusual for the person who 'found' the body to be the killer. They couldn't sit with the guilt, with the waiting. Did that chime with what she'd seen the other night? She had observed him possibly assaulting his wife, restraining her, and Beth had been crying a lot, and now a woman was dead and they were standing behind the police cordon. Dots were starting to connect. Something about the interaction that night had really bothered her. Not just Beth's permanently leaking eyes, but the low, vicious whisper she'd heard the husband use, and the way he had clutched her wrist. You didn't need training in coercive control to recognise that this wasn't right. And then there was the scream, of course, which Alison had noted the time of, police instincts kicking in—

Tom said, 'Oh, it's probably nothing. But I've just remembered where I've seen that bloke before.'

She was about to ask Tom what he meant, but instantly forgot when there was a flurry of activity around the body. White-suited techs had brought a body bag to seal her into, to carry her to a waiting ambulance. There was something obscene about all these eyes watching her, but Alison couldn't tear her own away either, looking for clues. A hand flopped down as they zipped her in – like a pale fish – and Alison noted some of the nails were missing, the others long and red. Several rings.

'Hello! *Hola, señor!*' She waved down one of the remaining police officers, a gum-chewing man in sunglasses. Was it bad that she suddenly felt much more alive than she had done for days, stuffing herself at buffets and idling by the pool? This was real. Someone was dead, and finding out what had happened was what Alison was good at.

Two problems. Well, three. She had no jurisdiction here. She did not speak Spanish (the Duolingo owl had even given up guilt-tripping her). And she was seven months pregnant.

'*Señora, no es posible*,' said the Spanish officer, who had a natty little goatee and smelled of strong cologne and sweat.

'But I'm a detective. In the UK. Wait.' She fumbled in her beach bag and flashed her warrant card, not missing the roll of Tom's eyes that she had brought this with her in the first place. 'He is too.' She gestured to Tom, who sighed.

The officer scanned it then handed it back. Contempt rolled off him even more strongly than the cologne. He spoke in heavy English. 'Is Spain, not *Inglaterra*.'

'No, I know, obviously, but I might be able to help. The tourists, they're mostly English, no?' She waved her hands around at the crowds gathered to watch, many filming on phones still. 'I can help you with the – scene. Controlling it.'

His eyes travelled down to her belly, eloquent in silence.

'Yes, that too, but I can still work. I'm working back home.'

He walked away. Put his phone to his ear and simply walked away. Alison gaped in fury, then felt Tom's hand on her arm. 'Come on.'

'But I want to—'

'I know. But this isn't the way to do it. To him you're just a sunburnt tourist about to pop.'

Alison looked down at her outfit – swimsuit, floaty wrap, swollen feet in Birkenstocks – and had to admit he was right. 'I'm not sunburnt,' she grouched, even though she was a bit pink. The touch of his hand had left white marks on her skin. 'Alright, so what do I do?'

'There's precedent for British officers helping tourists who get in trouble abroad. The Madeleine McCann case, for example. But we have to do it right.'

Her eyes travelled to Vince and Beth, huddled behind the cordon, and she marched over towards them. 'Hey!'

They jumped at her voice, both their faces stretched with anxiety. 'Are you OK?' she called.

Beth answered. 'Oh – it's awful, really. We found her. Both of us.'

That was a weird way to put it. *Both of us.*

'Can you tell me what happened? I'm a detective, Tom too.' She indicated Tom, who gave an awkward wave, his disapproval clear. Was it her imagination, or did they both stiffen at the mention of her and Tom being cops?

Beth looked away. 'I don't know, really. It's such a horrible shock. I woke up early – we woke up, and we went for a walk, you know, to see the sunrise. And then I saw her just – floating.

I thought it was just old clothes at first. Or – a big jellyfish, something like that.'

'Did you touch her?' The instinct was often to fish the person out, try to resuscitate them even if that hope was long gone. Alison blamed TV shows where people sat up and coughed water long after brain death would have occurred in real life.

Beth shot her husband a look. He was staring out to sea, clutching both of his elbows. 'Eh – no. We didn't.' There was a tinge of doubt in her tone and Alison knew right away she had just been lied to. But why?

'Have you been arrested? Cautioned?'

'No! Why would we – no, they just wanted to ask some questions. But we don't speak Spanish, so I don't know . . .'

God, why hadn't she kept up her Duolingo? 'Me either, I'm afraid. But you can ask for a translator if you don't understand. They most likely speak English, though.'

Beth wore a shell-shocked expression Alison recognised from people unexpectedly caught up in a crime. The safe walls of their world crumbled around them, revealing the whole thing to be paper-thin, a cardboard set. 'But – they aren't going to take us to the station?'

'Likely they will, yes.' This was a dangerous moment. British citizens tended to believe the laws of their country protected them everywhere, but the truth was they didn't. Once you set foot in another territory, you were subject to the rules they had set. 'If it gets hairy, you should contact the embassy. Ask for consular support.'

'But how do we . . . ?'

She couldn't help it. 'Here, give me your phone.' Beth hesitated for a moment, then handed it over. Alison keyed her number in, careful not to look at anything else, and handed it back over the cordon. 'You can call us if you need help.'

Officer Too-Much-Cologne was waving over. 'No, *señora.*' He was indicating she should step back, so Alison did – or at least part of her did. Another pace was needed to bring the belly back as well.

'Come on,' Tom murmured. 'We shouldn't be here.'

Alison let him lead her away with extreme reluctance, casting glances over her shoulder at the frightened couple, who were now being directed to a police car. Whatever they now feared, she was sure it would be a hundred times worse than they could ever imagine. Being questioned by the police was always a shock, let alone in another country and in a foreign language.

'Why did you tell them that?' Tom asked, as they traipsed back up from the beach. Alison suddenly felt very tired, clammy with sweat all down her back. 'That we'd help?'

'Well, it's the right thing to do, isn't it? They're British, they're scared and clueless . . .'

'You never thought maybe they did it? Or one of them?' He signalled to a waiter and ushered her to sit at a table under an umbrella. She collapsed gratefully into a chair.

'What makes you say that? They seem pretty normal.' Although that was a stupid thing to say. Plenty of normal-seeming people had committed murders, and worn exactly the same shocked expression as Beth when they looked down at their blood-covered hands.

Tom said, 'I never finished telling you where I knew him from.'

Beth – now

'Well, that was weird.'

They were in an Uber going home, a silent driver in the front muttering occasionally into headphones in a language Beth could not make out.

Vince said nothing. He was staring out into the South London night, the red lights of the Crystal Palace TV tower in the distance. She'd wondered if he was going to ask what she'd been doing in the bedroom, but of course he hadn't. To ask her anything might fracture the fragile pane of ice they were standing on.

'Don't you think?' she tried again.

He turned his head slowly towards her, as if she were the most boring and irritating person in the world. 'What?'

'It was a weird night.'

'I didn't think so. The food was good. Why would you say that?'

Of course the food was good. Everything Joel and Corinna did was perfect, aesthetic, curated. Where was the real them? She couldn't believe anyone actually lived in that flat. Where was all their stuff?

Now, as they drew up to their own place, she realised Vince was looking at her in the dark of the car, waiting for an answer. 'They just asked so many questions,' she said weakly. It had felt unseemly, she thought. Probing so much about the dead woman, about Vince's experience of being questioned by the police, those hellish few days when she hadn't been allowed to talk to him or see him, and then that police officer she'd met on the beach, the pregnant woman with no boundaries, had got involved, and somehow Vince had come back to her. But it wasn't Vince anymore. It was a stranger here in the car with her, soon to be saying the same Vince phrase, *Here on the left, mate.* It looked and sounded like Vince. But Vince, her Vince, would never shut her out like this.

Vince had said something. 'Sorry?'

'I said, someone had to ask questions.'

'What does that mean?'

He looked out of the window. Sighed. 'Well, you could have made more of an effort. Or not drunk an entire bottle of wine by yourself.'

'What are you talking about? I didn't!'

'Didn't you?'

'Vince, I've not even had that much to drink, don't be ridiculous.' They had all been drinking, hadn't they? She didn't think she was that drunk, but the darkness of the park outside dissolved as tears filled her eyes. It wasn't fair.

They reached home. Getting out of the cab, she stumbled a little and realised she had in fact drunk too much. She gulped some water, pressing the cold glass to her face in the kitchen. In the bathroom, Vince was running the tap and brushing his teeth. She took out her phone to look at the brochure she'd photographed in Joel and Corinna's so-called flat. There was a little x on it, and a number written there – 734. Maybe the number of their room, given to them when they'd checked in? Beth squinted, turning the paper around and trying to remember the layout of the hotel. Joel and Corinna's room had been in the building opposite, their balcony facing Beth and Vince's, the pool behind it. This didn't look right. In fact – wasn't 734 her and Vince's room?

Beth went into the office and rifled through the holiday documents she'd dumped there, dropping them on the floor and not caring. The invoice from the hotel was printed out neatly. Mr and Mrs Jones, since she made the booking. The kind of mistake they'd have laughed about once. And there was the room they'd stayed in – 734.

Why did Joel and Corinna have a map with Beth and Vince's room number on it?

Alison – then

She digested what Tom was saying, glad of the shade of the umbrella. She'd let herself get too hot and bothered – her head felt fuzzy and her stomach heavier than lead. 'So that was him – Vince?'

'Yeah. He's changed his name, but I never forget a face, as you know.'

She realised she was rubbing her bump through her sack-like cotton top. 'You reckon the wife knows?'

'Maybe. She seemed jumpy as hell, didn't she?'

'And she's covering for him?' Something did not smell good, and it wasn't her own sweaty pits. God, she hated not being in the middle of it all. She had a million questions. Did Vince have an alibi, apart from his wife? Was there CCTV of the beach? Were there any witnesses? Did the dead woman have ID on her (she'd be amazed if that floaty red dress had pockets)? Did Vince have a record of any other crimes?

'Ali,' said Tom patiently.

'I know, I know. But we can't just do nothing.' As if she could read a book on a sun lounger now that poor young woman was dead.

'Any chance it's an accident? Someone off a migrant boat?'

'In a dress like that? Doubt it. Also, did you not see her neck?' It had been listing to the side when the body was pooled on to the stretcher, boneless and lifeless. Alison guessed from the rising bloom on the woman's skin, the angle of her slender neck, that she had been strangled.

He was nodding, reluctant. 'Yeah. So it's a murder?'

'I think so.' A murder, on their holiday, in this plush resort. Management would be doing their nut.

'Could have happened miles from here, with the currents. Or she fell off a cruise ship or something, or was pushed.'

'Could be.'

They both knew, with a gut instinct nurtured over years of interviewing people who were lying, that this wasn't true. She could tell from the nervousness of Beth and Vince on the beach, the way Beth had looked to him before answering if they'd touched the body, that this was dodgy as hell. Those two knew something about the dead woman. The *murdered* woman.

'How do I get in there?' she said, having once again had the bulk of the conversation with him inside her head. 'I mean, we're witnesses too. Right?'

Tom nodded even more slowly, like the irritating toy bulldog one of her colleagues, Brian, had on his desk. 'We could certainly go by and tell them what we saw.'

'In fact, we should. It's our duty, you could say. You know, I heard a scream last night.'

'You did?'

'Yeah, around half two. You woke me up with your snoring, and I heard it. I thought, you know, just people messing about. But I did take note of the time.'

He looked at her, half-smiling in exasperation. 'Trust you to find a murder even on holiday.'

'Oh well. I never did like massages anyway.'

◆ ◆ ◆

The police station was just a few streets away from the hotel, once they'd got the information out of the startled receptionist. 'Did something get stolen, *señora*? If so, you can report that to us first.'

Alison was impatient. 'No – someone washed up dead. On your beach. You can't have missed it.' There were three police officers in the lobby for a start, drinking coffee from the free machine.

The woman's mask-like face closed up. 'It's just a local matter, *señora*, nothing to worry about. A migrant.'

'She wasn't a migrant, and even if she was, that's still worth investigating, isn't it?'

'It happens now. All the time.'

'Well, look, my partner and I are police officers back home, and we'd like to give witness statements. We saw some things that might be helpful, we think.'

The woman's gaze travelled down Alison in a way she was becoming used to. 'Surely you would rather rest, *señora*. The police station, it is very rough, some not-good people there.'

'I work in one, I know what they're like. Can you just tell me where it is? The detectives who were here earlier, where would they have gone?'

With great reluctance the receptionist took out a map and circled a location with a pen. 'Please, we don't want our guests to worry. This is nothing to do with the hotel. The tide, it brings things in.'

Alison wasn't so sure about that, but she could imagine management was probably panicking that guests would start asking for refunds on their 300-euros-a-night rooms. You didn't expect them to come with a floating dead body.

Tom insisted on her covering up in a straw hat and loose shirt before they set out into the hot car park. Outside the air-conditioned lobby of the hotel, the sun was so fierce she almost staggered. Was this the future of Europe, summers too hot to even go outside in the daytime? Outside felt threatening too. There was a group of people standing just beyond the gate, being chivvied away by a security guard. They held placards, some in Spanish and some in English, that said '*Tourists Go Home*' and '*Keep Your Drunks Away*'. The Spanish one said '*Las Canarias No Se Vende*', which she thought meant 'The Canaries Are Not For Sale'.

She felt Tom's arm at her elbow. He said, 'It's just some anti-tourism protests. You remember we saw about them on the news.'

'Oh, right.' She knew the locals weren't happy about rising prices and the Airbnb culture, meaning they had nowhere to live. Guilt pricked at her.

'Let's take the car, maybe?' he said.

'No, no, it's not far, and it'll be hell to park.'

As they headed down the street, she saw several men dotted about in the shade every few metres, all alone, watchful, sometimes murmuring things to passers-by. Selling drugs to tourists, most likely. They were right on the edge of Europe, almost in Africa, and the problems of the rest of the world were pressing hard on the barriers they had built, starting to strain and crumble. As well as anti-tourism feeling, there was anger at the migrants coming in daily, desperate people putting strain on an already struggling economy here. She was glad of Tom with her to take her arm as they walked along, shops shuttered up for siesta time.

The police station was an ugly concrete building in shades of terracotta and cream, cooler than the street, though not air-conditioned, whirring with old-fashioned ceiling fans and high, frosted windows. Their footsteps echoed on the stone floor as they approached the desk.

'*Sí?*' A balding man in a navy uniform, smelling strongly of sweat.

'Um . . .' *Oh dear, what to say now?* 'English?'

He rolled his eyes, disappeared through a door behind reception, and came back a few moments later with a younger man in a shirt and tie, dark hair neatly cut. 'Hello, can I help you?'

'Oh, thanks. You speak English?'

'Yes, I lived in London for several years. How can I help you?' His eyes were also fixed on her stomach.

'It's about the body. On the beach.'

His expression shifted, became wary. 'We cannot give out information about that, *señora.*'

'We're police officers,' said Tom. 'Back home. And we're staying at that hotel, so we thought maybe you'd like our statements.'

The police officer looked them over, as if deciding whether they were telling the truth. Alison, sunburnt and heavily pregnant, probably didn't look like a detective, but he must have seen some kinship in Tom, burly and emanating a quiet assertiveness that always calmed situations. 'If you like. Follow me.'

As he led them through an alarmed door and down a dark corridor, uncarpeted and windowless, Alison saw a door open in the distance and caught a quick glimpse of something – it was Vince Castries, sitting at an interview table, looking absolutely in terror of his life.

Beth – now

She worked from home the day after the dinner party, nursing a fuzzy head and a stomach curdled with anxiety. Ignoring the emails pinging into her inbox, she stared at the pictures she'd taken in Joel and Corinna's apartment. The pills seemed to be for a mood disorder, in Corinna's name, and again she felt vaguely ashamed she had been so nosey. But she was desperate. She studied the creased resort map, recalling the real-life version, the heat on her skin, the gentle hiss of water sprinklers keeping all that greenery alive, the ever-present crash of the waves. That made her think of the young woman's body, floating in them like rubbish.

Although she had promised herself not to, she found she was googling it. There wasn't much online, but she did find many other accounts of death in the Canaries, lots of capsized migrant boats, and even shark attacks, which surprised her, as that was not a worry she'd even factored into their time there. Drug deaths. Car accidents, people knocked off scooters. Several other murders. Eventually she found the death, Ana Garcia de Vasquez. The report was in Spanish, so she clicked the translate option at the top of the page. Initially it had been reported as a drowning, and then later reports called it a suspicious death. It was just the facts, that someone had been arrested but released without charge. There was so little here, as opposed to the high-profile true-crime cases that captured the imagination. Why did no one care that one young Spanish woman had been killed? Even Beth had not cared that much, if she was honest. All she had wanted was to clear her husband and get away from that place, back to their own country, where they had the privilege of being citizens and understood the law and language. And they were back. Vince had been released, and some young African men had since been arrested and questioned, fuel for the anti-migrant movement in the islands. Nothing to do with her.

And yet. Beth could not forget Ana, even if the internet had. The red dress floating in the waves, darkened by saltwater, the gold toenails. The memory of her alive, so pretty and talented.

She was up and on her feet before she had even admitted to herself what she was going to do. In the olden days, before all this, Vince had also worked from home three days a week, and if they coincided they would meet for lunch in the kitchen, bowls of home-made soup or cheese on toast, chat about their days, sometimes sneak out for a walk in the park, holding hands, kissing goodbye on the landing with reluctance. *See you later, my love.* How long since he had used a pet name for her? She couldn't even remember. He kept a desk in the spare room, while she preferred to be in the living room, as it was warmer, and she could look out the window at people going by whenever she got bored. Now, she pushed open the door to the room. Rarely used, it had a forlorn and chilly feel. This had been where their eventual baby was going to sleep, something that had not been mentioned for over a year now, by tacit agreement. There was a fold-up sofa bed, a wardrobe, a yoga ball left over from pandemic exercising. And Vince's desk, an old chipboard one with a scratched surface, an empty laptop stand. The laptop lived at the office now, and in any case she wouldn't be able to get into it.

Was this who she was now? Someone who went through her husband's computer?

She opened the top drawer and rifled through it. An old stapler, lots of receipts, several Allen keys and leftover screws. What was she even looking for? Some evidence her husband wasn't who she'd thought? A clue that linked him to a dead Spanish woman, or going further back, some more information on the incident last year, the thing at the wedding?

Snooping was addictive, it seemed. She found herself surrounded by piles of paper, sitting back on her heels on the carpet. People didn't leave incriminating evidence lying around in this digital era – photographs showing them with a murder victim they weren't supposed to know, letters from secret lovers. It was all on his phone, and that was never out of his sight, except when charging at night right beside his face.

But here was something. After going through about a hundred old bank and pension statements, she did take a cursory scan over one from the previous month. They had a joint account for bills, but kept their own for other purchases, so she didn't have a good sense of what Vince earned or what he spent. Did he have a gambling habit, like Janice's brother, who had re-mortgaged the house without his wife knowing? Or another woman? She ran her eye down it. Sainsbury's, petrol, online subscriptions – she should suggest going through and cancelling all those random ones they both had – and what was this? There was a payment, a large payment – £1,000 – going out every month. The payee was just a group of initials. EMF. What was that? A country? A person? She took out her phone and googled it, but nothing came up.

Beth sat back and thought about it, the quiet of the flat settling around her, a rattling in the pipes that said it was cold enough for the heating to come on. She hadn't really expected to find anything dodgy – in fact she had been hoping to quiet the worry that whispered down the back of her neck, growing stronger and stronger for months and screaming in her ear since the holiday

– but here it was. A payment she knew nothing about. It was almost as much as the mortgage, but that came out of the joint account, same with the bills. Carefully, she stacked up all the letters and detritus and put them back where she'd found them. Would he know she'd been through his things? Would he leave the statement for her to find if it really was a secret? Maybe he wanted her to see it. Maybe all of this, the coldness, the shortness, the silent treatment, and even Tenerife, had been to try and send a message. That her marriage was over.

Alison – then

'I don't understand why you are here.'

The detective – Alejandro was his name, and Alison kept singing the Lady Gaga song over and over in her head – sat scowling at them across the table of another small interview room. He had his shirtsleeves rolled up and sweat stains blooming, but he was undeniably good-looking. Barely thirty, by the looks of it.

Tom tried his man-to-man voice. 'We were on the scene not long after she was found.'

'But is not a murder.'

'How do you know that?' said Alison.

'She drown.' He said this like it was obvious.

Alison was impatient. 'Are you sure? You've had the post-mortem done already, have you? Quicker than the UK then.'

His scowl deepened. 'She is in the water. People drown here all the time. Strong currents.'

'She went swimming in that dress?'

'Maybe a boat or something. Who knows? Many yachts here.'

It was possible, but Alison had spotted her neck and recognised the signs of strangulation. 'Did you actually see the body, Alejandro?'

He hesitated. 'Not yet. I was not there.'

'Right. I understand you maybe don't want to say yet that a young woman has been murdered, but I don't think this was an accident. Right, Tom?'

He screwed up his face. 'Hard to say without the PM results.'

'Right. Also, why have you taken in a British tourist, if you think it's an accident?'

'Is procedure. They find the body, pull it out of the water. We need prints and so forth.' So Vince had touched the body. And they'd lied about it to Alison. Interesting.

Tom met her eyes. Touching her was a normal human reaction, trying to get someone out of the water. Of course, it might not be true. Vince might have been holding her under. 'Well, do you want our statements anyway?'

The detective sighed. 'Fine. OK. What did you see?'

They outlined their morning: walking to breakfast, seeing a small crowd gathering on the beach, then going down to find the cordon already in place. He wrote it down, but his raised eyebrows told Alison he was not very impressed, and she didn't blame him. They were no more than bystanders. 'This woman, you see her before ever?'

Alison shook her head. 'I couldn't tell. I would have remembered the dress if I'd seen her, I think.' Long, floaty, and with a gold chain belt, it was the kind of thing she could never pull off even if she wasn't pregnant. 'Did the hotel release CCTV? They have cameras everywhere, security guards too.'

'We will get it. But you assume she was even at the hotel. The tides wash things in, you know. From different places. Boats, other islands, even Africa.'

Tom said, 'Has anyone been reported missing? Fallen off a yacht or a ferry, that sort of thing?' Alison had a vision of a woman running barefoot along a deck, red dress flying – no, wait, that was *Titanic*.

'Many people are reported missing after a Friday night here. We will follow up.'

It was a wide net – not just the whole island, but the entire ocean nearby.

'She's not a migrant,' Alison said. 'Not in that dress.'

'We do not know anything for sure, *señora*.'

'Detective.'

His scowl became more of a growl. 'Thank you for your information, Detectives. If you think of anything . . .'

'There was something else,' said Tom, surprising her. 'The scream last night. Remember?'

Alison had almost forgotten. 'Oh yes! So I heard a scream last night, from our balcony. At 2.38 a.m.' The detective raised his eyebrows, wrote it down.

'You are sure?'

'Very sure. It sounded like a woman.' She had a horrible thought just then – what if she'd heard the dead woman being attacked? And done nothing to help her? Surely someone else would have noticed if she were being murdered right in the resort.

Tom said, 'There was a lot of activity in general last night. I woke up myself not long before you, and heard laughing, and music.'

'You did?' Alison couldn't help but say. 'Was it from a balcony in another building? If so, I heard them too, when I was up. Lots of racket.'

Alejandro was writing again. 'What time was this?'

Tom said, 'Just after two – 2.03 a.m. I looked at the clock too.' This was why detectives made good witnesses.

'Did you see who it was?'

'No, but there's one couple who've been generally making lots of noise since they arrived, and I assumed it was them.'

Something they'd said had intrigued the detective. She could tell from his newly alert posture and eye contact. He took out his phone and held it up.

'These?'

Alison peered at the screen, irritated already by the tinny sound of a TikTok video. It was the woman from the hotel pool, the one with big hair and a loud laugh, and her partner, who never seemed to button up his shirt, even for dinner.

'Yeah, that's them. I don't know their full names.'

It said on the video, though – Corinna Cooper. Lifestyle coach and wellness influencer. Could you describe yourself as an influencer? Wasn't that something other people had to decide on?

The detective seemed to be wondering how to phrase his question. 'Tell me, do you ever see this couple with the other – the ones who find the body?'

'Vince and Beth?' Alison thought it over. 'I don't know if I have. They only arrived a couple of days ago, I think, this lot.'

'I saw them,' said Tom, again surprising her. 'In the bar last night when we were going to bed – the four of them were drinking together.'

Alejandro wrote down some more things. Alison was disappointed in herself – had pregnancy destroyed her powers of observation? She was dead on her feet by nine every night at the moment, unable to see anything but the path to bed. She had no memory of the two couples being in the bar.

Alejandro pulled something from his trouser pocket and slid it over the table. A business card. Alejandro Costa. 'Please. If you remember anything else, call me.'

Feeling a bit smug that they had after all been helpful, Alison pushed back the chair and stood up, annoyed to feel Tom's hand on her arm but needing it all the same.

Tom said, 'There was some aggro round our hotel earlier too.'

The officer looked confused. 'Aggro?'

'Like a protest. No to tourism.'

His face closed over. 'Oh, yes. Our islands depend on tourism, but it is like a hungry animal. It eats up everything, all the houses, all the apartments, all the space. And the noise and rubbish and the drunk people falling over in the street and being sick in the gutters.'

Alison felt another twinge of guilt. She knew it was the British who were most guilty of such behaviour. 'Housing is expensive here?'

He flicked her a look. 'Many of my colleagues, and the staff of the hotel, they must live with their parents still, or in huts, there is no air-conditioning, no hot water sometimes.'

'Really?' Alison was shocked by that, perhaps naively. She imagined working in a hotel did not pay much, even one where a massage cost over a hundred euros.

'There is some talk that maybe a tourist kill her. Our local girls, not safe from these drunk men.' He checked himself. 'Though we do not know she was killed, of course.'

And Vince, a tourist, was sitting in the cells, their chief suspect.

'OK, well – thank you for your time.'

They exited the station and went back out into the heavy heat of the street. No further sign of Vince, or indeed of Beth.

'How did you notice all that?' she asked, as they walked along the tree-lined street. 'About them being with the other couple.' A thought struck her. 'Is it because she looks like a model, that TikTok woman?' She was like a wisp of a thing, compared to Alison's current beached whale.

Tom walked a few paces more. Then he said, 'No. It's because something weird was going on. With that lot. The four of them. Vince and Beth, and the other couple.'

Beth – now

Vince came home late that night, well after eight. Closer to nine. Beth had made dinner, vegetable stew with barley, but it had long since gone cold as she waited for him. Her mind agitated, she'd spent the time googling Joel and Corinna. The first thing she noticed was that they'd both locked their social media accounts, set them to private. When she'd looked them up out in Tenerife, they both had thousands of followers. He did mostly to-camera discussions of business issues – investing, savings, stuff that should have been boring, but he delivered it in a punchy, 'Here's how to beat the man' style, often topless, sometimes with his hair long and loose about his shoulders. He had some kind of investment fund that Beth didn't really understand. There were also yoga videos and fitness tips. He was irritatingly fit and could do an astonishing number of chest-to-floor press-ups.

As far as she recalled, Corinna's account had more memes, more arty shots of her hand clasping glasses or of her staring artfully out the window. There wasn't a single bad picture of her anywhere in existence, it seemed, and Beth knew that the reality was just as toned and taut. She wasn't sure how old Corinna was – could have been anything from twenty-five to a youthful forty. There was a stiffness around her lips that suggested work had been done. Why would they have locked their accounts? Corinna couldn't take a step without Instagramming it, it seemed. This, coupled with the early check-out, just seemed suspicious.

Beth heard a key in the lock, and realised she had spent hours on this, endlessly scrolling through the internet. In search of what? Proof that Joel and Corinna were good people, an explanation of their interest in Vince and Beth, answers about what had happened that night she had no memory of?

She went to the bathroom and washed her face, staring in the mirror at her haggard skin and limp hair. She had not been sleeping since the holiday, often waking up with a gasp and finding Vince's side of the bed empty, as she had in Tenerife. Usually he was in the living room playing games, but once or twice he was just gone, and she was too scared to ask where. Secretly, she had been looking at her finances and doing sums in her head. She couldn't afford the mortgage by herself, and the rent on a one-bed flat would also clean her out each month. It was so much more expensive to be single. She could probably move in with her mum and dad, but the commute from Sittingbourne would be gruelling, not to mention the cost of living back with her parents at thirty-seven. It couldn't be true, could it? They weren't really splitting up?

He was coming in now, and for a moment she felt something strange in her solar plexus – fear. She was scared of him. Her own husband.

'What?' he said, seeing her standing there, wringing her hands.

I know about the money you're paying out. What's going on, Vince? What's going on?

'Nothing,' she said nervously, bottling it again. 'I made dinner.'

'OK.'

'You're very late. I can heat it up.'

She waited for him to say sorry for his lateness, but he didn't, just took off his jacket and headed into the bathroom, phone in hand. Beth warmed up the stew, then called for him. She called five times before he came back out, a grouchy expression on his face.

As she pushed the tasteless food around her plate, she tried again. 'Are you OK, love? You've seemed really off since we came back.'

He stared into his dinner. His phone was beside him, never more than a hand's-length away.

'You can tell me if something's wrong. Whatever it is, I'd rather know. And maybe we can fix it.' Her voice wavered.

'There's nothing you can do.'

'So something is wrong?'

He sighed. Looked somewhere over her left shoulder. 'You don't think being arrested over a murder, racially profiled, abused, was enough to make me feel bad?'

'Of course. But even before that things weren't right. You know that. We barely spent any time together on the holiday.'

'We see each other every day.'

'But not quality time. Only to eat dinner, and sometimes not even then, plus you're always on your—'

Right on cue, his phone buzzed, and he reached for it right away. She watched his face watch the screen, reflecting on how often she had seen this view in the past few months. The top of his head, his eyes staring at something she couldn't see, a small frown puckering his forehead. What was he looking at? Who had messaged?

'Vince,' she tried, keeping her voice as soft as she could. 'The phone. You're on it all the time. I really – I find it really hard.'

No answer. He didn't look up; he was typing something. A response? Who to? Corinna?

'Vince.'

'What?' he snapped. 'Will you stop policing my phone use? You're not my mother.'

'I'm trying to say something here.'

'It's work. You want me to just ignore my work?'

'Well, yes? If it's dinnertime and I'm trying to talk to you.'

With an exaggerated sigh he put the phone down on the table. 'What is there to say? You've asked what's wrong, I've told you nothing. I'm busy. I went through something horrible. That's all.'

'But then we should get help, find you someone to talk to.'

'I'm not crazy, Beth.'

'I didn't – you don't have to be crazy to talk to a therapist!' Beth was starting to think she needed one herself.

Vince pushed back his chair, leaving the rest of his dinner. He used to clean up if she cooked, but she would stay in the kitchen and talk to him, respond to news items or songs on the radio, sweep the floor. Now he was just walking out. Didn't even say where he was going, but she knew it was to play games in the living room and ignore her all night. He picked up his phone to take with him, and for a second she saw the screen. He hadn't turned off his notifications, which maybe meant he had nothing to hide or maybe that he didn't care what she thought. Either way, she was able to see who had messaged him – an unknown number. She couldn't see what the message said.

Vince and his phone left the room, and Beth sat alone, feeling hot, salty tears run down into her uneaten meal. She dashed into the bathroom to hide her sobs, examined her face in the loo mirror for traces of what she was going through, finding them in the creases around her eyes and the grey, haggard tone of her skin. So much for a post-holiday glow – it had made things even worse than before.

Alison – then

'God, people die all the time here. Lot of non-suspicious circumstances.' It was later in the day, and the hotel staff were doing their best to cover up a dead body being found on the beach. Extra drinks had been offered round the pool, not that Alison could avail herself of this, and notes had been slipped under every door saying that support was available if anyone was disturbed by events. It had been described as a 'regrettable accident', much as the police had said, but Alison was convinced otherwise.

'I'm surprised how much violent death there is out here. Drunk tourists falling off balconies, going missing, drowning, coming off mopeds. Did you know there are sharks, even? Six people got killed by them!'

Tom was patient. 'That's literally fewer than I've seen die of dodgy vapes back home. But yes, it's a dangerous place. People let down their guard on holiday, drink too much. That's why it's not definitely a murder.'

Alison wasn't so sure. Of course the local police wanted to play it down. They wouldn't want word getting out that there was a killer on the island. If the TikTok crime lot got hold of it there'd be no peace ever again.

'They just both seemed so jumpy. Beth and Vince, I mean. I wonder if it's because of that old case he was involved in. Can you remember the outcome?'

Tom resettled himself on the lounger. For all his teasing, he also liked nothing more than a good gossip about cases. 'He was never charged with anything, but he was arrested, so it'll be on the system.'

'And what did you think?'

'Hard to say. I remember he was shit-scared – not much contact with the police before. Keen to dob the others in, clear himself.'

'You believed him?'

Tom shrugged. 'I was too junior to be doing the interviews. I didn't not believe him.'

Alison had tried googling the case, but there was nothing online about Vince's involvement, since he'd never been charged. She'd often wished there was a 'bad vibes' record that you could check when you first met someone, for those thousands of people who were 'just' cruel or abusive or controlling, or even those who raped and hit but it was never reported, or it was reported and the case never prosecuted, or it was prosecuted and then fell apart in court. The actual convictions were just the tiniest tip of an iceberg of harm.

Did Beth Jones know that her husband had been wrapped up in a murder before? Alison wished she could access HOLMES, but it wasn't allowed, even if she had been at the station. She picked up her phone again – sod unplugging, she'd had a shock and needed to soothe herself with some nice dopamine – and began to search for the name of the hotel across various social media apps. Lots of posts came up – the usual holiday shots of hot-dog legs, cocktails against the sunset, mind-numbingly banal captions like 'Annnnnd relax' or 'Not a bad start to the holiday'. She quickly came to the accounts of the other couple, the younger ones who seemed to be some kind of influencers. Lots of travel and lifestyle tips and annoying memes and challenges, and both of them too good-looking to be real.

'Enjoying yourself?' said Tom judgily, from behind his hefty book (the cover adorned with several squashed mosquitoes, because it was at least better for that than her phone).

'Yes, thanks.'

'Find out anything?'

'Well, Ken and Barbie are kind of low-level internet famous. I bet they got some of their holiday free.' She had gleaned as much from their posts marked *#spon* and bits of promoted content. Various gushing captions about the spa and pools and food. She'd seen them around the place, making their 'content' and forcing you to move if you were in shot, which she resented, and she had generally taken against the man's chirpy 'cheeky chap' energy and the woman's mid-Atlantic drawl and simpering facial expressions. But that didn't mean they were involved in this death, of course. They were on the balcony when Alison heard the scream below, if it had come from the poor woman who died. Tom had told the police the couple were with Vince and Beth the night before, all of them drinking together when he and Alison went up to bed. Chatting round the pool. Alejandro the detective had certainly seemed to perk up when she mentioned them. Why? 'What was it you found weird about them hanging out, the four of them?'

He screwed up his face. 'I don't know, really. They were too loud, drinking too much. Like there was something fake about it.'

She mulled it over for a while longer. There *was* something fake about it, but what? 'There's one thing I don't get,' she said out loud.

'Hmm?'

'Why would a couple like that be friends with the other ones? I mean, they're very different, aren't they?'

Vincent Castries. Beth Jones. Corinna Cooper. Joel Hardiman. Four people Alison would not have expected to know each other or become friends, and yet they had been hanging out the night of a woman's death. Was it just the phenomenon of holiday mates? Years ago she and Tom had gone on a walking tour in New York and made friends with what seemed like a lovely couple from Texas. They'd had such a laugh they'd agreed to meet for dinner the following night, only to be greeted by pamphlets and a lecture about letting the Lord into their lives and ending their sinful unmarried union. Since then she was always wary of people who tried to chat to you on holiday. They clearly hated their own spouse or family if they couldn't get through two weeks without roping in other people. Where were the other couple now? Their statements would be important, surely. Did the police here know about the connection, and would they think to interview them? She squinted about the pool but could see no sign of them, or hear the tinny sound of their videos recording.

She continued to google, looking for answers that might not exist. Suddenly she sat bolt upright. 'Tom!'

'What?' He took out his AirPod, which he'd put in perhaps to get some peace from her obsession with this case.

'They've identified the body.' She scanned the news article quickly. 'Ana Garcia de Vasquez, a local singer and musician. So she was from here, not a tourist or a migrant.' Likely not off a yacht or cruise ship then either. There was a picture of her, sultry in a low-cut dress, holding a microphone and standing beside a piano. Something chimed in Alison. She knew who the woman was.

Beth – now

She couldn't believe she was doing this. Going through his desk drawers was one thing; that could maybe be explained away as tidying. They weren't locked, so it wasn't that much of an invasion of privacy. She could have been looking for Post-its or a charging cable or something. But this – sitting in the car outside Vince's office – this was taking things a little bit too far. She was supposed to be in a meeting now, but she'd faked a double booking and let Janice cover for her.

Vince worked for a green-energy start-up which had its headquarters in a business park near Lewisham. He used to drive in, but since the return to work, post-Covid, he'd started taking the tram and was talking about selling the car. Beth had put her foot down on that, though it was getting harder to justify as their finances were squeezed more and more.

Vince had left at eight and should have been in just before nine. It was now nine fifteen, and there was no sign of him. If he'd arrived and spotted the car, she'd been planning to say he'd forgotten something – his wallet, which he hadn't carried now for months, and she knew it. There was a good chance he wouldn't see her, since he never looked up from his phone these days. But where was he? The feeling was back, the gasping for breath like she was being held underwater. What was going on? How could it take him this long to get here – had he stopped off somewhere, or had she somehow missed him?

By nine twenty, she knew she couldn't put it off any longer. Maybe he'd been injured or had an accident on his way in, and then wouldn't she feel bad with all her suspicions? She took a deep breath and undid her belt, marching up to the reception of the shared office space. The receptionist was not someone she knew, so she asked for Vince. The woman behind the desk, who had very long nails painted with little pumpkins – in September! – pressed a few buttons on her computer. 'Sorry, who did you say you wanted?'

'Vincent Castries. Vince. At Green Bulb.'

'Um, it's not coming up on the system. Hang on.'

Beth waited a few moments by the vending machine that only sold organic snacks, and then someone she recognised came out of the lift. Oh yes, it was the head of marketing, her hair part-dyed pink. She waved to Beth. 'Oh hi! Do you remember me? Vince's wife, right?'

'Yes, of course, from the Christmas party. Abeko, isn't it? I just stopped by to give Vince his wallet, thought he might need it.'

She couldn't read the expression on Abeko's face. 'Eh, sorry, Beth, this is a bit weird.'

'What? Is he OK?' Her pulse soared. Her chest had a weight on it.

'Well, the thing is, Beth – Vince hasn't worked here for months.'

◆ ◆ ◆

She gripped the wheel hard, aware that the world was detaching from her and peeling away like the skin of an orange, and the last thing she needed now was to crash the car too. Vince would only berate her about the cost of fixing it, and say once again they needed to get rid of it. But how could she ever listen to another thing he said? This man who had been chiding her for months, telling her she needed to be more environmental, pay more attention to cleaning, eat better, drink less, vote differently, he had been lying to her the entire time. He hadn't worked at Green Bulb since May, Abeko had said. That was the entire summer. So all those times he'd snapped at her and said he was working and needed to be on his phone, he wasn't, because he had no job. He had been leaving the house every day at eight but not coming here to this office, because he didn't work there. So where had he been going? And why had he left? Abeko had spoken of it very carefully, in couched HR language, with eyes averted, so Beth didn't know if he'd quit or been fired. *Moved on from here. Non-disclosure agreements. You should ask him. Really, Beth, you should ask him.* But why would he not tell her when it happened? And where was he right now, if not at work?

The facts sat inside her like cement blocks. Her husband had undergone some kind of personality shift over the past year, had become a stranger who snapped, and avoided, and would not look at her. He was paying out a large sum of money every month to someone, and getting texts from unknown numbers that made him stiffen up in anxiety, and he had quit or lost his job. He had been arrested for murder in Spain, and she had found him on the beach, cradling the body of a dead woman. What did it mean? What was going on? Who was her husband, really?

Beth gasped so hard in pain she almost swerved into the path of a bus. Getting a grip on herself, she blinked away the tears that clouded her eyes. Carrying on as carefully as she could, she saw that there were no answers to those questions that she didn't find unbearable.

Alison – then

Tom looked up in alarm. 'Where are you going?'

'Hang on a minute. I just need to check something.'

Moving faster than she had in weeks, she was on her feet and shuffling rapidly past the sun loungers towards the lobby. The cool of the air con settled on her like a fine mist, the whole place smelling pleasantly of flowers and lemon from the water dispenser.

The receptionist, the same one with the perfect make-up, spotted her. '*Señora?* Do you need help?' But Alison continued on like a cadaver dog.

Where had she seen it? Would they have removed it yet? No! There it was. There was a poster on a stand by the bar, listing the various events at the hotel. Kids' club, karaoke, and three times a week live music in the bar, with local singer Ana Garcia de Vasquez. It was even the same photo from the news article.

Breathless, the receptionist came up behind Alison, clacking in her heels. '*Señora?*'

'That's her, right? The dead woman. She sang here?'

Silence.

'I know she did, so no point in pretending.'

That poor young woman. Alison remembered her now, how pretty she was, how sweetly she had sung. And now she was gone.

'Yes, *señora*, very sadly we have learned that Ana did die. We are all very sad about this.'

'Are there cameras in the lobby? What time did her performance end, usually?' Alison checked the dates – she would have been singing the night she died.

'Of course, we gave all our footage to the police, we will do everything we can to help. She finished around 1 a.m., maybe. It depends how many people there are.'

Even now, Alison could see several portly, middle-aged British men propping up the bar and enjoying afternoon pints. Her mind was whirring. A pretty woman like that would attract a lot of unwanted attention from drunk tourists, she imagined. If anyone was seen talking to her on the CCTV, then they might have followed her out of the hotel.

'Did she drive here?' Alison asked. The receptionist looked confused. 'How did Ana get to work? She didn't live in, I imagine.'

'She has a car, yes.'

Which was probably still in the car park, assuming the police hadn't got that far yet. 'Can you show me?'

'Madame?'

'Can you show me her car, if it's still here? You have to issue parking badges, right?' She remembered this from when they arrived in their hire car, which they'd barely used so far since it was too hot to go out. A waste of money.

She was aware the receptionist had no need to help her. She was a young woman too, no more than mid-twenties, her dark hair smoothed back into a bun, and heavy make-up for such a hot day. 'I hear someone say you are a police lady, back in England?'

'That's right, I'm a detective. I'm just trying to help. I think maybe someone hurt Ana.'

The receptionist lowered her voice. 'The police say it is an accident. She drowned, she fell in the water.'

'But how could that be . . . ?' She glanced at the receptionist's name tag, pinned to her ample bosom. 'Maria Theresa, yes? Would Ana ever go to the beach after she finished working?'

'No, never. She would be in her nice dress. Not for sand and water.'

'Right. She'd go straight home, then?'

'Sometimes we all have a drink, the late-night staff and her and her piano man, his name is Eduardo. But not last night, I don't think.'

Alison would definitely want to speak to him as well. 'So you liked her.'

'Yes. She was a very nice girl.' Maria Theresa's voice wobbled slightly.

'I'm sorry for your loss. Now, please, if you could just show me whether her car is here still? I won't touch it, I promise. I'd just like to know her movements.'

Maria Theresa nodded. 'OK. I did not work last night, but I can ask who did, what time she leave.'

'Thank you. This way?'

Alison and the girl trooped out to the car park, back into the blinding sun, and she was shown a small red Mini, stylish, the back seat heaped with shoes, cardigans, sheet music. So Ana had not driven home last night. Maybe someone had given her a lift? Or maybe she never left the hotel. Alison fished out her phone from the pocket of her vast beach wrap and snapped a quick picture, feeling the unease of the receptionist beside her. But she was only taking a picture, not interfering with anything. Surely the Spanish police would tow this soon, search it for evidence.

'There you are! Can you not just take off like that, please? You can still put on some speed when you're after something.' Tom had come huffing over, his T-shirt wet with sweat under the arms.

'Sorry, sorry. This is her car. The singer, Ana. That's who died.' Tom eyed it, then Alison. He knew the significance of it still being here without her having to explain.

On his arrival, the receptionist had snapped back on her professional mask. 'Please, *señor, señora*, may I bring you back inside? Is very hot today. I can arrange for some drinks by the pool?'

'That's OK,' said Alison. She would be back when the time was right to probe for more info. She cast a final look at Ana's car, the detritus of a young woman's life, full of energy and activity, a little messy, some empty coffee cups on the passenger seat showing she likely drove alone most of the time. Who would come to claim it now, and these items she had needed, made at one stroke unnecessary, useless?

In the lobby, she saw Maria Theresa hesitate, recognising the look of someone who wasn't sure whether or not to share a detail. Alison prompted, 'Was there something else? Even if it doesn't seem important, you know, it could be.'

'There was a man. He was – bothering her, maybe. The last day or two.'

Alarm bells were going off in Alison's head like sirens. There was, so very often, a man who had been bothering a woman who later ended up on a slab in the morgue. 'Do you know who? One of the staff?'

'She said it was a guest. Someone staying at the hotel.' Like Vince Castries, who had grabbed his wife's arm, who had made her cry every day of their holiday that Alison had seen.

'Anything else you know?'

Maria Theresa shook her head, and Alison saw the hollows under her pretty eyes. 'I don't know. Just that there was a man and he annoyed her, hanging about to talk to her, trying to buy her drinks, but she did not drink when working, you know. There is always a man.'

Wasn't there just. 'I'm sorry,' said Alison, as gently as she could. 'She was your friend, yes?'

'Yes.' She gulped, the weight of the shock pulling her down.

Alison would love to tell her that went away, that you got used to people being gone, but she knew that sudden and violent death took years to process, if you ever did. The brain could not take it in, a young and healthy person suddenly not being there, turned to a slab of cold blue flesh locked away in a drawer in the hospital. All she could do – all she had ever known how to do – was try to catch the person who had done it.

Beth – now

'I've invited Joel and Corinna tonight.'

Beth stared at him. She had waited all day for Vince to come home so she could have it out with him, and now here he was when she came out of the bathroom, sorting his post in the kitchen, calmly telling her this. 'What? Tonight?'

'Yeah, we've nothing on, so I thought, why not?'

A spontaneous dinner invitation was so far from their normal way of doing things that Beth had no idea what to say.

'But – we've nothing in.'

'I'll go out now and buy things. Caribbean night. I'll cook.'

'What time did you say?'

It was already six o'clock, and she'd been planning a plain dinner of fish and veg, likely not to be eaten at all after the colossal row they would no doubt have about his lying and her stalking. She had even faced the possibility that this might be it, made mental plans to go to her mum's. And now instead she was hosting Corinna and Joel, who she did not trust at all. But. This was the most animated she had seen Vince for months, and he was offering to cook too.

'Half seven, eight maybe.' It was a Tuesday night. But then, he clearly did not have to be up for work.

Beth forced a smile. She would play along for as long as she could, and maybe she'd learn something more about what Joel and Corinna were up to, if their sudden friendship had anything to do with Vince's strange behaviour.

'Alright. Maybe some nice wine, since those two are so into it. I'll see what we have in and set the table.'

◆ ◆ ◆

'So it was really wonderful, quite transformational in fact. You should go.'

Beth did not have the money to go to the fancy gym Corinna was talking about, which offered sound baths as well as reformer Pilates and spa treatments. At least Vince's unemployment explained their financial hole and his debts. But why was he paying someone nearly a grand a month then? Make it make sense. Her mind kept churning over it, and she could barely focus on the wittering of Joel and Corinna. They looked out of place in Vince and Beth's run-down flat, their tans still glowing, both in fashionable, expensive-looking clothes, as if untouched by the autumn drizzle outside.

'Do you work out, Beth?' asked Corinna, in what felt like a pointed way.

She was wearing a cashmere jumper in an elegant oatmeal shade, gold hoop earrings. Simple luxe. Beth was still wearing the long-sleeved top and jeans she'd put on that morning, and make-up had proved beyond her, she was so worried and confused. Anyway, there was nothing she could do to compete with Corinna, who appeared in a perfumed cloud and curled her feet up on Beth's sofa with lithe grace. She had slipped off her loafers at the door and her feet were bare and brown, the red polish unchipped. Beth's socks had holes in them, and one uncut toenail was poking through.

‘Oh, I don’t really have time. Sometimes I go for a run. Vince and I did a half marathon once together, actually.’

‘You should do weight-bearing exercise, very important at your age.’

At Beth’s age? Not at our age? Surely she was not very much older than Corinna, though it was hard to tell. Beth fumed quietly into the delicious orange wine they had brought, but which no one had been allowed to drink until after a long lecture from Joel about the small organic vineyard he had invested in near Devon.

‘You see, with climate change, UK viticulture is really taking off, and of course a natural designation implies . . .’ Beth had stopped listening after that. The sound of her own panicked pulse was drowning out everything else. The wine was nearly gone now, and Beth was already thinking what to open next, if she was to get through this night.

What was going on? Why were these people in her house? The curry had turned out well, Vince clearly making an effort for the first time in a long time, and Corinna praised it to the skies, making Beth feel inadequate that all she had done was serve drinks. All the while she was thinking, *Vince has lost his job. He’s been pretending to go to work for months. Vince is paying someone a thousand pounds a month.*

Vince does not love me anymore. The worst fear, the one that made her breath catch in her throat.

Corinna dabbed at her full lips with a Christmas-patterned napkin, all Beth had been able to find in the cupboards. ‘Well, that was delicious. Could you direct me to your bathroom, please?’

Beth did a mental scan – was it clean? She didn’t want Corinna to see the damp stains on the ceiling or the threadbare towels she’d never got round to replacing. But she could hardly say no. ‘It’s just down the hall on the left.’ Difficult to get lost in such a tiny flat. And now they would never be able to move to a house, and that meant starting a family was clearly not on the cards anytime soon. Though if, as she feared, her husband was leaving her, that wasn't going to happen either way. Oh God. How did she get here? It was like a nightmare.

Leaving the men to chat about electric cars, she gathered the plates and took them through to the kitchen, leaning for a moment on the counter. The place was a disaster zone – curry splashed up the walls and cupboards, ingredients left out, lids off jars, salt scattered over the worktop. It felt like another little gesture of disrespect from Vince. Outside, the moon was full and yellow, like a malevolent eye. She'd rather be up there, cold and alone in a barren wasteland, than here in her own flat with these people, all of them strangers to her. Even her own husband.

She heard a noise from the next room, like a door shutting. That was their bedroom. She peeked into the hallway. Corinna was coming out of their room, her hand on the door, a guilty expression on her face.

'Were you in our bedroom?' Beth knew she sounded accusing.

Corinna was unperturbed. 'So sorry! I went in the wrong door, and then I couldn't help looking at your pictures, so nice. You have lovely taste.'

She dodged easily past Beth, who noticed that the bathroom fan was not on, meaning the light hadn't been switched on recently, meaning Corinna hadn't even gone in there. What was she playing at? Beth pushed open the door to the bedroom, but could see nothing amiss.

◆ ◆ ◆

It was only later, after they had gone – close to midnight, and Beth had work in the morning – and she was lying in bed beside an out-cold, snoring Vince, who had been asleep when she came back from the bathroom and not even said goodnight, that Beth realised what was wrong. There were no pictures in the bedroom. They'd been removed to paint it six months ago, but Vince had never got round to doing it. They were still stacked up in the office in a heap. So just as Beth had snooped in their flat, Corinna was snooping in hers.

The question behind all of this was – why?

Him

'It's nice, isn't it?'

She'd said this about five times already. He clenched his jaw, took a second to suppress the eye roll and calm down the contempt in his voice.

'I've said it's lovely, you don't need to keep asking. Calm down, OK?'

'Sorry.' Her eyes darted about. Why was she so goddamn nervy? Couldn't she tell that it only aggravated him, this servility, the fevered agreeableness? He wanted some bite, some pushback, like at the start. Sometimes he could feel himself crushing her to see when she'd rebound, like a rubber ball. These days, she never did. Even his most egregious betrayals or cruelties were met only with a wavering voice and misting of the eyes, a choke in the throat.

Say something, he wanted to urge her. *Tell me I'm being a bastard. Don't let me get away with it.*

Please, somebody, stop me.

He looked her over, in the unforgiving sun by the hotel pool. She had been picking the skin around her nails again, and it was ragged and sore. Behind the sunglasses he knew her eyes were also red, and her scalp was beginning to show through her hair. The drain was clogged with it every day, though she'd started cleaning it out once he'd complained. She was not OK. And yet he could not stop himself from pushing, from poking, from stripping everything away from her. Seeing her so broken, shaking with nerves and looking old and sad in the unforgiving light, it made him hate her. So much that it almost frightened him.

Maybe someone else would pull his focus, allow him to find some kindness for his wife again. Scrabble back into the mask he had been horrified to find slipping, which he could not now seem to put back on. His eyes scanned the poolside like a predator on the savannah, feeling his contempt grow as they rested on bimbo after bimbo, ill-educated chavs with a bit of money but no class yelling out to each other that they wanted a *facking umbrella* in their cocktail *innit*. Slurping from giant water bottles and playing tinny music on their phones. He'd wanted a place with class, and this wasn't it. Actually, he was annoyed now that she had chosen this hotel. At least there weren't any children, splashing and squealing and floating, gormless, in their swim nappies, urgh.

She was watching him again. 'OK?'

'The music is annoying. It's too loud and it clashes with the bar's.'

'I can ask them to turn it off?' She was already raising herself from her lounger.

'No, no. I'll put my headphones in.' He did, blessedly drowning out the world, marooning himself on his own little island of silence. Now back to the women. Chav, chav, too old, too old, too lovey-dovey with her partner – now *there*. A beautiful woman was sitting alone by the bar, one slender foot dangling and tapping in time with the sound system. She had bangles all up her arms, and long hair, dark with gold highlights. Something in him sat up and began to hyper-focus. Yes, this was better than the sunburnt, overweight or over-enhanced tourists round the pool, dressed in tiny unflattering bikinis or sack-like cover-ups. She was elegant, tastefully made-up, leafing through what looked like a book of sheet music. He could tell right away she was not British, from the way she held herself. Local, probably. A singer, perhaps? He remembered now seeing a sign for live music in the bar later. His wife had commented on it with that tremulous tone in her voice. *Might be nice, what do you think . . . ?* No opinions of her own anymore, always waiting to hear what he thought. He'd groaned at the idea of sun-stupid tourists listening to bad soft-jazz covers, but if this was the singer then he might reconsider.

He continued to watch her as she sipped a sparkling water and concentrated on her music, a small smile playing around the corners of his mouth as the holiday regained meaning and colour. Yes, she would do nicely. He especially liked the dress she was wearing – long, red, and floaty. Like an Ancient Greek priestess, ready for the sacrifice.

Alison – then

She didn't sleep much, what with the heat and a trapped mosquito and Tom's continued snoring and her worry about Beth Jones, who she hadn't seen since the beach that morning. Had she been arrested too? Did they have the wit to ask for consular assistance, or take it when offered? Tom would say it was none of their business, but Alison felt responsible somehow. She'd seen how scared and sad Beth was, witnessed that moment in the dark below their balcony. And then there was poor Ana, her life choked out. Surely the Spanish police wouldn't dismiss it as a drowning? A post-mortem would clear that up, assuming they were routine here. It was so frustrating not being able to exercise her powers. Ana's car was gone when she looked out the front of the hotel, so that was something, at least. But she so much wished she could find out the results of the search.

The next morning, the hotel was waking up as if nothing had happened. As if the day before had not begun with a woman being dragged from the water. There was a queue for the omelette station, and people were already ordering cocktails at the swim-up bar – at ten in the morning – and the towels were being stacked, the ice being shaken, the umbrellas being moved, as always. But Alison could not pretend. They were heading to breakfast when she saw Beth Jones sitting wanly in the pool bar, her head in her hands.

She was wearing linen trousers and a long-sleeved top, her outfit put-together, but her face was raw with tears. Alison motioned to Tom to go on without her, mouthing, *Get me some sausages.* He went with only a slight headshake.

'Beth? Are you OK?'

The waiter brought laminated cocktail menus, but Alison shook her head. It amazed her how much people let themselves go on holiday, drinking all day long. Even Beth had a half-finished mojito in front of her.

'They've kept him in,' she said dully. 'I've not even been allowed to see him. They gave me a list of lawyers, and I tried to call them, but no one can understand me.' A gulp of tears – Beth was on the verge of full-on sobbing.

Alison said, 'You need to contact the British consul if you haven't already; they'll be able to help you find an English-speaking lawyer, at least. Vince will have an interpreter already. And you need to document everything that's said. The laws are different here.'

'I just don't understand it. Why did they even arrest him in the first place? Just because he found the body? It could have been anyone.'

He, she'd said. Not *we*.

'Beth, you need to tell me exactly what happened that night and morning, or I can't help you. Do you understand?'

Alison couldn't really help her anyway, but at least she knew how murder detectives thought. She could perhaps steer the couple through the maze of traps they had found themselves in. Though why would she? She wasn't at all sure Vince was innocent. She just wanted, as always, to find out the truth of what had happened. It was what drove her. A deep curiosity about why people did what they did, a strong sense of justice, and a distaste for the dark, squiggly twists of untruth.

Beth nodded, tearful. 'I thought it was an accident. I don't understand why they'd arrest anyone at all. She just drowned, surely.'

'It wasn't an accident. Oh, I know they said that, but come on. How did she get in the water in a dress like that? Someone did this, Beth.'

Beth gave a gasp of horror, hand to her mouth. In doing so, her sleeve fell down and Alison could see a large purple bruise on her forearm. Beth saw her notice it, and blushed, pulling the sleeve down again. 'That poor woman. It's so awful. I heard it was the singer, from the bar?'

'Yes. Ana was her name. Did you ever speak to her?'

'No – I don't think so. She was good. Very pretty, in that lovely red dress. God, I can't believe it. You're saying someone killed her? On purpose?'

'I believe so. Clearly the police do too, whatever they're saying, or they wouldn't be keeping Vince in.'

'But they haven't said it was a murder.' Beth dropped her voice on the last word.

'Not yet. Likely under pressure not to upset the tourists. But they will, I'm sure of it. Now, did the police speak to you yet? You said you were with him when he found the body?'

Another hesitation, and she fixed Beth with the gaze that had broken much more hardened criminals. Beth faltered, 'N-o. OK, the truth is, I don't know where Vince was overnight. I woke up in our room with the most awful hangover, and he hadn't come back. I don't think so, anyway. I went out to find him and he was on the beach with her. He'd just seen her and waded in, and he was in shock, I think, really upset. He didn't know she was dead, he was trying to help her. Then there was a hotel worker, and he called the police, and a mum with a little kid too, I think. They would be able to back that up.'

So Beth had lied before. In Alison's experience, small lies usually concealed bigger ones. 'You need to tell the police all this. What time did you last see Vince the night before?'

'I – honestly, I can't really remember getting back to the room. It's a blur. We were drinking in this bar here for ages.'

'You left him here?'

'I think so, yes. Pretty late. We'd got talking to this other couple from the UK.' That fitted with what Tom had noticed.

'The influencers?'

'That's right. Corinna and Joel. I guess we all had too much to drink.' There was pink around Beth's mouth now, not just from crying. Embarrassment. Something had happened that night, but what?

'They need to go the police then, and make a statement about when they last saw Vince. Do you know where they went?'

'No. I haven't seen them since that night. I think they checked out. Their room's empty.'

Alison frowned. She'd feared as much. 'No one should have been allowed to leave without being questioned. Do you recall anything about that night, any strangeness? Did you see Ana at all? She didn't come to the bar?'

'I don't think so. No.'

Alison sat back in the uncomfortable wicker chair, which she could feel leaving indents on her legs under her kaftan. 'Beth – be honest with me here, if you can. Has Vince ever shown any signs of violence, anything like that?'

Most wives would not admit to that, she knew, but one as unhappy as Beth might open up. She thought of the grasped wrist she'd seen the first night. The bruise. Alison didn't want to refer to it directly. Abused partners were rarely able to admit to the truth right away. They'd make excuses. He was stressed. He'd had too much to drink.

'No, absolutely not, he's never even been in a fight. I'm just so worried they're going to pin this on him somehow and he'll go to prison and I'll never see him again. He doesn't speak Spanish, he won't know what's going on.' Now she was crying, proper shoulder-shaking sobs. Like a woman who was genuinely distraught and worried for her husband. Or something else. 'And I heard them say something when they took him, about him being black. All this migrant stuff going on, what if they're prejudiced? Is he even going to get fair treatment?'

Alison made soothing noises as best she could. But there was something Beth said that had stuck in her mind, and she sorted back through it to find out what. Oh yes. Beth had mentioned Ana's red dress, how pretty she'd been in it, but how would she have known that unless she'd seen her wearing it, alive? So she must have seen her that night. The night she'd died.

Beth – now

Her sister licked the cupcake wrapper and balled it up on the plate. 'Well, Bets, you know what I think.'

'Yes, Tan, I know you never liked him, but that's not particularly helpful right now. Do you think something dodgy's going on?'

She'd outlined the various odd happenings, aware as she did that nothing Vince had done was in itself conclusive. Not telling her he'd lost his job was pretty weird, though she was starting to wonder if he'd found another one and somehow not said. Or he had said and she'd missed it? Was that completely insane? No more so than him pretending to have a job for months. She felt like she was losing her mind. God, she'd kill for a glass of wine. She'd mooted going to the pub for this Saturday afternoon catch-up, but Tanya was on some irritating 'sober-curious' kick and had insisted on a café instead.

'Probably. It usually is.' Her sister had an unrelentingly cynical view of male behaviour, bolstered by a ceaseless supply of anecdotes about her many friends and acquaintances and the various ways men had screwed them over. 'I told you about Jane's husband, didn't I – he was on three different dating apps and using their wedding photos for his pictures, the stupid twat. And Cath's ex, Michael, he slept with her sister.'

Tanya's own husband, Gary, was far too cowed to ever dream of doing anything untoward, but she still went through his phone on a regular basis in search of *kompromat*. Beth had heard many of these stories over the years, but never thought it would be *her* man who ended up as a cautionary tale. Maybe nobody did.

'But Tan, even if he's up to no good, it doesn't mean he – killed someone.' She lowered her voice so the patrons of the Waterstones' café didn't hear. On this cosy, rainy autumn day, the coffee machine hissing and low hubbub of conversation, the idea of murder seemed ridiculous outside of the colourful crime novels piled high on the islands. The thought that earlier in the month they had been in the heat of Spain, fearful sweat inching down her spine, Beth wondering if she'd ever see Vince again as a free man. Surely it was all some kind of fever dream.

Tanya looked up shrewdly. She'd had a nice balayage or something done, and Beth thought that she should get her own roots attended to. All this proximity to Corinna had made her feel old and frumpy. 'So what is it you've found out? There's money going out, and he's also lost his job? That could be gambling, you know, like Jodie's ex.'

'Plus there's this couple who kind of latched on to us, out of nowhere.'

'But you never met them before the holiday?'

'Not as far as I know.' Was there a chance Vince already knew Corinna? That he'd faked the meeting in the hotel? No, surely you'd have to be a sociopath to act that well. Not Vince, who could barely even lie about liking an ill-chosen Christmas gift (one of the many reasons Tanya wasn't a fan). 'But they were the ones who alibied him. And they left the morning she was found. Like, just vanished, early on. That was weird. I thought they were staying the week.'

'And this girl who died, did you see Vince talking to her, anything like that?'

'Well, no, but he did go to the lobby bar a few times while I was asleep. Said he couldn't drop off.' And hadn't she felt a rumble of panic at that, which she'd tried her best to push down? Their relationship was nothing but fault lines, tectonic plates moving further and further apart.

'It's hardly a smoking gun, Bets.' No one but Tanya called her Bets, a childhood nickname that even her mother had long given up. Vince had once called her *baby*. Not for a long time. 'Has he ever raised a hand to you?'

'No! No, of course not.' But. There was that time before the holiday where he'd shoved her when she'd gone to hug him, but that was just distress, wasn't it? He'd had a stressful day, he said – maybe that was when he'd lost his job? He hadn't meant to hurt her, even if she had fallen against the door and caught her arm on it. Then there was the night on holiday that she'd been trying not to think about, when he'd lost his temper and grabbed her wrist. Beth realised she was biting her lip, hard enough to hurt. 'It's just – he's not been himself. For a long time, even before the holiday. I thought it would help, but it just made it worse. I don't know what happened. But since the summer, definitely, he's like a different person.'

Tanya took a deep breath and pushed away the remnants of her matcha latte (Beth could not understand why anyone drank those, they tasted like grass clippings). 'OK. If I tell you something, you can't get cross I waited this long, alright? And you can't shoot the messenger.'

'What? Oh my God, what are you talking about?'

'Promise, alright? Cos I'm not to blame for stuff your husband may or may not have done.'

'Jesus, will you just tell me?' Panic was yawning in her stomach. What could it be? Knowing Tanya, it could be anything from murder to forgetting to like one of her Instagram posts.

'OK. You know Kayleigh that I work with, the one with the giant fake lashes? So she sends me this message a few months ago, after she friends me on Facebook. And it's a screenshot from your wedding, you and Vince. Came up on my Facebook memories.' There weren't many photos online of Vince, who refused to have social media, but even he couldn't escape being pictured at his own wedding.

'And?'

'Well, she says, "Is that your brother-in-law?" And I say, "Yeah, he is now," I mean, I keep forgetting, but yeah, you're married so he is—'

'TANYA.'

'Sorry, sorry. It's just hard to tell you this. Anyway, she says – "I've seen that guy before, but he had a different name then." He's from the same place as her – near Reading, right?'

'Yeah . . .' Not that she had ever been to Vince's family home, or met his family.

'Well, she said people used to talk about him in town. They said he'd been accused of something – criminal. Something really bad.'

The background had dissolved, like one of those dreams that drill through to your core with horror, and then you wake up and almost sob with relief that it wasn't real. But she wasn't waking up. 'Please, just tell me.'

'She said she was pretty sure Vince – or whatever he used to be called – had been involved in a murder.'

The word seemed loud as a gunshot in the café. Everything shrank to a pinpoint, then sound rushed back in. The memory of a wedding last year, a friend of Beth's from university, at a country hotel in Buckinghamshire. Someone coming up to Vince as they queued for the bar, a drunk man with his tie around his head, saying, *Excuse me, mate, did you go to Reading High School back in the early 2000s?* Seeing how Vince's face had changed, turned ashen, and he'd hustled her away even before the cake was cut. She'd never been able to get an answer out of him about that. He'd just said he was feeling sick, wanted to beat the traffic, they'd both had enough to drink. At the time it had only been mildly strange. But thinking about it, could she trace his behaviour back to that night, to last summer?

Beth grasped for answers. She couldn't ask him. No one else could know about this, so family and friends were out. Who could help her, give her answers, a way through this storm? Then she pictured something very clearly – a business card, tucked into the inside pocket of her handbag. The raffia one she'd taken on holiday. The meddling police officer from Tenerife, who had ended up being so helpful to them.

She was going to contact DI Alison Hegarty, and ask her what to do.

Alison – then

'Madame. Madame!'

They had attempted to leave the hotel for lunch, quickly realised it was too warm to walk more than a few metres, and ended up having some disappointing paella in a tourist-trap café. She was crossing the lobby, tired and huge, when she heard the urgent whisper. Maria Theresa was beckoning her from behind reception. Alison handed her bag to Tom. 'I'll meet you at the room?'

Tom heaved a sigh, but went off without a word. Alison lumbered over. The young woman whispered, 'Do you want to see the CCTV from the hotel, *señora*?'

'Oh my God, really? Yes. Yes, please!'

Maria Theresa slipped off her headset and said something in Spanish to the other receptionist, a heavily made-up blonde, nodding Alison towards a door behind the desk. 'I ask the night receptionist about Ana. They say she leave with her piano player as normal, but then she came back in. She had lost her keys, for her car.'

'Ah.' That explained why she hadn't left. 'And then?'

'He did not know. We can check, though.' Past the door was a small, windowless room where a burly man sat at a desk, chewing gum and scrolling on his phone. Maria Theresa said, 'This is Luis, the security guard. He can show you the CCTV.' Luis pushed back his chair, gave Alison a brief nod, then went back to his phone as he leaned against the wall. At least he had the sound off.

'Oh, great. You're sure it's OK?'

Maria Theresa shrugged. She looked immaculate again, her skin poreless, beige skirt skin-tight and wrinkle-free, hair as smooth as Barbie's. 'We all liked Ana a lot, and want to find out the truth of what happened. *Sí, Luis?*'

He nodded again, moving aside to let Alison sit down at a computer terminal. 'You know how to use?'

'I think so.' Alison was familiar with such terminals from her days as a DC. She scanned it quickly – a computer with lots of small squares on its screen, from different parts of the hotel. The feeds were numbered, and after a moment she could make out which was which. The lobby. The bar. The restaurant. The pool. She reached for the mouse like a kid in a sweet shop. 'How long do I have?'

Maria Theresa glanced through the ajar door to reception. Her voice was low. 'Ten minutes, maybe. The manager is on duty but – he takes a long time always in the bathroom. A long, long time. I think maybe he is looking at the football.'

If Tom was anything to go by, she probably had more like half an hour, but Alison got a move on. Ana had died on the night of the third, so she'd look at the feed from then and the day after as well. With occasional interventions from Luis, and Maria Theresa anxiously standing guard by the ajar door, Alison found her way to the lobby bar footage from that night. There was Ana, and there was her piano player, arranging their mics and music. Alison watched it sped up, the dead woman moving jerkily, like an automaton. A break where she sat at the bar and looked at her phone, sipping a sparkling water. No one approached her – there were only a few people in, mostly couples who applauded sporadically, and one or two lone men probably escaping their wives. She went to the previous day and kept going until someone came into shot that she recognised. 'How do I go back?'

Luis pointed to the rewind button – and she painstakingly scrolled to the night before Ana died. Yes, that was him. Unmistakable even without the Hawaiian-style shirt. Vince Castries. He came into the bar, ordered a pint, sat on a stool watching Ana, his phone by his side. He picked it up approximately every ten seconds. Onscreen, Ana's mouth moved silently, and Alison wondered what song she was singing. Then the time stamp showed 1 a.m., and she was bowing, people were clapping. Her set must be over. The piano player was packing up his music. And Vince Castries was going up to Ana.

Alison slowed the footage down to half-speed and watched every second, every gesture. They were talking. He was moving his hands. She was smiling. She pressed her hands to her heart, as if to say thank you. And then? She turned to her pianist, picked up her bag and pashmina, and went out of frame. Vince Castries remained at the bar, staring into space. Then he got up, drained his pint, and left. Alison sighed in frustration. So he had spoken to her the night before she died. But not on the actual night.

'OK, I need to see the lobby footage now of the third. From, let's see – 1.05 a.m.'

Luis cued it up for her, and she watched. Various people coming and going, couples staggering in drunk, some even stopping to kiss in the lobby, overpowered by holiday spirit.

'There!' she breathed.

It was Ana, walking with her pianist – Eduardo was his name, apparently – her scarf trailing on the ground. He picked up the end for her, draped it over her. She smiled at him, adjusted the large leather bag she held over one shoulder. They were chatting, heading to the car park. Alison scrolled on another few minutes, but there was no sign of Vince Castries or anyone else following Ana out. She fast-forwarded to about ten minutes later, when Ana came back into the lobby, holding up her skirt to reveal high, strappy shoes. She was gesturing to the receptionist on duty. Then she headed in the other direction. Towards the pool, and the bedrooms. And the beach, where she would be found dead six hours later.

Alison moved on to the restaurant footage, zipping past an image of herself and Tom eating dinner. She could see she was slumped and sunburnt, exhausted from the heat. What had they talked about that night? – she seemed to recall an intense debate about where to spend Christmas, when, all going to plan, they would have a third person to consider. They had eaten early, and she'd been asleep by nine. Practically lunchtime by Spanish standards. She had slept until woken by Tom's snoring and that scream at 2.38 a.m. Beth and Vince had eaten around nine, no obvious signs of tension between them for once.

She scrolled on several hours, and there they were together in the bar – Beth, Vince, and the other couple, the influencers. Alison noted that the woman, Corinna, was in a long red dress, not dissimilar to the one Ana had been wearing. Was that significant? Several empty drinks on the table in front of them, lots of big gestures and faces screwed up in laughter. Even Beth smiled a few times. Growing impatient, Alison zipped on further – 1 a.m., 1.30 – and then Beth got up and left, staggering slightly. She leaned in to kiss Vince goodbye, but on the tape he seemed to pull away from her embrace. After a few minutes, Joel stood up and also went out of shot, the same way Beth had gone.

Vince and Corinna sat at the table talking for a while – almost forty minutes. Then he also got up and left, presumably to find his wife. Corinna stayed, looking at her phone and finishing her drink, then the waiter came over, perhaps to say the place was closing, so she also stood up, gathering her little bag and slipping her feet into the flip-flips she had kicked off.

So far, this gave Vince a partial alibi. He was with Corinna until around two. If there was any way to be more sure about Ana's time of death, this might exonerate all of them. If not, it was clear that the four of them had been up late on the night Ana died, all of them wandering around the hotel in various groupings, or alone.

Beth – now

This was, she reflected as she waited on hold, the first time in her life she had ever called the police. She almost had in Spain after poor Ana was found, but the hotel employee was already on it. There had been some aversion in her, some fear of the police coming. A long-ago memory of blue lights and the buzz of radios. *You are under arrest . . .*

But she wasn't thinking about that now.

A click, and finally a human voice after a maze of dialling options. 'Oh, hi! I'm hoping to speak to one of your officers, DI Alison Hegarty?'

'She's not in.' A bored female voice with a London accent.

'Oh, do you know when she'll be back?'

'Not for a while.'

'Did something happen?' Maybe she'd had her baby already?

'I can't give out those details, madam.'

'OK. It's just – she gave me her card and said to call if I had information about – something.'

'If it's a live case I can put you through to another officer.'

'No, it's – something else. Kind of personal, I suppose? Any chance you can put me in touch with her?'

'I can't give out the private information of officers.' The voice was becoming cross.

'I know, I know. Maybe you could tell her I called? It's Beth Jones, from Spain. She'll know what that means.'

Beth could hear sounds of clicking. 'I'll make a note, but I wouldn't expect to hear from her anytime soon.'

The phone was hung up, and Beth highly doubted Alison would ever get the message. She shouldn't be on mat leave yet, should she? She'd mentioned she had another month or so to try to clear her caseload.

Restless, she looked around the spare room. What Tanya had told her was crazy. Was it really possible her husband had changed his name, and she didn't even know? Wouldn't it have come out when they got married? She tried to think back to that time, when she'd been in a fog of alterations and confetti, fighting with her mother about chicken versus lamb, handling the fallout over Tanya's typically strident organisation of the hen do. Vince had dealt with the legalities, and hadn't she felt proud that she was marrying a man who actually took an interest, helped to plan the wedding? She seemed to recall there was a section where you had to say if you'd been married before, or known by another name. Would she even have been aware if that were the case? She'd not exactly looked at the paperwork.

Thirty seconds later she was on her knees, pulling all their important documents out of the plastic file box they kept them in. Hers were disordered, the manual from the new dishwasher mixed up with work contracts and old P45s. But Vince had always been very organised. She hesitated, looking at the box where he kept his information. It was locked, which had never seemed strange, although hers was spilling open, documents shoved in haphazardly. Now that she thought about it, it was strange. Why lock up boring old documents? But she was pretty sure she knew where the key was.

Yes, there it was, in the top drawer of the desk. A small and flimsy one, the kind of object you see every day but don't really notice. Was she going to do this? This was how you went insane. First a small betrayal. Looking in an unlocked drawer. Then a bigger betrayal, that you could still tell yourself was innocent – taking him something at work. But this – opening his private document case and looking inside – this was a step beyond. The next thing was to go through his phone, should he ever put it down for long enough. Would she do that? She'd always prided herself on giving him privacy, not being paranoid or jealous. But who knew what she'd do? She had already gone much further than she could have imagined, and nothing she had learned so far had set her mind at ease. She took a deep breath and unlocked the box.

God, it was neat. Pathologically so, even. Car, mortgage, pensions, insurance. And there was a divider marked *Important Documents*. She took out the sheaf of papers. There was the valuation for her engagement ring, their marriage cert. That was in the name Vincent Castries, as expected. At the bottom was a small piece of paper, old and much folded. A birth certificate.

Beth stared at it. She knew, somehow, deep in her bones, that this was the smoking gun she had been looking for and hoped not to find. That this piece of paper was going to prove her entire life was a lie.

She opened it, and read the name on it.

A few moments later, she stumbled across the room and picked up the business card again, searching for a personal mobile for Alison Hegarty, but not finding one. Shakily, Beth put it into her pocket. What would she say anyway? *You helped get my husband out of prison – but I think he might have been guilty after all?*

Alison – then

She had been trying for the past minute or so to identify the tune that Eduardo the pianist was playing. Something that was usually faster . . . what was it? She realised she was humming it to herself.

'It's "*The Final Countdown*",' said Tom, in an extremely long-suffering voice.

'Thank you! Finally all those pub quiz music rounds come in handy.' Tom was much sought after in the hotly contested London and South-East Forces Christmas Quiz.

He nodded to the pianist, draining his pint. 'Are you going to go and talk to him? You've overdone it for today. Don't need me to tell you that. You're knackered.'

'Fine, fine.'

There was hardly anyone else in the bar anyway at this time, and she was aware it looked odd for a heavily pregnant, very red in the face woman to be in there. She lumbered over to him as the final notes died away. He was a small and dapper man in a black suit and shirt, with a natty silver beard and swept-back locks.

'Hi – I'm Alison, did Maria Theresa—?'

Furtively, he leaned in and shushed her. 'Not here, *señora*. One moment.'

He finished the song with a flourish and people clapped in a lacklustre fashion, Alison too. She said, 'Can I buy you a drink?'

He nodded. 'Coca-light. Thank you.'

He joined them at their table, after neatly stacking his music into a case. Alison introduced Tom, who nodded in a pained manner. Alison said, 'So, Eduardo, we saw on the CCTV that you left with Ana the night that she – that she passed. Did you see where she went after that?'

He sighed, staring down at his drink. 'Ana, she is like a daughter to me. A lovely girl. A wonderful voice. This is very hard.'

'Of course. I'm sorry.' Alison had to admit her police officer's mind had already considered the sweet old man as a suspect too. Everyone was always a suspect, that was the rule. But he seemed genuinely cut up. 'Can you tell me when you last saw her?'

He played with his bottle, hardly drinking. 'She was at her car, I think. Looking in her bag for keys – she can never find the keys. I drove away in mine, we waved. My wife had made dinner, so I wanted to get back. I said, "See you tomorrow."' He stared down at his pianist's hands. Alison wondered had the police checked with the wife, made sure he had an alibi? Surely. She caught Tom's eye and saw he'd had the same thought.

'And you never heard from her again?'

'No. The next day the receptionist call me, crying, tell me it's Ana in the water. I don't know how she could get there. I just do not understand.'

'You thought she was driving straight home?'

'Of course. That's what I thought.'

'Maybe – you said she was looking for her keys? Maybe she went back for them, if she left them here in the bar, or somewhere else?'

'Is possible. Often she lose them.'

'Did the police speak to you yet, Eduardo?'

'Of course. But they do not ask about this, the keys, the car.' They would probably assume the keys were in her missing bag. But that was just because no one had asked the right questions.

It was frustrating. How to find out what had happened to Ana after Eduardo waved goodbye to her in the car park? Alison knew she had come back into the hotel at least, to talk to the receptionist on duty. She'd nudge Alejandro to check the pianist's story, but surely he would already have done that. 'Is there anything else you could tell me – us – that might be helpful?'

'There is the man,' said the pianist, taking a sip of Coke. 'I did not like him.'

Alison and Tom exchanged a quick glance. She said, 'Oh? Which man?' Was it the same one Maria Theresa had mentioned?

'He come in every night. Always looking at phone, and at her. At her, and at phone.'

That sounded like Vince Castries alright. The exact behaviour you'd expect from someone who was obsessed with Ana, who might have followed her out to the car park after her set, found her as she rummaged for her keys in the dark. 'Would you be able to identify him, if I show you a picture?'

'I think so, yes.'

She handed him her phone, open to Beth Jones's Instagram. Although Vince seemed to shy away from being photographed, he had been caught in the back of one of Beth's pictures, head bowed over his phone as she bravely tried to project that they were having a lovely time. *38 degrees in the shade! Phew!*

'Is that him?'

Eduardo frowned at it. 'No . . . I do not think so.'

'How about this?'

She found another shot of Beth's, her and Vince by the pool, him in sunglasses and a cap, so not very easy to identify. Her face was pressed to his shoulder, but his expression was totally blank. *Sun and fun!* Poor Beth. Trying so hard to hide the truth, even from herself.

The pianist carefully enlarged the picture, peering at it. 'Wait. That is him. There. That one.'

Alison took it back. He was pointing not to Vince Castries but to someone else in the background of the picture, sitting at the swim-up bar. Head turning to say something to the barman, face clearly visible. It was the man from that influencer couple. Joel Hardiman.

She gave Tom a significant look. 'Is it possible Ana's keys are in the bar somewhere? If she just went straight from here to the car park? Does the place get cleaned every day?'

He made an 'ish' movement with his hand. Alison signalled to the barman, a bored-looking young man with an earring. 'Any chance you found a set of keys in here yesterday? Like for a car?'

He shrugged. 'Nothing was found.'

'OK, well – mind if we take a quick look?'

Tom drained his beer and stood up. 'I'll do it.'

He approached the piano Eduardo had been playing and began to methodically search the area around it. It was years since Alison had performed a good fingertip search and she was almost nostalgic for it. Being a DI involved so much coordination, so many meetings. Maybe that was why she was so caught up in this case.

Not long after, Tom moved the heavy curtains that sealed the bar in from the outside sun. He came back, grabbed a napkin from the holder on the bar.

'Did you . . . ?'

'One sec.' Ten seconds later he was back, holding a set of keys with the napkin. 'These hers?'

'I think so, yes.' Eduardo sighed. 'Always I tell her to be more careful. She has this big bag, you know, the things always fall out. Needs a zip. A backpack, maybe.'

Ana could hardly carry a backpack with her pretty dress and high heels. And where were her shoes, and where was the bag he was describing, which she'd seen on the CCTV too? At least they'd found the keys. Alison felt faintly vindicated, and wondered if the police here would have got round to searching the bar. Of course, it might not be relevant, but it explained why Ana had not gone straight home that night. She had come back into the hotel, gone out towards the pool. And then what? What had happened to her after that? Or who?

Beth – now

It was something that came up from time to time, an unusual little fact that might be trotted out at dinner parties, or which friends might pass on to other friends. *You know Beth? Well, she's never even met her mother-in-law.* Someone might laugh and say she was lucky, before telling a story about something egregious their own mother-in-law had done. She might laugh along, but secretly she had always felt wistful at the idea of having one herself, maybe one who wore statement necklaces and would meet her at the V&A for lunch and an exhibition.

Vince always just said he wasn't in touch with his family. There was no big reason. They weren't in his life, that was it. Very different people. Under probing, he would simply shut down, so over time Beth had learned not to bring it up, but she'd picked up a few things over the years. His mother was the one with the Caribbean heritage. Her name was Brenda, Beth had gleaned. His dad was never mentioned, but as far as she knew Vince also had a sister, who she'd imagined meeting as well. Now she was searching Facebook for details of these never-met in-laws.

The birth certificate she'd found had told her that her husband's name at birth was in fact Darren Charles. Vincent was his middle name, and Castries was his father's name, true enough, but he had not been given it at birth. Brenda Charles, his mother's name when he'd been born, was yielding nothing so far. What was the sister's name again? She'd seen a few childhood photos before, old pictures from the nineties of a skinny young Vince and a girl with the same eyes. She tried to remember if she'd ever heard a name mentioned. *Christina*. That was it. Darren and Christina.

Searching for Christina Charles immediately got her someone with her husband's eyes, which made her heart squeeze. This total stranger who was Vince's sister. *Darren's* sister. And she typed out a message.

Facebook could work fast on occasion. Entirely sacking off her day's work and the communications plan for a new recycling collection schedule, a few hours later Beth was pulling up at a semi-detached house outside Reading. All this time, her in-laws had been living just hours away, and Vince had barely even mentioned them. Was that a red flag too, that someone could cut off their relations so entirely? Here she was. The home her husband had grown up in. A very normal mock-Tudor semi with bay windows and two cars parked outside. She left hers on the street and walked to the front door, heart hammering in her chest.

It was opened before she could knock. A tall, slim woman with Vince's features and skin tone, her hair in locs and tied up in a bun.

'Beth?' Same accent as Vince too.

'Hi. Yes. It's me.'

They regarded each other. Sisters-in-law who had never met. 'Well, you'd better come in, I suppose.'

She was brought in, sat down on the squashy sofa, supplied without being asked with a cup of tea and a plate of Fondant Fancies. Christina sat opposite, and on the armchair was Brenda Philips, Vince's mother, who had taken her new husband's name after marrying him five years before. She had never been married to Paul Castries, the kids' father, who'd left when Vince was three and Christina was five. They had never been called by that name until Vince had adopted it at the age of nineteen, for reasons Beth did not understand.

'It's nice to meet you,' said Beth nervously. This was so weird. She wished she'd brought Tanya with her to even the score. Tan would have been wolfing down thc Fondant Fancies and examining the curtains by now.

'What was your wedding like?' said Brenda, who had grown up in Grenada and retained a Caribbean accent.

'Oh! It was lovely. Yeah, really nice. All our family and friends.' She realised her mistake as it came out of her mouth. 'Eh. I asked if he wanted to invite you. But he said – well, you weren't in touch, he said.'

It had been sad too, to look over at his side and see only a few friends and workmates, no family at all. They'd told people his parents were dead, and he was an only child, but that was a lie. These people were right here and very alive. Though it hadn't been her fault, there was guilt.

'Listen, I'm here because – Vince doesn't know I'm here. He wouldn't like it if he did.' And even taking this step said something about how things were between them, because she knew she was causing irrevocable damage to her marriage, and she'd been driven to do it anyway. 'I'm just really worried about him. He's been acting strangely for a while now, and I only found out recently he changed his name. He never told me. Also there's the – well. He doesn't talk to any of you, his family. I'd just like to know why.'

There was more she could have said. That he'd been acting off for months now, that he'd been arrested for murder in Spain and only released on the word of a strange couple who had become attached to them, that he was paying a large sum of money out to someone or something every month. That someone random Tanya knew said he had been involved in a crime, a terrible one.

'Also – he's quit his job, a while back now, and he didn't even tell me.' She halted, aware that what she'd said was more than enough. 'I'm sorry to bring this to you. I just didn't know what else to do.'

Christina and Brenda exchanged a look. Beth picked up her mug of tea to cradle, for the warmth, the comfort.

Christina said, 'So he didn't tell you any of it, then?'

Alison – then

Alejandro the detective heaved an enormous sigh on seeing her in the station reception yet again the next morning. Tom hadn't even come in with her this time, clearly sick of the whole thing. '*Señora*. You are back.'

'You're not really surprised, are you? You'd do the same if you came across a murder on holiday. Right?'

He inclined his head to acknowledge the point. 'You have some information for me?'

'I do. And maybe you have some for me too?'

He regarded her over the reception desk of the police station, scowling slightly. Then he sighed again. 'Fine. Follow me.'

Alison looked at the pictures spread on Alejandro's chipped desk, in the depressing windowless basement where he had his office. She was amazed he had actually shown her the post-mortem report, and while it wasn't pleasant, she'd seen enough photos of dead bodies to remain objective, look for what should not be there, or what should have been there but wasn't. The first thing was glaringly obvious, even with Alison's bad Spanish.

'Her hyoid bone was snapped? Is that what it says?' Thinking he might not know the English word, she put a hand to the base of her throat.

He nodded. 'Correct.'

It was a telltale sign of strangling. 'I take it she didn't drown, then.'

He tapped the report – no water in the lungs. She had been dead when she went into the sea, as Alison suspected.

'I was right, so.' She couldn't resist.

He rolled his eyes. 'Yes, *señora*, you were right. Now what else are you right about? Help me, if you can, please. I will gladly accept.'

Alison had already handed over the keys Tom found, sealed in a Ziploc bag the hotel barman had reluctantly provided. Apparently, though, the car had yielded nothing of interest. She scanned the pages of the post-mortem report, struggling with the unfamiliar layout.

'No forensics recovered?'

Of course, the water would have washed off fibres and DNA, if there was any. There was seaweed tangled in her hair, even the wrapper from a chocolate bar. She had been thrown away like rubbish.

And the question they had to ask every time: 'No sign of sexual activity?'

'No.'

That was something, at least, though she was dead either way. The hopelessness of it weighed Alison down. This woman, with all her beauty and talent and her hopes and dreams and thoughts, someone had killed her. Deliberately choked the life and future out of her.

'None, *señora*.' He checked himself. 'Detective.'

She'd be senior to him back home, but she had no jurisdiction here, she had to remember. He was doing this only as a courtesy, and perhaps because he thought she had something to contribute. They had found the car keys, but where was Ana's bag, for example? Had her shoes come off in the water, or were they somewhere to be found still?

Alison pushed away the pictures. She'd seen enough of blue, lifeless skin and staring eyes, the sodden red dress that had been so stylish a few days before.

'So. What's your current thinking?' She had shared all her findings with him, the influencers having drinks with Vince and Beth that night, Ana's car still being there, and what Eduardo had told her about Joel talking to Ana a lot. His eyebrows went higher with each revelation.

'You view the hotel cameras, even? *Señora*, I do think to do these things also, you know.'

'I'm sure. I was just – nosey, I suppose. Curious. The other couple seem to have gone, by the way. Checked out already – I asked the receptionist.'

He nodded. 'This I am aware of also.'

She couldn't help it. 'You didn't want to interview everyone before letting people leave?'

According to Maria Theresa, they'd gone very early on the morning Ana was found. That niggled at Alison. Out drinking so late, then up and gone first thing? Why had they checked out in what seemed like a hurry, earlier than planned? If it was her, she'd be focusing all her resources on finding that couple. But it wasn't her. This was not her wheelhouse, and she hated that.

He looked annoyed. '*Señora*, we have forty arrests on this small island every day. Mostly your people. British tourists. They drink so much, they fight, they urinate in the street, they vomit, women get assaulted, they lose their bags and wallets and phones, they punch each other. We are overwhelmed, and also we have the migrant crisis, the local people sleeping in cars because they cannot afford homes.'

'I can imagine. I deal with some of that back home as well.' And she knew people behaved much worse on holiday. Let out the beast within. That was what she was worried about. 'But a murder, that's something else. No sign of Ana's handbag? Or shoes?'

'Not so far. The security guard says he saw her going down to the beach though, with a man.'

'He did?' Alison had seen guards loitering near the path to the beach, usually on their phones also. They were there to keep undesirables out of the hotel grounds, and probably wouldn't stop a guest going down to look at the sea by night. 'Any info on him?'

'Not someone the guard recognised. British, though, he say. Speaking English.'

'Did you show him . . . ?'

'I show him the pictures of Vince Castries, yes, he does not remember anything about the man. It was dark, he did not look closely.' And presumably he had not heard a scream or seen anything happen to Ana.

'What time?'

'He says around three, maybe later. He did not know exactly.'

Typical. 'You have Vince Castries in custody still? Surely you've asked him everything by now?' He'd been in for over twenty-four hours. Back home they would have to charge or release him, or ask for more time if they had solid evidence. What did Alejandro have on Vince?

He stacked the pages of the report. 'We have asked. He does not answer.'

'What? He's refusing to cooperate?'

'Correct. He has his interpreter, he has a lawyer now also, and he will not tell us anything. Not if he knew Ana, not what he did that night, not if he can provide an alibi.'

Alison had not yet shared what she'd learned about Vince's involvement in another, long-ago murder case, or about his name change. She wasn't sure what the right thing to do was. If Alejandro was any good at his job he'd find out at some point. Would her offering that information jeopardise Vince's chance of a fair time in custody?

'Did the consul get in touch?'

'He is receiving all the attention he's entitled to, *señora*.' He shuffled the documents back into their manila folder. She had annoyed him.

'Sorry! I'm sure you're doing an excellent job, Alejandro. I'm just interested, as I saw them around the resort in the days before this happened, him and his wife. It felt like something was up with them.'

'Up?'

'Something was wrong. They were fighting a lot.'

That got his attention. 'He hurt her?'

'Maybe. I don't know. I saw him grab her wrist once.' She encircled her own to demonstrate. 'And she's been crying a lot. All the time, almost.'

'You see him with her? Ana?' He tapped the folder with the grisly post-mortem pictures.

'No – just on the camera in the bar, like you did. Look, I think he made some stupid mistakes. Wading into the sea and touching the body, that was dumb, but maybe he was trying to save her. It's a natural reaction. Is that all you have on him?'

'He cannot account for his whereabouts during the time she died. And he is the one found with her body.'

'Fine, fine. Have you tried to look for the other couple – the influencers? Do you know where they went? They flew back?' The couple were the only ones who could potentially free Vince Castries now, if they'd been with him at the time of the murder.

'We do not know. They were not on any flight manifests; not by these names, in any case. And there are many hotels to check on the island.'

'What about Beth, Vince's wife? Did you talk to her?'

'She also is not much help. She does not remember, she says.'

'Could I see Vince? He must be terrified.'

He sighed. 'You can look but not talk. To see he is alright and that we do things properly here in Spain. OK? Come.'

Alison lumbered to her feet and followed him down another dank stone corridor, through various locked doors that buzzed in their wake. She was aware of all eyes on her; she was chronically out of place in the environment where she'd always felt most at home. Even a foreign nick was still a nick. He led her into a darkened room with a two-way mirror along one side, looking into an internal room where Vince Castries sat, unable to see them. He was staring into space, rubbing nervously at his hands, the nails picked and red, his eyes bloodshot and hooded. He had big hands, Alison noticed. He wasn't tall, but he was burly, strong. Strong enough to choke the life from a healthy young woman? And if he hadn't done it, who had?

Beth – now

'Are you sure this is OK?' she said, nervously.

'He's not been here in years, love. Go ahead. It's time you knew the truth. There's a box of his things in the wardrobe there.'

She was standing in her husband's childhood room, which under normal circumstances would have broken her heart a little. The peeling wallpaper and remnants of old Sellotape on the wardrobe doors, the torn corners of posters. A framed picture of a teenage Vince, his hair in an Afro, hugging his mum. They looked so close, so loving. What had gone so wrong?

His mum moved away from the doorway, and Beth heard her step creak on the stairs. Alone, she looked around the small room with the white built-in wardrobes. What was she even looking for? Downstairs, Christina and Brenda had given her sparse details. *He didn't tell you, then.* Didn't tell her what? They'd refused to say. Just that she was welcome to look around his room for some answers.

Answers to what? Beth had asked again. At which the mother and daughter exchanged a look. Christina had spoken reluctantly. 'When Darren was at school, he got into a bit of trouble.'

'Like with the police?'

She'd nodded. 'There was this group of boys he played football with, and this girl got hurt one night down by their clubhouse.'

Beth had let out a gasp. It was like that detective had said to her. *Has Vince ever been accused of anything like this before?* And she'd said no, no, of course not. But he had. He had. And Tanya's friend had mentioned this too. That he'd been involved in something as a teenager, when he was called by a different name.

'But how was he involved? Did he get arrested?'

'He did. But not charged. The other boys went to prison.'

'Prison?' It must have been bad, then. From the delicate way they were speaking, she inferred that the girl had been assaulted, raped maybe. 'Was she – how badly hurt was she?' Murder, Tanya had said. Was that true?

A pause. Both were looking in different directions, not making eye contact. 'She died,' said Brenda. 'God rest her soul. And they – did things to her. First.'

Beth's mind rebelled. Dead. Just like Ana the beautiful singer was dead. 'Oh my God. That's awful.'

'It was nothing to do with my Darren!' The response was fierce. 'He wasn't even there! Just the wrong place, wrong time.'

'They were racist,' said Christina. 'They saw a black boy, and he was the only one, and they just assumed. He wasn't even there when it happened, he'd gone home already.'

Beth tried this thought on – he'd been a scapegoat, he hadn't been involved – and found it did not calm her much. Then it had happened again somehow, in Spain? A woman dead and Vince right there at the scene? It seemed very unlucky.

'Well, that's really tough. It was after that he left home, changed his name?'

'People talked. Racists, the lot of them. And the girl's family, they had plenty to say for themselves. I mean, my heart goes out to them, of course it does. But it wasn't my boy who did it.'

'What was her name – do you remember?'

'Of course. Lucy Brady. Poor child.' The name of a dead girl, like Ana. Beth would google it as soon as she could.

'But why did Vince cut you off? I'm sorry – Darren.'

'Oh darling, I wish I knew!' cried Brenda. 'I told him over and over. We don't blame you. We know you, that you wouldn't do a thing like that. This isn't you. But he went off to college and we just never saw him again. Changed his number. Changed his name – that was hurtful to me, darling, I can tell you. He never even met that man whose name he took. I even phoned the university, and Christina went round to his student house one day. He wouldn't let her in.'

Christina looked away, tears in her eyes. They were saying the same things Beth had over in Spain, that she believed him, she knew he was innocent. But did she, really? That was when they'd offered to let her see his old room, and she couldn't turn down the chance, though it seemed like a violation. The Vince who had lived here – not even Vince then – was long gone.

Tentatively now, she opened the wardrobe, not knowing what she was even looking for. There was a box full of things. Old clothes, a faint smell of sweat and cheap deodorant. Empty canisters of hair gel and shaving cream. Then she found them – photographs. From the days when people actually got theirs printed out, from a roll at the chemist – another industry that had entirely dried up since Beth's youth.

There was Vince, in a line with four other boys. His five-a-side football team. There in his school uniform, getting an award, beaming with pride. Where had that boy gone? School reports, essays with red As inked on them. This version of Vince had the brightest of futures. Something rustled under her fingers, and she pulled out an old sheaf of newspaper clippings. The top one made her gasp again.

Police appeal for info in slain Lucy case. There was a picture of the girl, who had been sixteen and in the year below Vince and the other boys at school. A sporty girl, with blonde hair in a high ponytail, smiling in a netball uniform. Beth stared at the picture. She didn't recall even hearing about this on the news. You'd think such a horrible death would merit more coverage, but then Ana's hadn't either. Maybe there were so many women and girls being hurt there wasn't space for people to care about them all.

She leafed through the other cuttings. They were all about the case, the gory details of the murder, how she had been left strangled and 'interfered with' on the grass beside the football field where they played, how the boys had all been interviewed separately and betrayed themselves with stories that didn't add up, with stupid lies. How DNA evidence could link some but not all to the crime. One of the five was released without charge, it said. Had that been Vince? Had he given evidence about his friends, how he'd left them there at the field in the dark of a November night, and perhaps Lucy Brady was there too, chatting, hopeful, and he had sensed a turn in the mood, or just needed to get home for dinner? Walked away with his hands and conscience clean? If so, how could he then be accused of strangling another woman over twenty years later, in another country?

Alison – then

Sitting by the pool, Alison realised she had shaken off her holiday torpor and felt energised for the first time all week. In her notebook she had made a list of things she wanted to know.

Ana's handbag – where did it go?

Shoes? Where?

The body had been barefoot, so Alison wanted to know if there was a pair of high heels somewhere along the beach that Ana had perhaps carried over the sand. In her experience, male officers did not always think of such nuances.

And what the receptionist had said, about a man. Was it Joel who had been hassling Ana, or someone else too? And where were Joel and Corinna now – why had they left in such a hurry? Was there other CCTV that covered the accommodation blocks and the lifts – any way to prove people went to bed when they said they did? How did Beth get that bruise on her arm, and had she lied on purpose about finding the body, or was she just trying to protect Vince?

Alison had also been busy researching the Spanish detention system, and could now have conducted a short training session on it for her colleagues back home. She had been regaling Tom with facts as he tried to read his book in the shade.

'So they can hold him for up to seventy-two hours before charge. That would be useful, wouldn't it? Not having to go before the mags' court for more than thirty-six?'

'It would. You reckon they have enough to charge him, though? Surely not.'

'As far as I can see, they have nothing but circumstantial. But it would be good to help him find an alibi. If he has one.'

It was pretty unhelpful that Vince wouldn't offer one for himself, or even answer questions about what he had been doing that night. She didn't understand why, if he wasn't guilty. He couldn't remember from all the drinking? He was ashamed? He had some kind of death wish? Although what about Beth Jones? She'd seemed very drunk on the CCTV, and by her own admission. Surely she had just passed out not long after being caught on camera – it was a miracle she'd even made it back to the room.

Or, and Alison had to consider this, as unpalatable as it was, Vince really was guilty and she was assisting a murderer.

'We need to find those bloody influencers,' she said out loud.

Tom shut his book. Despite himself, he had now been drawn into the ad hoc investigation, and had clearly decided to accept what he could not change and change the things he could. 'I was wondering about that. You spoke to your receptionist mate, yeah?'

'She said she didn't check them out because they left so early. But they were booked in for the week, so it was a bit strange. They lost all the money on the booking. It wasn't gifted after all, they did pay.'

He nodded. 'I was asking myself, how did they leave? Must have got a cab, right?' She smiled. He was getting drawn in despite himself.

'Or an Uber. That would be harder to trace if so. Hmm.' She looked at Tom expectantly.

He sighed. 'What?'

'How would you feel about being my wooden-top?'

He glared at her. 'I've been out of uniform for ten years.'

She coaxed, 'It would save me running about. Just a few little questions?'

He sighed. 'Fine. What are they?'

'No harm in asking the taxi drivers out front if they drove them, is there?' At such a big hotel, there was usually a queue of taxis outside waiting for pick-ups.

'No harm. You got a picture of the couple?'

'Yeah, hang on.' That was one advantage in people being extremely online; you could always find recent pictures of them. She looked them up quickly, and frowned. 'That's weird.'

'What?'

'Their accounts are down. Both of them.' She searched for the usernames, which by now she had memorised, but nothing came up. For people like Joel and Corinna, who lived their lives online, this was very suspicious. Alison searched for them on Google, finding a cached shot of them together and WhatsApping it to him. His phone pinged with the message. 'Alright. I'll just nip out to the rank.'

'OK. Be careful, though.'

On their way back from the station earlier, she had seen more of the protestors gathering. The crowd had seemed bigger this time, the sounds of their shouting audible through the windows of the car. She couldn't make out the Spanish, but the gist was clear. They weren't welcome here.

Tom stood up, stooped to kiss her sweaty cheek. 'I'm fine. You just rest, OK?'

'Or I was thinking I could ask the room cleaners. You know, was anything left in their room. Since they left in such a hurry.'

He rolled his eyes. 'Fine. Just not too much exertion, please, love? It's pushing forty today.'

He didn't often call her *love*, and her heart twinged. 'I promise. Sorry. But to quote *Hamilton*, you know who you married, or rather, didn't marry.'

Tom hated musicals even more than spas. 'Be careful.'

He flip-flopped away, and she heaved herself very slowly to her feet, leaving her wrap spread over the loungers. There were some beady-eyed lurkers who'd snap them up in a heartbeat if they looked unoccupied.

Beth – now

Lucy Brady murder. Lucy Brady conviction. Lucy Brady killers. Drinking from an overly large glass of red on their old threadbare sofa, Beth clicked endlessly through more and more horrors. The case had been long enough ago that there was not a lot online about it, but she found some archived stories on local news sites. Lucy had been a shy, quiet girl who had gone to meet the boys after their football match, the other team and the coaches long gone, the boys remaining to drink illicitly under the trees that bordered the ground. Late November, dark by three, a chill in the air, the football pitch glowing with light and drawing out the shadows around it. Beth could too easily imagine it; after all, this had been her life too. She had been the same age as Lucy, Vince one year older. All of the boys but one, Peter Johnson, who'd been eighteen already and judged the ringleader, had escaped being tried as adults by the skin of a few months. The other three had been shielded, their names and pictures not released, and she wondered where they were now. Only Johnson had been convicted of murder; the others of assisting an offender and attempting to pervert the course of justice. They'd be out by now, surely. She should have asked Vince's mother for their names, but she had been so shocked by what she'd learned. Nowadays you'd find the identities leaked on internet forums, but back in 2002, before social media, secrets could remain secret.

The door slammed and she jumped, hastily clicking out of her laptop screen. Did he check her devices too? If so, she'd have to wipe her search history or he'd know what she'd been doing. Was that who they were now, a couple who spied on each other? Where all trust was gone? Vince poked his head in the door, dressed in his work clothes of trousers and a pressed shirt, and Beth felt a surge of rage. She had ironed that shirt for him last week, trying to be a supportive wife. Look at him, pretending he had a job. Pretending he had never been arrested before Spain. Or known a girl who was murdered.

'Did you forget?' he said, looking annoyed at her already, before she'd even said a word.

'Forget what?'

He sighed unnecessarily. 'We're going out. Joel and Corinna's.'

'What, again?'

'What do you mean, again? I told you the other day.' He glared at her glass of wine. 'I guess you aren't going to be driving us, then.'

'Oh Jesus, I totally forgot.' She had no memory of this plan at all, but could not summon the energy to invent an excuse. He knew she wasn't busy. Seeing them was the absolute last thing she could face now, in the middle of all this. 'Vince – will you talk to me? Please?'

'What about?' He already had his phone in his hand, checking something.

'I mean – are you alright? You've seemed so – off, recently.'

This was her chance. Say *I know you lost your job, and I know you changed your name, and I know you were arrested once before for killing a girl, and you turned on your friends and they all went to prison for it.* But she couldn't. His eyes caught hers for a brief second, snagged, pulled away to the phone again.

'Corinna says is tagine OK. I'll say yes?'

'Vince! I'm trying to talk to you.'

'And as usual you're choosing the worst possible moment. I'm tired, I just got in, and here you are, springing some big emotional conversation on me.'

Tired from what? she wanted to yell. *You don't have a job!* But she chickened out, as she had so many times before. Failed to ask the questions, because she couldn't bear what the answers might be. 'But are you really alright?'

'What do you want me to say, Beth? I'm exhausted, money is tight, I'm still under suspicion for murder in Spain. Of course I'm not alright. I'm doing my best.'

'I'm doing my best too,' she said, and tears thickened her voice. She wiped them away with the heel of her hand. He looked at her for a second, and she begged him silently to come over, touch her, kiss her, talk to her, look at her.

Instead, he said, 'I'm going for a shower. Hurry up, I don't want to be late.'

She heard him go into the bathroom, and the water start up. Her tears quickly dried into a quiet fury. He'd been treating her like an idiot all this time, making her feel responsible for their lack of money, while all the while he'd been paying out thousands to someone, and he'd lied to her over and over. Clearly, she did not know a single thing about her husband, the stranger in the bathroom next door. Including what he might be capable of in his darkest moments.

Alison – then

Alison had spotted cleaners around the place all week, discreetly coming in to leave the rooms smoothed out, bleached, and freezing cold by turning the air con to arctic. Being British, she was already worried about whether she should leave a tip when they went, and if so how much. She made her way to the block where Joel and Corinna had stayed. Maria Theresa had given her the room number, a little guiltily, but since they'd already checked out it wasn't a huge data breach.

Alison was in luck – the cleaners were turning over the room at that moment, an older woman and a younger, both wearing the white T-shirts with the logo of the hotel on it. They regarded her warily. She tried, '*Hola – eh, hablas inglés?*'

They exchanged looks. 'Little,' said the younger woman.

Alison held out the picture of Joel and Corinna on her phone. The older woman reached for the phone, pinched the picture to enlarge it. 'Ah, *sí*.' She said something Alison didn't quite understand, but she made out the word *Sábado,* which she thought was Saturday. They were supposed to stay until Saturday, but had done a flit.

'Did they leave anything – *algunas cosas aquí*?' She gestured to the room behind them.

'*Sí*,' said the younger woman. '*Los zapatos. De mujer*.' Alison didn't know the word, but with some pointing towards her feet, she gathered that it meant shoes. Women's shoes had been left behind.

'*Qué tipo?*' Alison was feeling quite proud of herself with the Spanish. Maybe she'd get back on Duolingo during mat leave. The shrivelled little owl and its passive-aggressive reminders made her cross.

The woman said another word she didn't know, indicating with her hands high heels, very high ones. '*Muy bonitos*,' she said. That meant pretty, Alison thought. So fancy shoes. High shoes. Not the kind you'd wear on a beach.

'*Dónde está – están?*'

'*No le sé*,' said the older woman, shrugging. She stood back, indicating Alison could go inside, and so she did, not one to let an opportunity for nosiness pass.

The room was just like hers and Tom's, though facing in the opposite direction, towards the beach, which Alison seemed to recall was more expensive. Their room only had a view of this building. That room opposite, with the swimsuit hanging on it, was that Vince and Beth's? Alison squinted over, spotting a cleaner at work in there too, and realised that she could quite clearly make out the furniture and decor in the room. Especially at night, backlit, you would be able to see everything. So Corinna had left behind some shoes and they were now missing. Was that significant? Maybe they were in lost property or something. But she didn't seem the type to wear heels. Too much of a hippie.

Trudging back down to the pool, she settled on her lounger and sipped from the cool juice the waiter had brought her earlier. This wasn't so bad. Maybe she could install a lounger in the station and spend the rest of her pregnancy lolling while her DCs ran about doing her legwork. Not that she would trust them to ask the right questions. But she did trust Tom, from their days working as partners in Kent Police, and that was a nice feeling. To know that her boyfriend was not the kind of man who'd grab your wrist or make you cry or hassle an innocent woman just trying to do her job, as poor Ana had been.

When he came back, he did a double take at her expression. 'What?'

'I'm just smiling at you! You know, like with fondness? Is that so weird?'

'A bit, yeah. Alright, ma'am, your answers. Yes, there is more CCTV, police have requested it, but it's a lot to get through. No one has handed in a bag or shoes.'

Was there any chance the shoes left behind were the same ones Ana was missing? But how did they get into Joel and Corinna's room if so? And where were they now? There were too many connections missing. God, what she'd give to get her hands on the rest of the CCTV.

'Anything else?'

'I called it,' he said, with that mild smugness she remembered from their days as partners. 'They got a taxi, to a hotel in the north of the island. The driver remembered Corinna because she was filming on her phone the entire time.'

Beth – now

It was amazing how much normalcy could remain in a relationship that was dying. Like a human body still eating, breathing, as the cancer ate it up. Here they were with all these lies between them, and they were still discussing what kind of wine they should bring to Joel and Corinna's, and the best transport options to get there. Beth had still put on her nicest dress, since Corinna would obviously be looking amazing, and had even straightened her hair. She looked over at Vince, his body so familiar, his hands, his hair, even the shirt she'd bought him for Christmas, the shoes that were scuffed but he refused to throw out as they were no longer made in that colour. She knew every inch of him, and yet he was a stranger.

She sat next to him on the bus, their legs held carefully apart as if with a stranger. He scrolled through his phone the whole time, not even trying to hide what he was looking at. It was nonsense anyway – football analysis, TikTok videos, tweets about the upcoming election. She didn't try to engage him like usual, either by actually saying, *Hey could you put that down for a sec?*, or by pointing out things through the window or asking him bright upbeat questions that often went ignored. It was exhausting. She had never felt so tired in her life, and so she gave up, and they didn't speak a word the whole journey.

When they arrived at the right stop, he stood up without saying anything and walked down the aisle without even looking at her. For a second Beth was tempted to stay on, end up in Peckham Bus Depot, but she didn't. They walked down the road under a light drizzle, also in silence. Inside she was screaming. *Say something. Say something!* He didn't. Neither did she. They reached the building and he buzzed, and she heard his voice for the first time the whole trip, so normal and pleasant it sent a shock through her.

'Hi! It's us!'

She could hear Corinna's voice, also upbeat and carefree. 'Great! Come on up.' The lift ride also took place in silence, their wan faces reflected side by side in the mirrored interior. A child had left tiny handprints further down, which made Beth think of her own phantom kids, the ones she would never have now that would be half her and half Vince. Because this was the end, wasn't it? They weren't even speaking now. It could not be anything other than the end.

She went to fix on her smile before the lift door opened, and for a second faltered. She couldn't do this. This was the Emperor's New Clothes, only worse, a thousand times more toxic, and she had to be the one to say *Stop, this is a farce. What the hell is going on? What do you people want from us?*

Instead, she said nothing. Corinna opened the door in a cloud of scented candles and perfume, her shoulders bare and brown in an off-the-shoulder jumper, tight jeans underneath, bare feet again, this time her toenails painted golden.

With a lurch she stepped forward into the warm flat, the windows steamed up from cooking. Corinna and Vince were talking about the weather and the wine – he'd insisted on buying a bottle in the fancy grocery that had opened up in Crystal Palace, thirty quid splurged, even though he had no job and they might lose the flat. Beth had wanted to get two – it was the only way she'd make it through the night – but not at that price. Though money was the least of her worries. At least she had pre-loaded, the several large glasses of wine she'd drunk at home making her fuzzy and clumsy.

Joel was coming over now. He was shaking Vince's hand and taking the wine and examining it, making impressed noises, and no one had even looked at Beth yet. She could likely just get back in the lift and leave and they wouldn't even notice. She could go home, pack a bag, take an Uber to Tanya's and just never see him again. Walk out of the fiasco her life had become.

But she didn't. She took off her coat instead and looked for somewhere to hang it. Joel was saying something about Moroccan ceramics, and she didn't care, she just did not care and could not sit through another lecture about spice provenance or biodynamic wine. Beth's breath felt stuck in her throat. Maybe this was a panic attack. Her feet were rooted to the doormat, and she knew she had to take her shoes off if she was staying, but she couldn't bring herself to bend down. She was still holding her coat, wet with drops of rain on the wool. It was then that she saw it.

The bedroom door was ajar, and she remembered going in there before, and how there had been no pictures or personal items left out, nothing that seemed to belong to Corinna, but now she saw a framed photo on the dressing table. It was a photo Beth recognised from somewhere else, of a group of boys in football gear, and one second later she knew why. She had seen it earlier that very day, in a box at Vince's mother's house. A place Beth was never supposed to go, a picture she was never supposed to see, of Vince and four boys he had helped send to prison. And here it was, in another place it never should have been.

Alison – then

The rest of the day passed frustratingly slowly. Tom went to the station to pass on the information about Joel and Corinna's whereabouts, so hopefully they would be picked up soon and interviewed. Alison kept refreshing the local news sites, and the couple's social media, waiting for answers. If only she could be down at the station instead of here by this lovely pool with waiter and towel service. She was aware that this might mean there was something very wrong with her. Tom was back now, reading his book, but she could tell from how often he looked up that he was distracted too.

Around six, just when her British stomach was starting to think about dinner, she got a ping on her phone, and opened the message so quickly she almost gave herself whiplash. 'It's Alejandro!'

'Yeah?' Tom put down his book, pretence of reading gone.

'He says Vince Castries was just released from custody.'

Tom sat forward and shuffled into his flip-flops. 'Do you want to get changed, or go straight there?'

How comforting to have a partner who knew her so well. 'Straight there. I have to know what's going on.'

◆ ◆ ◆

'So what – it's just not going to get solved?' She glared at the Spanish detective. He'd just told her that Joel and Corinna had been located and had alibied Vince, insisted he'd been with them until dawn that night, then headed back to his room only minutes before finding the body on the beach. Just an unlucky man, in the wrong place at the wrong time.

Alejandro shook his head in frustration. 'The English man has been alibied, *señora*. We have no other suspects. People think it's a migrant who did it, you know? A homeless person. They are undocumented, naturally, so we don't know who is even on the island.'

'But there's no evidence of that. Did Ana really not get picked up on any of the CCTV, in the whole resort? Or can you corroborate when they all went to bed?' She'd yet to see anything from the lifts, but surely that would be relevant.

'There are many hours of footage. Will take some time to view it all. But so far, no one has seen Ana after she goes back into the hotel, except maybe this security guard.'

It was frustrating. What had happened to Ana between 1 a.m., when Eduardo left her and she headed out towards the pool, and her body being found just after seven? If that was her screaming at 2.38 a.m., where had she been the rest of the time? There was so much Alison wanted to know, and she had no way to find out. It was like having both hands tied behind her back.

'I mean, it feels a bit dodgy, doesn't it? Vince was with them all night?'

'I am aware, *señora*. They both say that he was. Ana, she must have gone for a walk on the beach maybe, and someone attacked her. Could be from any other hotel, or anyone passing by, or sleeping down there.'

'But why would she do that alone, in an evening dress? It doesn't make any sense. It wasn't even sunrise for hours. Why would she go down there in the dark? When she was about to head home?'

'We cannot know. Maybe she wants to see the sea. Or she thinks she dropped her keys on the beach.'

Alison heaved a huge sigh, feeling the truth slip from her fingers. 'And where are Vince and Beth now? They left?' She'd been hoping she might catch them, but it seemed they had gone already.

He glanced at the clock above her head. 'I think their flight leaves in one hour.'

'They went straight to the airport?' They hadn't even said goodbye.

'*Sí, señora*, I think they do not want to stay here, now he is free to go.'

That made sense, she supposed. But something about it felt very, very off to her. And her instincts were usually right.

She left the police station still frustrated. Tom was waiting for her by the door and clocked her expression. 'What?'

'They've gone already. Getting the first flight out.'

'Suppose you can hardly blame them. Come on, you look knackered.'

He was right. She couldn't stand to be in this smelly, dank building another second. She needed a shower and a lie-down. Outside, the street was baking, and Tom took her hand as they walked.

'Car's not far off. You look dead on your feet.'

'Yeah. I've overdone it, I know. I'll even admit it.'

'So I can skip the lecture.'

'You can.' As they walked a few steps, Alison was aware of shouting voices that got louder and louder. She had time to think – *what* – a fight?

They turned a corner and suddenly they were in the thick of it. Another anti-tourism protest, but this time hundreds of people waving signs and shouting angrily, marching towards the centre of town. They had taken up the entire main road, and cars were honking and blaring.

'Oh no,' said Tom quietly. 'Where did this lot come from?'

Alison backed off. 'Let's go down the side streets.' She didn't want to get caught in it and stranded under the hot sun. She could already see police officers putting out bollards, blowing whistles. 'What do we do?'

'Come on. Nip down this way.' They did, and for a second the street was cooler and quieter, then the protest surged in from the opposite end. They were being hemmed in – kettled, maybe. 'Shit,' muttered Tom, who rarely swore. 'They've shut off both ends.'

It happened so quickly. The press of bodies was at one moment annoying, then it tipped and was frightening. Tom's hand slipped from her sweaty one, torn away by the crowd, and her thoughts went *Oh, this is bad.* She could not shield her body in the usual way, the way she'd learned to when she'd been a beat cop, policing riots and demonstrations like this one, which could so easily turn ugly in the space of a heartbeat.

'Help!' she tried. 'I'm pregnant!'

Her voice was swallowed up in the noise, and anyway she didn't know the Spanish word for 'help'. *Ayuda*, was that it? She shouted it. No one seemed to hear, and there were backs to her, an elbow catching her upper arm, someone's boot on her ankle, and she yelped in pain.

This is bad. This is really bad.

'*Tom!*' she yelled, but he was gone, she could see him nowhere in the mass of bodies, all looking away from her, it seemed. No one had noticed her. The chanting was reaching its peak, and no one could see her, and then she was up against a stone wall, and her newly enlarged body had nowhere to go, and someone's back was pressed right into her. Alison opened her mouth to scream, felt the air knocked from her, and the patch of hot blue sky she could see was suddenly blotted out, and she was falling.

Beth – now

'What the hell is going on?' she exclaimed, bursting from the bedroom into the open-plan living room. Joel was in the kitchen, cooking, in a roll-neck jumper that the flat was too warm for, and didn't seem to hear her over the music he was playing from a small speaker. The other two were on the balcony, despite the horrible weather, Corinna perched on the edge of the balcony wall, sleek and beautiful, a vape in her hand. Vince, her Vince, rain on his glasses, nodding along to whatever she was saying. Like the two of them were a unit, not Beth and Vince.

She charged out of the balcony door and waved the photo in its frame. 'This picture. That's Vince, right, in the middle? Why do you have a picture of my husband, Corinna?'

Vince had turned pale. 'Beth, what are you talking about? Where did you get this?'

'Ask your new friend Corinna why she has it. I talked to your family, Vince. I found out that Spain wasn't the first time you got arrested, was it? A girl, Lucy Brady, she was killed when you were at school. And your friends, these guys in the picture, they went to prison for it, but you didn't, you turned on them and gave yourself an alibi.' She caught Corinna glance over to Joel, who still hadn't noticed what was going on – had they known this about Vince? They must have. Why else would they have the picture?

She moved forward, wildly gesturing with her arms, out on to the balcony, feeling the damp night air settle on her skin. She was out of control, like the world was spinning. 'So what's going on, Corinna? Why did you befriend us on holiday? Tell me what you're up to.'

Corinna made a noise in her slender throat. Disgust, even amusement. 'Honestly, Beth, you can't just come into someone's home and start barging about in their bedrooms. Still, I shouldn't be surprised you have no manners, after how you behaved in Spain.'

This was like a nightmare, a mirror world where nothing made sense. 'How *I* behaved? I did nothing!'

'Oh, didn't you?'

Somehow, Beth was still walking towards her, to where Corinna sat, unsafe, on the edge of the balcony. Her feet – bare in the rain and cold! – were propped on a flowerpot. In that moment, Beth hated her, her flirtatiousness, her feigned dishevelment, her angry little smirk.

'I have no idea what you're talking about. You came over to us at the hotel, you "bumped" into me in Sainsbury's, you're the ones pretending you live here in this . . . box of a show home!'

How had she walked so far towards the edge? Beth could feel the whoosh of the wind on her face, hear the cars on the road three storeys below. All she could see was Corinna's slim neck, her bare shoulders.

Rage had reduced the world to a pinprick. The picture clattered to the ground and shattered, broken glass spilling at her feet. She heard it crunch under her. She heard someone call her name – Vince? Joel? – but she took another step forward all the same.

Him

Sometimes he had these moments. *Blackouts* seemed a bit extreme a term, but it was something close to that. Just a few seconds, like when you fall asleep on the motorway and wake in terror a micro-moment later. Stress, the doctor had said. Drinking too much, not sleeping. Easy to say get more rest, as if the hustle ever stopped for a second. The struggle to keep his mask on.

He blinked his eyes. He'd been gone, but for how long? It had felt longer than usual. He was here on the beach still, the sand gritty beneath his bare feet, the waves crashing nearby. It was dark, a faint grey in the sky telling him dawn was close. Christ, how much had he drunk? Vague memories of slamming shots, a taste of tequila in his mouth. Soft, tanned skin, a woman's voice.

He put out a hand to try and stand up and gave a small gasp as it landed on something. Someone. A human leg, a woman's leg. She was spread out on the beach, her red dress billowing in a faint breeze from the sea. Hair tangled and gritty with sand, eyes open and staring. Of course, the singer from the lounge. More vague memories – the smell of her neck, the sound of her breath – a scream—

He shook her. 'Hey, get up.' Her body moved at his touch, but not independently. 'Come on, we need to get ourselves together, it's nearly morning.'

Nothing. He laid his head on her chest. Unmoving. And her skin was icy, and he could now see in the rapidly dawning light that it had a blue-tinged pallor.

His entire body flushed with cold. Oh no. No no no. This could not be happening. Not again. He got to his feet, looking down at her. Should he do CPR? No, it was clearly too late, and that would only leave DNA behind. Had anyone seen him with her? His sluggish brain tried to work through it.

Come on, you twat. You'll go to prison this time for sure.

The jolt of adrenaline woke him up. There was still a chance to get away with this. No one could have seen them together, and even if they did there was no proof he'd hurt her. She could easily have overdosed or had sudden heart failure. That did happen. Even he didn't know he *had* hurt her, after all. He had no memory beyond coming down to the beach. She'd lost her keys and he said he'd help her look, or he'd call her a cab. He tried that story out. Nothing to do with him. Just an unfortunate coincidence. Wrong place, wrong time. Maybe a little dodgy to be on the beach with a strange woman when he was in a relationship with someone else, but that could be explained away too. Poor me, innocent bystander.

The words left a sour taste in his mouth, because he knew in his bones this had been his fault. He wasn't sure exactly how, but he had caused this woman's death. And if he didn't act fast, he'd lose everything, the life he had clawed back together after it happened last time. A wave of nausea hit him, but he choked it down, because that would be more DNA and he wasn't stupid.

He seized hold of her bare brown legs, her shoes missing – where? – and began to drag her to the shore. She was a slim woman, but a dead weight was a dead weight, then he had to wade in until her body began to float. He panicked. He didn't want her floating – ideally she'd just never be found again. He searched around under his feet, the water clear and still warm even at night. Found a large flat stone, placed it on to her stomach. Watched as she slowly folded and sank. The last thing to go under were her feet, the toenails winking gold. With luck the tide would carry her out and sink her far and deep.

It was almost a beautiful scene, he thought, as he stood up to the edges of his shorts and waited for her to disappear. The sun coming up, tinging the calm water red, no one else around, just the lap of waves and sound of morning birds. A sense of calm washed over him. She would be gone, and he could go back to his life as if nothing had happened. He looked around him for any evidence. There was her handbag, a large leather tote, lying some way off, and a pair of flip-flops too. He dipped them into the water to wash off any prints, then, being careful not to touch them with his bare hands, shoved the bag and shoes deep into an overflowing bin at the edge of the beach. It would be emptied first thing, he knew, likely before she was even found. If luck was on his side, as it had been before, she never would be found. The fish could pick clean her bones and her pretty red dress would rot and disintegrate.

He dusted the sand off himself and turned to go back to the hotel, leaving the woman to the depths of the ocean.

Alison – now

Two weeks later

Bang. Bang. Bang.

She reached for the old umbrella by the bed, and slammed it three times off the floor. Nothing. Three times more. Then she heard steps coming up the stairs, Tom laden down with a full water bottle, a cup of tea, and a packet of Jammy Dodgers held in his teeth. These he released on to the bed. 'We need to get a tray.'

'Sorry. I feel like I should ring a bell or something. Like you're my butler.'

'Just enjoy it, because after this you'll owe me about six thousand breakfasts in bed.'

Alison snorted as she reached for the biscuits and tore them open. 'I think I'm safe then, since you could never tolerate the crumbs. Are you going to work first?'

Tom was heading to a conference for the week, but was in his detective uniform of a mid-priced navy suit and blue shirt, no tie.

'Where else? Too much to get through.'

She sighed. 'God, I miss it.'

'What, even the smell of drains in the downstairs corridor, and the microwave no one ever cleans, and the coffee machine that makes everything taste of mould?'

'Yep. All of it.'

'The crims and weirdos and personal hygiene issues – and that's just our colleagues?'

Thinking of Brian's BO made her feel queasy, and she pushed away the biscuits. 'God, this absolutely sucks. Another six weeks of this?'

After the incident in Spain, the terror of the crush, Tom's hand being ripped from hers, the sky turning dark with bodies over her head, the feel of feet landing on her legs, she'd been kept in hospital there for a terrifying twenty-four hours, unable to speak to the doctors or nurses and worried the whole time she would lose her baby. Maybe she'd even have deserved to, with all her grumbling about mat leave and not being able to drink. Thankfully, she'd been able to come home and was on strict rest for the next two months. Two months! Now she knew how the crims she sent down felt.

Tom was combing his hair in the mirror and caught her reflected gaze. 'Please, Ali. I can't go through that again. Thinking I'd lost you, lost both of you – please will you just listen to the doctors and stay in bed?'

'I'm staying in bed! It's just so boring.'

He'd moved the TV up for her, but there was nothing she wanted to watch. She could finish off some of her work on her laptop, but much of it needed to be done at the station.

'I know. It'll prepare you well for life with a kid, they say.'

She scowled at him. 'Bye then. Be careful.'

'You be careful.'

'You're the one going to a place full of lowlifes. What's going to happen to me here, I get crumbs in my bra?'

'You're not wearing a bra, mate. I could always skip the conference?'

'No, no, it'll look good if you go for promotion, and I'll be fine. It's only a few days.'

He bent to kiss her, in a cloud of aftershave, and went out, leaving her alone with her thoughts and *This Morning*. She pulled her laptop towards her and tapped away at some paperwork. But her mind kept being dragged back to Spain, the unsolved mystery of that week. Vince Castries had been alibied by the influencer couple, yes, and he and his wife had flown home a few days before Alison and Tom. In the terror of her hospital stay, she had lost track of the case and not been able to follow up with Alejandro.

She found his email now and sent one off, pretending to offer further assistance but really wanting news. There were too many loose ends for her to feel comfortable. If Vince really had just found the body, why had Beth initially lied about being with him when he did? Furthermore, had she lied about ever speaking to Ana? And did she know that her husband had been a suspect in a long-ago crime, that he had given evidence to convict his friends and then changed his name? Why wouldn't Vince answer questions or alibi himself? All highly suspicious behaviour in Alison's book.

Idly, she googled the names again. Annoyingly, Tom could not remember what Vince's original name had been. She put in Vince Castries. Beth Jones. Corinna Cooper. She let out a gasp, jerking so hard she knocked her tea and spilled some of it on the duvet cover. There it was in black and white. *Police probe influencer fall.* A glamorous picture of Corinna, and in the text the news that she had fallen from a balcony of a rented flat the night before, and was in hospital in a critical condition. The area was in Alison's patch, barely a mile away, which was strange because she'd got the impression from their socials that they lived out of town, in a rural idyll where Corinna could peddle her all-natural tradwife bullshit.

The short article from the local paper gave scant information, except to say that a man and woman in their thirties were helping police with enquiries. Could that be Beth Jones and Vince Castries? Was it possible that whatever had happened in Tenerife was still playing out even now, and had not yet reached its conclusion?

Beth – then

Two weeks earlier

'It's nice, isn't it?' She was aware that she'd said it several times now and he would be getting annoyed. Vince sighed, not looking up from his phone, as they sat in the reception of the hotel waiting to be checked in. They'd been given wet, cold towels handed over with tongs – she wasn't sure what for – and welcome drinks that seemed to be disappointingly non-alcoholic. Beth was running through all the possible pitfalls in her head, things that might annoy him. 'Like I said, there's three pools, and you have to pay extra for the spa, but I guess that's fairly standard, and we can hire dinghies and paddleboards too. If we want.'

No response.

'We can just relax too. Whatever you like.'

Still nothing. Her anxiety was soaring, her chest tight – they were early, so their room was not ready, and now they were waiting, sticky and tired from the early-morning flight, and she was worried he might explode. Where had this fear come from? Vince had never been an angry man before, never shouted at her, but somehow tension had grown up between them like mushrooms. She realised her hands were digging hard into the raffia of the chair when, thankfully, the receptionist came over. She was young, mid-twenties perhaps, with dark, shiny hair slicked into a high bun, and lots of make-up hiding the fact she was naturally very beautiful. Her name badge read Maria Theresa.

'*Señor, señora*, your room is now ready, if you will follow me?'

Beth's chest loosened as she lifted her tote bag and went to reach for her wheely case.

'They'll get it,' snapped Vince. 'You'd think you hadn't stayed in a hotel before.' He followed the uniformed bellboy off into the hotel's central courtyard, and she trailed behind, biting her lip to keep back the tears. These days she was always just one sharp comment away from crying. Like a woman carrying a bomb in her outstretched hands. It was going to be a long week.

The room was smaller than she'd imagined, the sea view only there if you stood on the balcony and craned your neck. The bellhop hovered a bit, but she had no cash, and Vince simply turned his back on the man until he left.

'Is it OK?' she asked anxiously. 'There were nicer rooms, but I thought . . .' He'd been on at her for spending money for months now.

'It's fine.' His voice seemed heavy, scratchy.

'So, what shall we do? Beach, pool? Or lunch?'

'I'm not hungry.'

He had taken his phone out and was scrolling through it. The plane ride had been a welcome break from that, but he had downloaded some episodes of a stupid show about elves and put his headphones in anyway.

'Oh. Well – we can sit by the pool? Get a drink?'

'It's barely lunchtime,' he snapped.

'No, but – we're on holiday.' She heard the pleading in her own voice, and hated it.

'I'm going to stay up here for a bit.'

'You are? Why?'

'I want some time to myself, is that a crime?'

She recoiled at his tone. 'Um – no. OK, I'll go to the pool. Come down whenever.' She gathered her things, suncream and book and hat, and managed to hold her anxious smile until the door had shut behind her.

On her way downstairs, the air-conditioned cool of the lobby settled on to her bare shoulders, making her shiver. She was going to cry, she realised. The tears leapt up in her throat like vomit, and she side-stepped into the ladies, leaning on the sink until she could get a hold of herself. Little gasps like a dying fish.

'Can I help you, *señora*?'

Someone had come out of the loo and was standing at the other sink, washing their hands. A young woman, perhaps in her late twenties, heavily made up for the afternoon and with shiny, dark hair twisted into an elaborate do. By contrast with her glamorous head, she was wearing cut-off shorts and a vest top, showing tanned, slender limbs. This just reminded Beth that she was nearly forty and her husband seemed to be disgusted by her, and she let out a fresh sob.

'Sorry. I'm OK. Just – a rough day.'

'I understand.' The young woman pulled some hand towels from the dispenser and passed them over. Her warmth made Beth want to cry even more.

'I don't know what's wrong with me. I'm in this beautiful place, I should be happy.'

'Ah well, sometimes that is the way. When you should be happy it just shows you are not. Like the New Year's Eve, you know, or Christmas?'

That was so true that Beth gave a watery laugh. 'Thank you. You're very kind. Do you work here?'

The woman turned to the mirror, fixing her hair, lifting her arms above her head in a gesture that highlighted her high breasts and flat stomach.

'Hmm, in a way. I am the singer for the bar. Ana.'

Alison – now

The email from Alejandro came back with surprising speed, as if he too had been ruminating over the case. He wrote in an annoying font with random capitals, but his English was good. There had been no developments, he said. There was pressure to charge some migrant man with the murder, but he did not believe any of the ones pulled in were guilty. Meanwhile he had dozens of people to charge over the tourism demos, and an entire industry to salvage. Reading between the lines, there wasn't time to get to the bottom of a case where everyone seemed to be lying.

She sent him a link to the story about Corinna's fall, with the subject line *The Influencers*, and he wrote straight back with a surprised-face emoji. *That is very interesting. Thank you, Alison. Who are the suspects mentioned?* She didn't know yet, but she was going to find out if it killed her. Not all that easy when she had to crawl to the loo on her hands and knees, but it wasn't like she had anything else to do.

She rang the MIT, getting through to Carmel, the seen-it-all desk sergeant, who specialised in Heather Shimmer lipstick and was entirely unfazed by anything, from a serial rapist in her cells to a full-scale riot. 'Oh, hiya, love. You alright?'

'Bored out of my skull, Carmel.' She made some dutiful chat about Carmel's various troublesome kids and grandkids, then went for it. 'You any idea who's on this balcony-fall case? Us or CID?'

'Oh yeah, the influencer? We've had the press ringing here and all, you know. Seem to think maybe she fell taking selfies. Apparently, she did that.' Alison did recall seeing posts of Corinna perched on the side of very unsafe drops, in places like Santorini, or on the edge of cliffs. 'CID have it, but might end up being an attempted murder, not sure yet, so we're liaising.'

'But there's been arrests?'

'One female arrested. Nigel's on it their end.'

Alison groaned internally. 'Would you ask him to call me? It might link up to another case I've been looking at. I have some info that could help him.'

Carmel paused, as well she might. Usually Alison would cross the road to avoid helping Nigel. 'Ain't you supposed to be off your feet?'

'I'm talking to you horizontal.'

'Just take it easy, alright?'

'I will. Any word on the victim?'

'Well, she's alive. They're saying she got lucky and might wake up, even.'

'How far did she fall?'

'Three storeys. Not always fatal.'

That was true. Alison had known of people falling even further, usually while drunk, and making it out relatively unscathed. It was true Corinna liked to sit in dangerous positions, but it sounded like other people had been present – was it Vince and Beth? So could be an accident, could be attempted murder, or an actual murder if Corinna didn't make it. 'Can you just confirm the names of the witnesses, please? You'd be doing me a big favour.'

'Go on then.'

'Beth? Vince? A Joel too?'

'How'd you know that?'

'A strong hunch. Thanks, Carmel.'

'Oh, by the way, love, someone rang here the other day, looking for you. Some woman.'

Could that have been Beth Jones too? Alison had given Beth her card out in Tenerife. What had been going on in the two weeks since they returned from holiday? She hung up, her mind racing. Was Vince Castries now in a police interview room for the third time in his life? That was more than just bad luck, wasn't it? That was a pattern.

Beth – then

She started awake, for a moment unsure of where she was, expecting to see the familiar edge of her dressing table in London. But no. They were on holiday, they were in Tenerife. These days, there were a few seconds on waking when she felt alright, and then it would hit her in the solar plexus. Things were not OK at all. Something was wrong with her husband, and she didn't know what. She looked over at him, curled in on himself as far away from her as possible in the small double bed, smaller than their king at home. In sleep his tension had ironed out, and he looked more like his old self. She felt the urge to reach over and stroke his hair, with that curly bounce in it she'd always loved. But he might wake up and be angry. She'd heard him get up in the night and go somewhere, muttering that he couldn't sleep and was going for a walk, then she'd lain awake for a while, worrying. She didn't know what time he had come back, but at least he was here now.

The clock and the light creeping under the thin hotel curtains told her it was after seven, so she decided to get up, extracting herself carefully from the bed in case she woke him up and he was angry. In the shower she practised upbeat thoughts. They were on holiday! Nothing to do but sunbathe, drink cocktails, and read. She'd brought along a book by a well-known therapist, and hoped Vince would not take that as a slight in some way. Maybe she could put a different slipcover over it. No, that was ridiculous. Why was she having these thoughts? Things weren't as bad as that.

She got dressed in the semi-dark, and he still didn't stir, an arm thrown over his face. She sent him a message for when he woke up, to say she was going to breakfast and to join her, adding two self-conscious kisses. They didn't really do that anymore, when most of their texts were about milk or the loo blocking again.

Downstairs, the buffet was in full swing, a small child being held up by his mother to laboriously pour cereal into a bowl from a dispenser. Beth threw them a smile. For years now, seeing a baby or toddler had ignited a tiny, warm flame inside her, thinking of the ones she and Vince might have. Maybe with his dark eyes or her fair hair, or a combination of the two. But was that ever going to happen? Or was he going to leave her when they got home, if this holiday wasn't a success?

She found an empty table and opened her bank app, scanning the figures. However she spun it, she couldn't afford the mortgage by herself. They'd have to sell, or maybe he'd buy her out. And then what? A studio flat, or sharing a house, almost in her forties? Or worse, in with Tanya and Silent Gary and their three loud teenagers? No, she had to make this holiday work. It really was make or break.

After forty minutes or so, she had finished her fruit, granola with yoghurt, and a fresh omelette from the station with the chef, and there was still no sign of Vince. Getting up, she went to look for him, and was startled to see him at the pool already, sprawled on a lounger in full-body shade, looking at his phone.

'Hi,' she said. Both loungers next to him had towels on them already. 'Is one of those for me?'

The pool was very crowded, music from the bar going full blast, lots of fit-looking people sitting in or beside it drinking coloured cocktails. It was just after breakfast, but Beth felt some relief at the thought of ordering one. It was OK on holiday to drink before midday, and it might help her relax a bit, curb these gnawing thoughts of hers.

He glanced up. 'No. Didn't know where you were.'

'I texted you; did you not see?'

'Yeah. Wasn't hungry.'

Beth stood above him, her own shadow casting her feet into darkness. Was this how it was going to be? Their make-or-break holiday was going to be spent largely apart?

He made no move to find her a lounger, or to get up himself. Timidly, she asked, 'Where did you go last night?'

'What?'

She could see herself reflected in his sunglasses, looming above him. 'You got up in the night.'

'I couldn't sleep, so I just went downstairs for a bit. Had a drink. What's the big deal?'

'No big deal.'

Silence fell. He took his phone out again.

She said, 'OK – I guess I'll just – I'll be over there.'

She found a spare lounger, with no shade, and put her sunglasses on. She got out her book, but there was no way she could read it through the tears that instantly filmed her eyes. The panic was gripping her belly even tighter. *Something is wrong. Something is very, very wrong.*

Alison – now

Tom was going to be so mad at her, she knew. But when they said to rest, they didn't mean she was supposed to actually lie on her back for two months, did they? That was insane. She'd lose all muscle tone, not be able to stand up once she had a baby to cart about. No, it was surely better for her to get some gentle exercise and fresh air. And so she was in an Uber heading to the police station. Tom still worked for Kent Police in Sevenoaks, so he wouldn't find out unless one of their mutual friends blabbed about seeing her at work. And even if they did, so what? He wasn't the boss of her. Thank God, they'd never had that type of relationship.

Her hands rested on her belly as the car drove along, and she was thinking furiously. She recalled the feeling she'd had that first day in Tenerife, her eyes drawn to Beth's energy somehow, a feeling of fear for her. *Help that woman. She's in trouble.* When she'd seen Vince grasping Beth's wrist, she'd assumed it was that particular kind of trouble, but then a different woman had turned up dead. And now another had been hurt, but Alison just didn't know how.

She thanked her silent driver and got out, with difficulty, hoping her pass would still work. It did. There was Carmel in her uniform, sleeves rolled up to show the tattoos of her kids' names, a cup of tea in each hand. 'Didn't expect to see you.'

'I know, I know, I'm not really in. Colette here?'

‘She’ll have your guts for garters, my love.’

‘I know.’ She made her way to her boss’s office. DCI Colette Milton had never been seen without full make-up and high heels, and was currently sitting at her desk pumping cute pink hand weights while listening to a podcaster Alison recognised as one who encouraged you to eat raw meat and immerse yourself in ice water. ‘Got a minute?’

‘Alison!’ Colette put down her weights and rebuttoned the sleeves of her trademark silk blouse. ‘You’re not supposed to be here.’

‘I know. I can’t just lie at home, though.’

‘Eh, that’s exactly what you can do. Does sick leave mean nothing to you?’ Colette had three children, and had been responding to emails within minutes of the birth of each.

‘Can I sit?’ She was tired even from the short walk from the car park.

‘You’d better. Water? Here.’ Colette placed a glass in front of her, from her own elegant carafe. ‘Now I assume you have a reason to be in? I told you Brian could clear up your cases.’

‘Yes, well, I question the truth of that, Colette, but that’s not why I’m here. You know I’m just back from holiday, and there was a murder out there?’ She outlined her involvement in the case, Colette’s expensive eyebrows lowering further and further into a frown.

‘So your inability to stay out of things isn’t just restricted to this country?’

‘I could hardly help it. I practically found the poor woman. And the couple were so confused and scared, I couldn’t just abandon them.’

Colette hmphed. ‘But he was released without charge in the end?’

‘Yeah. The other couple alibied him, said he was with them the whole night. Joel and Corinna.’

'But you think someone's lying?'

'Someone. Maybe all of them. Pretty sure the wife didn't tell me the truth. Is that who you have in custody, Beth and Vince? Corinna Cooper's the victim?'

Colette sighed, then nodded. 'We have arrested Beth Jones on suspicion of attempted murder, yes.'

'So there was intent?'

'Alison, please . . .'

'I might be able to help! I know these people.'

'Fine, OK. Corinna Cooper is in hospital with a serious head injury, yes. There was some kind of altercation at their flat – or at least, the flat they were staying in – and she fell from the balcony. We don't know anything else yet. Corinna's partner isn't very helpful, says he didn't see what happened.'

'And Vince? You have him in custody too?'

'Vincent Castries has yet to be located.'

Colette said all these names crisply – they meant nothing to her. Whereas Alison was way too involved.

'What does that mean – he wasn't there?'

'Apparently he was, but left the scene. He's not at his home, and so far we can't trace him. His supposed office says he hasn't worked there in months. Apart from Beth, the only witness is Joel Hardiman, and he's at the hospital with Corinna.'

How strange, Vince running like that. It made him look guilty as hell – had he been the one to push Corinna? She had to ask. 'Please. Can I interview Beth Jones, or at least sit in? I think she'll talk to me. We built up a rapport, I helped get her husband out in Spain. I'm not officially off duty yet, right?' She knew they wouldn't have processed the paperwork yet.

Colette closed her eyes for a second, no doubt asking herself what Brené Brown would do in such a situation. 'When was the last time you even did an interview?'

'I know, but I'm good at it, you know that.' It was the thing she missed most now she was a DI. Alison tried, 'Come on, Colette. You really want Brian doing it? Remember the pig's ear he made of that suspicious house fire? I'm still tracking down the evidence he didn't bother logging at the time.' She thought with a pang of Diana Mendes, her former partner, who was on a temporary secondment in North London. She wouldn't feel so bad about going off if she could hand things over to Diana.

Colette sighed. 'Fine. But you better get something worthwhile out of it.'

Alison almost leapt from her chair in delight at having this chance, at being able to get in there and work at the puzzle. Then a wave of exhaustion swamped her, and she had to shut her eyes for a moment. She put her hands on her belly, trying not to show weakness. It was OK. She'd be sitting down the whole time, after all. It would all be fine.

Beth – then

Vince sighed hard. 'I thought the booking was for nine.'

'It is. I'm sure they'll seat us soon.' There was that soothing, wheedling tone again in her voice. They'd been waiting at the restaurant for five minutes now, and Beth's body was in knots with the tension, as if this was somehow her fault. Trying to smooth the world out for him. The first proper day of their holiday had not been relaxing at all. All she could think about was Vince, what was wrong with him, why he was treating her this way. Where he had gone last night by himself.

Then she saw someone waving at her. It was that nosey woman from the beach earlier today, the pregnant, red-faced one, who had marched over to Beth while she was crying and started asking some rather pointed questions. Almost like she knew something was wrong.

'Who's that?' said Vince, catching it.

'Just some woman I got chatting to.' A detective, apparently. Vince would not like that, she knew instinctively. He didn't trust the police, and she respected that, assuming it was because of his skin colour. He hadn't even wanted to call them when they'd had a break-in at their last place and her laptop got nicked. 'I suppose I better go and say hello.' Beth had been embarrassed after the encounter, to be so obviously upset in such beautiful surroundings.

Why couldn't she just enjoy herself? Maybe Vince was right to be fed up with her.

Vince sighed. 'Why do you always do this? Pick up random people?'

Because you won't talk to me! Beth bit her tongue, stared at her pedicured feet in her new gold sandals. She had made such effort for this trip, spent too much money on new clothes. And it had got off to such a bad start.

Their waiter was finally there, with a smile and menus ready, small talk about how their holiday was going. Beth smiled and lied, said it was all lovely. They followed him to their table, which had a clean white tablecloth and a flickering tealight, a bunch of dried lavender, the lapping waves beneath the deck. It was all so nice, and so awful. Beth set down her wrap and bag. 'I'll just go and say hi. Come with me?'

'Why?'

'Just to be polite. Please?'

Vince sighed deeply, but followed her to where the woman from the beach was sitting with a burly man in a white linen shirt. They were holding hands across the table, and Beth felt a surge of jealousy at that. They looked so happy, and they were having a baby too. Why did some people get all the luck? She could feel Vince standing awkwardly beside her as they made stilted introductions. Tom was the name of the woman's partner – Alison was hers, Beth remembered now. Both police, and it was obvious now that she knew. Something in the way they held themselves, the sense they were watching everything all the time. She saw Tom's eyes flick to Vince, who now had his phone out, as always. Looking him over, as if assessing him. And not liking what he found. Vince did not seem to notice.

They made some small talk about the food, the holiday. Then she said, 'Well, we'd better go and get our orders in!'

They retreated with an awkward wave, she already anticipating Vince's annoyance. As they sat down and the waiter came over, explained the specials and took their drinks order, he did not look up from his phone. She tried not to spy on him – he'd told her off more than once for that – but she couldn't help seeing what was on his screen. Sports news. Was it really essential he look at that right now?

'Vince,' she prompted, as the waiter hovered with his notepad. 'Do you want a drink? We could share a bottle of wine?'

He sighed. 'A Peroni will do me. I don't want to drink too much.' He wasn't even saying please or thank you now. He who'd once made conversation with waiters, called them *mate* and swapped football chat.

'A large glass of white then, please. Thank you.' She tried to make up for him by smiling widely.

The scene was beautiful. A soft violet light as the sun went down, the clear sea lapping at the deck they sat on, fairy lights glowing, smooth jazz playing, a smell of garlic and meat. But she was miserable. This was miserable. She waited for him to put his phone down, and had counted to fifty by the time he did.

Finally, he looked at her, if only briefly. 'So what kind of things did you want to do on this holiday?'

It was a pathetically small crumb, but she'd take it. She was starving to death, so even a crumb was food. As she launched into a description of all the activities they could try – hiking, boating, vineyard tours, spa treatments – she happened to glance over to the police officers, and saw that the man, Tom, was staring right at Vince, and frowning. As if they had somehow met before.

Alison – now

Beth Jones was sitting in the oldest interview room, the one no one ever wanted because the recorder tended to malfunction and it had always had a faint smell of drains. She was rubbing her hands together compulsively, her eyes red and her face shiny with tears. She looked up as Alison went in. 'It's you! Oh God, thank you, thank you. I was trying to find you, and they said you were off, and . . .'

Alison lowered herself into a seat. 'I am supposed to be. But I heard you got arrested. What the hell, Beth?'

Beth's eyes darted around, terrified. 'Is this an interview?'

'Not yet. I'm talking to you here as a friend. But there'll be an interview later, under caution, and you should have a solicitor for that.'

'I don't know what happened. It just all happened so fast.'

Alison held up a hand. 'Don't tell me anything important until the interview. Seriously, get a lawyer. Where is your husband?'

'I don't know. He – Joel – rang the police after it – happened – and they took me away.' She lowered her head, tears dripping on to the old, chipped table. 'I don't know where Vince is. I haven't spoken to him. Do you know?'

'We've no idea either, but we do need to talk to him. Any thoughts on where he would have gone, if not home? Friends, favourite places?' Beth shook her head helplessly. Alison sighed. 'Now, here's how it's going to work. You haven't been charged yet, but the clock is ticking. I'm going to conduct the interview, and I highly suggest that you have a lawyer present, and that you tell the truth. The whole truth, Beth. About everything that's relevant. And by that I mean everything that happened in Spain too. OK?'

Beth's face split in incredulity. 'I don't understand how this happened. I just don't. I don't remember anything. It's all a blank.'

Alison had heard that refrain often, sometimes from people who still had their victim's blood on their hands. It was true she'd first identified Beth as a potential victim of abuse herself, a suffering woman, driven almost mad by her husband. But there was no one as likely to snap and commit terrible acts as a victim who had simply had enough. Why would she target Corinna, though? Was it possible the woman had been having an affair with Vince? That didn't seem to make sense, when Corinna's own partner, Joel, was so sculpted and tanned, but stranger things had happened. She heaved herself up. 'Think about whether that's going to be your official statement, Beth. I'll be back in an hour or so. If you need any water or food, just ask. It's not a police state, OK? You have rights.'

'Where are you going?' said Beth, tearily. She seemed to think Alison was still her friend, the saviour who had helped them out of a catastrophe in Spain. But she wasn't. She was on the side of whoever had been hurt, and right now that was a woman who'd fallen from a third-floor balcony. However annoying Alison might have found her, Corinna was the victim here.

'To the hospital,' said Alison, lumbering out and shutting the door behind her. Much like her now-missing husband out in Spain, Beth Jones clearly had no idea of just how much trouble she was in.

◆ ◆ ◆

It was tempting, once Alison got there, to avail herself of the wheelchairs that waited by the door. A nurse who was vaping outside looked her up and down. 'Maternity's in another building.'

'I'm not here for that.' She was only seven months pregnant; did she really look ready to pop? 'Intensive Care?'

The man pointed with a disinterested elbow, and Alison lumbered on. Reception was predictably chaotic, with a TV showing the news at what she felt was an unnecessary volume, children crying, people stretched out grey-faced across chairs, and of course the ubiquitous phone cacophony. She asked for Corinna and showed her warrant card to a receptionist who was also watching loud videos on her phone, resisting the urge to remind the woman she was working, and in an important job at that. What was wrong with people?

'Date of birth?' said the receptionist, tapping laconically at her keyboard.

'I don't know her date of birth. How would I?'

'Patient middle name?'

'Again, how would I know that? She's the victim in an attempted murder inquiry, and if she's conscious at all I need to speak to her urgently.'

With a sigh, Alison was directed to the lifts, through some double doors that opened in her path, and made her way to Intensive Care. She nodded to the officer outside the door, one of Nigel's, she assumed, showed her ID.

The contrast was marked – this place was sombre, hushed. She had only seen Corinna a few times, always in tiny bikinis or floaty, floral dresses that showed off her yoga-cised body, hard as a bullet. Now she looked like a child, a tube taped to her face, her lungs rising and falling with machine-made breath. Her tawny hair was lank, dark with grease, and her face pale, unmade-up. Alison had not liked her one bit, and hours of watching her videos had only deepened this, but you felt sorry for anyone in a hospital bed. They were so vulnerable. She almost reached out and patted the sock-clad foot that had escaped from the hospital blanket.

Joel was beside the bed, head in his hands, for once not on his phone.

'Remember me?' Alison said. 'I'm sorry for what you're going through.'

He looked up slowly. His face was also grey and exhausted, as if he'd sat in the chair all night. 'You were out in Spain, weren't you? I recognise you.'

'Right. I'm actually a police officer, as it turns out, and this is my area. So, Corinna's fall is now my case.' Well, sort of. Nigel from Borough wouldn't be happy she was stepping on his turf, but he was nowhere to be seen. 'Has anyone spoken to you since? Did anyone take a recording or notes at the scene?' Paramedic testimony could be very useful in a case like this.

Joel shook his head, as if struggling to understand how this had happened. 'I don't know what's going on. I was in the kitchen, cooking – it's this chicken dish and you can't leave it or else the flavour . . .' He caught her eye. 'I didn't see, anyway. Just heard this scream from Beth. They were out on the balcony, the three of them. I had the music on. I didn't notice. And then I went running over, and Beth was just like howling, over and over, and Corinna was – gone.'

'And Vince Castries?'

Joel looked confused. 'I think he called the ambulance. But then – I don't know where he went.'

'So you didn't see an actual push?'

'No, but what else could it have been? Beth was screaming. Like, in her throat. Like a wild animal. There'd been some kind of row, I think. Before Corinna – fell.'

'Corinna liked to sit on the edge of balconies, didn't she? I saw her do it myself.'

He looked at the woman in the bed, distracted. 'I suppose. But it was always safe before.'

'Unfortunately, it just takes one tiny slip.' Alison had dealt with enough grisly falls in her time. People thought they were invincible, right until they plummeted.

She had so many questions. Like what had caused mild-mannered Beth Jones to finally lose it. Whether he really hadn't seen what happened or if he was lying.

'You've no idea what caused the row?'

'I really don't. They'd only just arrived, I think Beth went to the loo or something, then when she came back she was shouting. I didn't really notice, I guess. I was distracted with the food. And then – well, it was too late.' He stared, aghast, at the woman in the bed. 'Can she, like, hear us?'

'Possibly. People do hear things in comas, sometimes.'

'You think she'll wake up?'

'Also very possible. The doctor said her GCS number is four, which is quite promising, especially given how far she fell. So, tell me more about that night in Spain, Joel. The one in the bar.'

More confusion on his handsome face. Not the brightest bulb in the box. 'What's that got to do with it?'

'Well, someone died out there, and now Corinna's injured too. They might be linked. You gave a statement to police that Vince Castries was with you all night?'

Was that a slight hesitation? 'Eh, yeah. He was just kinda wrong place, wrong time, wasn't he?'

'You tell me, Joel. It was only your and Corinna's word that gave him an alibi.' And she wasn't going to be talking anytime soon. 'You spoke to the dead woman a few times, right? Ana?'

To his credit, he was smart enough not to lie. 'I was in the bar once or twice, yeah. I thought she was a good singer, offered to, like, link her up with a few people I know in the business.'

'Did you see her that night?'

No hesitation this time. 'No, not then. We didn't go to the lounge, just the pool bar.'

'What happened after Beth Jones went to the loo? Do you remember?'

'Um, yeah, she was pretty pissed – she can really put it away, you know. I went to the loo as well, checked on her, but she said she was going off to bed. I'd have walked her, but she kinda shook me off.'

'And where did you go then?' There'd been no sign of him on CCTV returning to the bar.

He screwed up his eyes. 'Um, I met up with Corinna and we went to the room, had a few more drinks on the balcony.'

'With Vince too?'

'That's right. With Vince.'

Alison watched him steadily. 'And have you any idea where Vince went after he left your flat? He's missing.'

Joel shook his head. 'No idea. He must have taken off before the paramedics came. I was kind of preoccupied, you know.'

'That's all you can tell me?'

'Yeah. That's all.' His eyes jumped away, back to Corinna. He was definitely lying, as was Beth. She just had to find out why.

Beth – then

She'd been snapping pictures of everything to send to Tanya and Janice, plus her various group chats. The spa, the pool, the other pool, the beach, the buffet spread of fresh fruits, her hand holding a cocktail up to the sunset, or a mimosa at breakfast. *It'd be rude not to.* She uploaded many to Instagram too, getting some comfort from the comments. *Beautiful! Enjoy!*

Everyone thought she was having such a great time. But she wasn't. Because she had somehow come on holiday with a stranger instead of her husband. Last evening in the restaurant, they'd made some desultory chat over dinner, but he'd become irritable when she asked him timidly about how work was going, and he'd stormed off early to the hotel room, claiming his stomach was upset. Beth had been left to finish her meal alone, tears in her eyes, sure that everyone was looking at her and wondering who the sad woman was. Luckily, Alison and her partner had already left before that, as Beth could not endure any more sympathetic questions.

When she'd gone upstairs, thinking that they could at least fall asleep in each other's arms, or even more, he was locked in the bathroom and sulkily said he needed some space. When he came out at last, he was asleep by the time she'd taken off her make-up. She had nudged him very gently with her foot. 'Babe?' They were on holiday, weren't they? And not even forty? Didn't normal couples have sex on their holidays?

He'd grunted, then turned away from her and started snoring. She had lain awake for hours, biting her lip to keep from crying. Tomorrow would be different, she told herself. He just needed to relax. But this morning she'd woken up to find him already gone, and she could not locate him for over an hour, since he didn't answer his phone or reply to her messages. Eventually she found him on the beach on a lounger, staring out to sea. 'There you are. Are you OK?'

He had started, looked at her like she was a stranger. 'What do you want?'

Beth had gaped at him. 'What do I want? I want to spend time with my husband, that's what. We're on holiday. I want to have breakfast together, and sit together by the pool, maybe read our books. I want you to *talk* to me.'

He'd said nothing for a moment, his eyes hidden behind his reflective sunglasses. After a moment he said, 'Alright. Let's go to the pool then.'

They were there now, a cocktail melting beside Beth. Vince was at least next to her on the adjoining lounger, but he might as well have been on Mars for all she could speak to him. His headphones were in, and he was drinking a sparkling water, though she had tried to cajole him into a beer, thinking he might at least relax and talk to her that way. She was pretending to read her Philippa Perry book, but the warm, wise advice seemed to trickle over her like cold water. No one could advise her on this. She was in big, big trouble. Everyone else was just sitting around the pool, skin pink, eyes shut, either scrolling on phones or reading, slurping down lurid sugary cocktails or just asleep. Even Alison and her partner were over there, but Beth had studiously ignored them, reading and scrolling contentedly on their phones, sometimes stopping to show each other things. She wanted to scream at people. *How can you be so calm? Don't you know the sky is falling in?*

She was sitting there, in this state of outwardly calm utter panic, when the other couple arrived. She noticed it first because they caused a minor disturbance, as if celebrities had shown up. The woman was tiny, barely five foot, surely, in big sunglasses and a chic linen cover-up, and the man was so muscled it barely seemed real, with two full arms of tattoos and a head shaved into complicated patterns. The receptionist, the pretty one, was showing them around, gesturing with her manicured hands towards the beach, the spa.

'I wonder if they're famous,' she said, forgetting that she wasn't allowed to talk to her husband anymore.

But Vince actually looked up from his phone and took out his headphones. He even took off his sunglasses.

'What?' said Beth. He had a strange look on his face. 'Vince, what's up?'

'Nothing. Nothing at all. It's just – I thought I knew her from somewhere, that's all.'

'You do? Is she on TV or something?' Maybe they were off some reality show that Beth didn't watch. Reality was overrated, she felt.

'I don't know.'

Beth didn't know what to say. Vince had turned pale for a second, and was trying to cover it now, putting his sunglasses back on. 'But where could you know her from?'

'I said I don't *know*, Beth. Maybe off TV or the internet or something. Or just imagining it.' Vince didn't really watch TV, except for *Top Gear* and documentaries about the Second World War. Why would he know some tiny, beautiful young woman? Beth had a hollow feeling in her stomach and put down the raspberry-flavoured cocktail she was drinking, so sweet it set her teeth on edge. She'd lost count of how many she'd had, but they were so watered down it barely mattered. And you had to get your money's worth at an all-inclusive.

She tried again. 'If it's someone from the internet, you don't really go on it, do you?'

'I don't post, but I do sometimes look at stuff. Anyway, I said I didn't know. I probably don't recognise her at all. For God's sake, does everything have to be policed now?'

And just like that their brief window of conversation was over, and things were terrible again. He did not speak to her for the rest of the afternoon. But every time Beth looked up from her book or her own phone, she'd see nosey Alison staring over at them, gaze trained on Vince. Did she know something Beth didn't?

Alison – now

She was very glad to find a lift up to the penthouse flat, actually opening into it, very swish. And she was amazed Corinna had not died from such a fall. Apparently she'd landed on the shrubbery downstairs, and was very lucky to be alive, even had a chance to recover. The place seemed very sterile, though, with the kind of cheap, mass-produced art and knick-knacks you got in Ikea or somewhere. It didn't seem like someone's home. Joel had spun her some story about having dry rot and needing to move out of their own place. She'd taken the supposed address but was not at all convinced they even owned property in the UK at all. Why would they lie about such a thing?

She felt wildly out of place at the crime scene in her floral maternity dress while everyone else was in white forensics suits or police uniforms. She'd been given the biggest suit they had, and it was still hard to zip it up over her belly. The DC on the scene looked about nineteen, pink-faced and bum-fluffed. His name was Gavin, she had gleaned.

'OK, so this isn't their place?'

He shook his head. 'It's an Airbnb, rented just for a month.' Joel had made it sound like a longer rental.

'But don't they live in London?'

'Apparently not, ma'am. We couldn't find any address for them in this country.'

Very strange. Why on earth would they have rented a place in this nondescript corner of South London, and why just for a month? She walked towards the balcony where the crime had happened, if indeed it was a crime. The remnants of a dinner party sat on the table – half-drunk glasses of wine, salad wilting in bowls. Joel had not been allowed to return, of course.

'Show me the balcony, then.'

Outside, the wind was high, and the walls around it seemed worryingly low. She could imagine all too well Corinna plunging over. There was nothing much else to see. Some half-dead plants in tubs, a patio table.

'The lights were on,' said Gavin. 'We switched them off. You know. For the environment.'

'That was very thoughtful of you.' She stepped closer to the edge and looked down. She could see flattened bushes below, and a dark circle on the patio where Corinna's blood had been washed off after Forensics did their thing. 'I can't believe she's still alive.'

Gavin was keen. 'Actually, ma'am, it's not unknown for people to survive falls even higher than this, if there's something to break it. I've heard of someone falling forty-seven floors and not dying, and—'

'Yes, I'm sure you're right. Point is not that she's alive, though. It's did someone try to kill her – and if so, is there any way to prove that?'

There were two witnesses to what Beth might have done, since Joel claimed not to have seen anything. One was currently unconscious, and one had absconded. She felt a fresh surge of rage at Vince Castries for leaving his wife like this, to face the damage he'd begun. She was about to go back in when she spotted something.

'Gavin. Have you logged this?' It looked like broken glass, a few shards of it on the balcony.

'Oh yes. It's not from the window or any of the glasses. Joel Hardiman said he didn't know where it came from.'

Strange.

'Get it lifted for testing, will you?'

The rest of the flat had hardly any possessions, which fitted with it being a temporary rental. Most of the drawers in the bedroom were empty. Thinking of the detritus she and Tom had accumulated over the years, Alison wondered where Joel and Corinna actually lived. Their whole life was some kind of facade, clearly. She'd seen videos recorded in beautiful homes in indefinable countries, sometimes that kind of huge, bland American house, sometimes chic flats in beige and white. What a scam. She felt a bit of rage at Joel and Corinna too, even if Corinna was unconscious.

In her rustling suit, she turned in a circle in the bedroom, the bed neatly made, a few items on each side table. An Apple Watch, a charger, lip balm, a paperback book that Alison had read herself and enjoyed. She always liked to take a moment like this in an investigation to stand among the ruins of a person's life and look for the telling detail. Even if there was a dead body bleeding on to the living-room floor, she found there were often more clues in the things people didn't expect to be seen. The normal bits that made up their lives. What was there here to see, with so few possessions?

She opened the bedside drawer, and struck gold. It was very rare nowadays that people actually printed out photos and left them as handy clues. But here was a wallet of them, with a Spanish brand printed on the side. Joel and Corinna's holiday snaps. But not of them. There was Beth and Vince by the pool, obviously arguing. Beth walking away in tears. There was a balcony, at night-time, Corinna's silhouette framed against the sky as she sat dangerously on the edge. Alison leafed through with her gloved hands, but there was nothing more incriminating. Why would they take pictures of Beth and Vince, and why go to the trouble of printing them out? It didn't make sense.

Now here were some at the beach the next day. Ana's body could not be seen, thankfully, but there were Vince and Beth again, white-faced, her hand clamped to her cheek. Looking extremely guilty indeed. Alison caught sight of herself, and sighed at how huge she was, not to mention red as a tomato and sweating all down her back. And who was that? There was a man standing to the edge of the crowd who'd caught her eye, but she wasn't sure why. Just a normal holidaymaker, a man of around fifty in a short-sleeved shirt and shorts, sunglasses perched on his head. She might have seen him around the hotel in fact; he looked vaguely familiar. He was staring straight out of shot, at where the body must have been still bobbing in the waves. Right at the dead woman.

Clearly, Joel or whoever took the picture had been aiming it at Vince and Beth, and this man had just wandered into shot. But a well-honed instinct told Alison that this was important. She had to find out who he was.

'Gavin. Here.' She directed him to remove and log the pictures.

She heard voices in the hallway and opened the door to see one of her least-favourite people. DS Nigel Heptonspagh, who'd never got over Alison's elevation to DI. 'Hi, Nige,' she said, on purpose.

Nigel was the kind of man who wore waxed jackets even in the most urban areas of London. 'Ma'am. I thought this was a CID case?'

'Could be attempted murder, don't you think?'

'Maybe. Unclear at the moment.'

'Right, so I thought I'd check it out. Plus, it might link up with another case I'm looking into.' He didn't need to know the case was in Spain and therefore very far from her patch.

His eyes travelled down her. 'Aren't you on desk duties? I thought I heard you were.'

'I can manage a bit of fieldwork, thank you. Though I might borrow Gavin here to come with me.' Gavin beamed. Alison could hardly remember being such an eager beaver, before cynicism had set in.

'You'll keep me in the loop?'

'Of course, DS Heptonspagh.' He scowled as she used his title, a reminder that she'd been promoted above him.

She noted that he was losing his hair, which she would be sure to tell Tom about. After an incident during the Christmas Pub Quiz over the difference between an administrative and a legislative capital, Nigel had also become one of his least-favourite people. It was these little shared grievances that kept a relationship alive, Alison felt.

Beth – then

See, this was nice. She'd booked them into the spa's 'thermal suite' for the afternoon, and had suggested a couples massage, but Vince had refused, saying he was too sunburnt to have someone touching him. So she wasn't having one either. They were sitting in an outdoor jacuzzi, the bubbles foaming up around her face. Vince was staring into space. 'Enjoying it?' she asked, hopefully.

'Mmm. It's a bit hot for spas, isn't it? Must be nearly forty today.'

Why did you let me book it then? Beth bit her lip. She had to say something. This couldn't go on. 'Look, we can just go home if you aren't having a good time,' she tried.

'What?' His brow furrowed.

'This whole holiday. You've been absolutely miserable from the minute we got here, and you don't seem to want to spend any time with me.'

'What are you talking about?' His eyes darted about, voice lowered – Vince had a terrible fear of public confrontation.

'Last night, for example. Where are you going? I keep waking up and you're not even there. It's so lonely.'

'I haven't been sleeping! I told you that. I just go down to the lobby, get a drink, try to calm my nerves.'

'But what nerves? Are you going to tell me what's going on?'

A slight pause. He looked away, the water from the jacuzzi slapping near his ear. 'Nothing's going on. We've been a couple for eight years, Beth. Do we have to spend every waking minute together?'

'No, but some time would be nice.'

'What's this, then?'

'You're complaining even about this. Nothing I do is right.'

He turned to glare at her, and the look in his eyes – haunted, almost – hit her in the solar plexus. She even gasped. He began, 'Look, you've no idea—'

'Hi! Mind if we join you?'

It was the couple from the pool earlier, the Instagrammers. Beth hoped they hadn't heard the argument, and hastily rearranged her face. She recalled seeing them the night before, the freedom of their movements on the balcony, their ease with each other and in their own bodies. She stammered, 'Oh, hi, of course.'

Vince was looking away again, his body turned to the side. The jacuzzi was not large, so as the other couple slid in, it suddenly felt like quite close quarters. The woman was tiny, in a cut-out red swimsuit that showed almost every inch of her lithe body, her big curls gathered on top of her head, various chains and rings and bracelets adorning her limbs. The man was big, with gym-honed muscles and tattoo sleeves, the sides of his head shaved.

'Hi,' he said. Handsome. They were both so good-looking they didn't seem real. He reached over to shake Vince's hand. 'Joel, hi, and this manic pixie here is Corinna.'

Corinna held her hand out to Beth, who shook it, a bit nonplussed at this formality. It was surprisingly cold, the nails sharp. 'Hi.'

'Hi,' she said, feeling embarrassed about sitting beside strangers in her control-stomach M&S swimsuit in sensible black. 'I'm Beth. This is Vince.'

The woman turned to Vince, hand out again. 'Hi, I'm Corinna.'

'Hi.'

Somehow, Beth did not like the moment they touched fingers. He must be thinking, if only my wife were this toned and tiny and beautiful.

She said, 'Where are you guys from?'

He sounded British, Essex maybe, but her accent was unquantifiable, wandering all over the Atlantic.

'Just outside London,' said Corinna. 'How about you?'

'Oh same. South-east London. Thornton Heath?'

'Oh yes, I know it. We're out west, but I guess you could call us digital nomads. Content creators.'

As if that were a real job. 'Oh, right. Sounds interesting.' Beth didn't think *works for the council* and *manages a green energy firm* would impress them. 'Nice spa, isn't it?'

'Lovely. Between you and me . . .' Here the man leaned in conspiratorially, so close his solid leg touched Beth's under the water. She jerked hers away. 'The hotel asked us to make some posts in return for a few perks, so we're just reviewing it, and the other facilities. All honest feedback, of course. Our followers expect it.'

'So you got to stay for free?' Vince suddenly spoke.

'Yeah, well, in exchange for making content! And that's a lot of work.' Corinna beamed. Vince was still staring at her.

'Corinna, did you say, is that your name?'

'Yeah, why?'

'It's just – you look kind of familiar, that's all.'

She reached up to release her bun, the curls snapping loose and tumbling out towards the water, the ends of them turning darker. She smiled. 'Oh, we get that a lot. You've probably seen us online.'

But Vince didn't go online – though Beth remembered his reaction the other day, when they had arrived at the pool. He had gone pale for a moment, on seeing her. Was it possible that, during all those hours glued to his phone, he had started to scroll through Instagram, TikTok? Following women who looked like Corinna?

She reached for the railing and hauled herself out of the jacuzzi, causing Corinna to blink water from her pretty face. 'Sorry. Got too hot.'

Vince was following her. 'Yeah, think we've had enough now, in these temperatures too.'

'Nice to meet you!' chirped Corinna, nestling into the curve of her partner's arm now they had more space. Happy, in love.

Beth muttered the same back, barely able to speak over the lump in her throat. The grief that there was no longer her and Vince, and likely never would be again.

Him

'We should leave today, maybe,' he said over the breakfast table, as nonchalantly as he could.

She looked up from the grapefruit she was digging at, spurting juice on to the tablecloth in a manner he'd already told her he didn't like. 'What? Why?'

'Well, there's been a death! It's creepy, isn't it?'

'But it's nothing to do with us. There must be hundreds of people in this resort. And we've paid for another three days. Think of the waste.'

'I don't like it. It's ruined it for me, all these police about the place.' He sighed and adopted a guilt-tripping tone that usually worked. 'But if you can really enjoy yourself and drink cocktails while some poor young woman is lying dead . . .'

He left it for a few seconds, and she started nodding like that annoying dog from the TV ads. 'You're right. I suppose I wasn't thinking of that.'

'You see what I mean, don't you? It's just – bad energy, you know? Sad. And scary – what if the killer is still out there? I worry about you, you know. Anyone could be next. I'd like to be home in our own nice house. Wouldn't you?'

He saw how she lit up at the unexpected warmth, and it curdled his stomach. He even slid a hand over the table and held hers, sticky as it was with sweat and juice. She smiled. He took his hand back – overdoing it would be suspicious. She said, 'Alright. Should I try to change the flights? I don't think they're refundable.'

Usually he hated wasting money, made her account for every pound, so he had to play this carefully. 'It's OK. We can book some new ones if it gets us home safe. Budget ones, mind.'

'Of course.'

'I'm sorry. We can go on a nice trip later in the year, maybe. I just – don't want to be around this.'

Her face became stricken with sympathy, and he averted his eyes from the sunburn on her nose. 'I'm so sorry, I didn't even think that it must be bringing back terrible memories.'

'Right. Exactly. Thank you for understanding.'

They went on eating their breakfasts, though every part of him was screaming to be away, watching for a flash of navy uniforms as every new person came into the dining room. But he knew how to hide it. He sipped his terrible machine coffee and watched her fiddle about with her phone on the EasyJet website. With luck, they would be home tonight, and out of danger. It was a shame the extradition laws between the UK and Spain had changed from the eighties, when you couldn't be brought back to face charges, but who would think to chase up a random couple who had nothing whatever to do with such a terrible crime? As she'd said, there were hundreds of guests in this hotel.

He thought back to the night before. He had deliberately approached the woman in an area that wasn't covered by CCTV, having scoped out the cameras beforehand. And there weren't any on the beach, as far as he knew. She had been looking for her car keys, frustrated and annoyed, and he'd offered to help. That lazy security guard had been sitting on a lounger scrolling on his phone, and he was pretty sure had not seen them pass. She hadn't wanted to go to the beach, not in her nice dress, but he'd convinced her that her keys might be there. Then he'd persuaded her to have a drink to calm her nerves, from the hip flask he always carried, which had proven useful over the years. She hadn't wanted to – wasn't a big drinker, she said – but she had done it to keep him happy. To appease him, as they always did. That much he could remember. Her red dress fluttering in the slight night breeze, the moon illuminating her from behind as he pretended to take her picture for 'headshots'. After that he couldn't remember what had happened. Of course, he had not intended for anything to go wrong. Of course not. Checking out the camera locations was just something he did everywhere he went. An old habit. He was sure he had not hurt her on purpose. He wouldn't do a thing like that. It was just an unfortunate accident, but now that it was too late and she was sadly gone, he was going to do whatever it took to protect himself, and be away from here as soon as possible. Once they were gone, he would be able to breathe more easily.

Alison – now

God, she would miss this, the peace of settling down in front of HOLMES with a cup of tea and a biscuit. Of course, this time she could barely reach the keyboard over her belly, and the tea had to be decaf and the biscuit had to be non-existent. But still. She had always enjoyed the research bit of her cases, shining a light on every corner of people's lives and seeing what scurried. Vince Castries; she knew his dark secrets already. One of Tom's first cases, Vince had been just a teenager then. The girl had been left to die on the outskirts of a playing field, an open-and-shut case where the five-a-side team who had been practising there were the only ones who could have done it. The dead girl had even told her sister she was going to see 'the team'. It was determined she'd had a crush on the captain, Peter Johnson, and had thought she was only going to meet him. She'd thought wrong. The next morning her strangled body had been found, as was so often the case, by a dog walker. It was one of the many reasons Alison would never get a dog.

Vince Castries had been one of the football team. He had left early, he claimed, when he saw what they were planning, but had not told his mother or done anything to help the girl. He'd immediately turned on his friends and helped send them down. Alison checked their whereabouts now. Peter Johnson was still in Belmarsh. The other three boys would only have served a few years, being underage at the time. She wondered about the men who were now free, who had Vince Castries to blame for the fact they had spent years of their lives in prison. If they might want revenge. And where was Vince now? For a man who seemed to have no friends and no contact with his family, he'd somehow gone to ground. She was waiting on the information from his phone company.

There was nothing on the system about Corinna, though Alison suspected the couple might not be using their real names. She fired off a message to Alejandro, remembering how he had perked up when she and Tom mentioned them back in Tenerife. Had he suspected them of something already? The name Joel Hardiman brought up a hit for minor credit-card fraud, which was interesting given he was always plugging his investment expertise on his profile. She didn't trust those two one bit.

Beth Jones was another matter. Surely this mild-mannered public servant, this reader of self-help books, would not have a criminal conviction? But Alison had been a police officer long enough now that she never believed anyone was definitely innocent. Even sweet old grannies could have long-ago arrests for shoplifting or fraud. She put the name into the database, plus the date of birth, which they had since Beth's recent arrest. The information would remain on here even if she was never charged. Alison always enjoyed the moments waiting for the system to tick away, searching its files and throwing up goodies. When the results came up for Beth Jones, she took a sharp intake of breath.

'Found something good?' said Samir, the civilian analyst, whose desk was covered in boxes of different Pukka teas. Alison was not a fan, and her current estrangement from proper brews was almost harder than giving up booze.

'Oh yes,' said Alison, hearing the pleasure in her own voice and remembering people's lives were at stake. And this didn't prove anything – having a record was more common than people thought, and it could just be an unfortunate coincidence. But it did suggest a history, a capacity for violence that you couldn't guess from speaking to the shaking, crying woman. Alison hated it when people didn't tell her the truth, and several things had now proven Beth Jones was most definitely guilty of that. So what else had she lied about?

Beth – then

They were having a desultory drink at the bar pre-dinner when they saw the couple again. Topics of conversation Beth had tried and given up on included the weather, what colour they should paint their bedroom walls, which still had the stripes of sample shades on from months ago, and brands of beer popular in Spain. Vince responded to everything with grunts or a few monosyllables, or by picking up his phone and swiping through it. She was going out of her mind. Earlier she had looked up the cost of a last-minute flight to London, fantasising about dashing the phone from his hand to the ground. *I'm going home. I can't live like this anymore. But don't worry, I doubt you'll even notice.* The cheapest she could find was over five hundred quid, and anyway, she wasn't one for the grand gesture. Too scared he'd take her up on her offer.

'Mind if we join you?' A cheerful voice broke through her reverie, and she looked up to see Joel and Corinna sitting down at the table beside theirs, each of them holding two drinks in various lurid shades.

'Um, no, please.'

Corinna was absolutely stunning in a clinging red dress with spaghetti straps and a cut-out showing her honed stomach. Joel had his shirt undone almost to the waist, displaying his own abs and near-total tattoo coverage. Beth felt a bit as if Brad Pitt and

Angelina Jolie had joined them. They moved the table closer, suddenly on top of Beth and Vince.

'You went for something more sensible, I see, mate.' The man nodded to Vince's beer bottle. 'Wise, very wise.'

Vince looked confused. 'Not into all that sweet stuff.'

'Well, me neither, mate, but when in Rome.'

Corinna giggled. 'He loves them really. Just thinks it's not manly to have an umbrella in your drink.' She reached out and took the little paper one from his cocktail, then tucked it behind Joel's ear. 'Gorgeous. Let me get you.'

He adopted a demure pose, hands under his chin, and she took several pictures with her phone. 'OK, enough. Phone down, babe.' He said it with such rueful adoration that it almost made Beth gasp with jealousy. Imagine having a partner who noticed you, who teased you, who asked *you* to put down your phone because they wanted your attention. No wonder Corinna took so many selfies, when she looked like that. As opposed to Beth's own pink-faced, double-chinned attempt of earlier.

'So,' said Joel, a strangely big smile on his face. Why were they so happy? Maybe because they were on holiday, she acknowledged. It was Beth who was strange, weeping into the swimming pool. 'Who's up for a great night?'

He leaned over and clinked Beth's glass, meeting her gaze in a sudden moment of intensity that made her stomach turn over. His eyes were very blue – closer to green, really – in his tanned face. But why on earth did two such beautiful creatures want to talk to miserable old Beth and Vince?

◆ ◆ ◆

Her head was spinning. She was laughing hard at something Joel was saying about boomers on Facebook, and she couldn't remember exactly what, but it was very funny, whatever it was. How many of the lurid cocktails had she had, and what was even in them? Joel kept signalling to the waiter, dark-haired and handsome, who whisked away evidence of empty glasses and brought new ones, crunchy with ice and sweet on her tongue.

This was what she'd hoped for from their holiday, for Vince to be smiling and chatting, and his phone not even in sight. Of course, she'd hope he would be smiling at her and not at a younger, more glamorous woman, but maybe his happiness would benefit Beth in the end. And she had Joel, who was being strangely attentive, laughing at her lame jokes, staring right into her eyes with his piercing ones, even brushing her hand with his when he handed her a drink. In fact, the touching had increased with each round. Corinna kept laughing and putting a hand on Vince's arm, swatting him playfully, and Joel had his arm draped over the back of Beth's chair. If she leaned back an inch, she'd be touching him, and she could feel the heat from his heavy, muscled limb, glowing through his tattoos and the seat and her thin cotton shirt. He looked like Tom Hardy a bit. Tanya was mad about him. Beth wondered what she'd think of Joel, with her famous Dickhead Radar. It was a bit weird that they wanted to talk to Beth and Vince, but maybe they were just bored on holiday. It did get boring, didn't it, a solid week of the same person you saw every day at home. No need to be paranoid.

She met Vince's eyes over the table, and tried to smile, but his gaze passed over her, like she was someone on the street. She saw a shadow cross his face again, and wondered what it was he was thinking of when that happened. *Please, please, why won't you talk to me? I'm your wife.*

She was very drunk, she realised. Walking all the way to the loos by the beach seemed insurmountable, but now Joel had a cocktail umbrella behind each ear, and was talking like a Southern belle, and she was going to wet herself if she didn't go soon.

'Excuse me.' She wobbled to her feet. 'Loo.'

Vince did not look up as she left, and the sadness was back, numbed out by alcohol and the chemicals flooding her system from flirting with someone else. It was nice, for a minute. Was this why people had affairs? But she didn't want anyone else, not even the handsome younger man with his shirt unbuttoned. She just wanted Vince. Beth peed, staring at the sand spilled on the floor of the loos, realising how very drunk she was. In the mirror she looked sweaty and wild-eyed, and splashed some water on to her face, which only made her make-up run further.

She stumbled back out into the warm Spanish night, hearing the roar of the waves and the distant music of the bar.

'You OK?' Someone loomed out of the darkness and took her arm. 'Just wanted to check on you.'

She smiled up at him. So he did care. 'I'm fine.'

'Here.' He stuck out an arm and she took it. Then Joel said, 'Can't have anything happening to you now, can we?'

Beth let herself enjoy the brief walk back, the strength of his body, the smell of his aftershave. Of course he wasn't interested in frumpy old Beth, when he had Corinna. But it was nice to pretend, even for a second, that someone was.

'Where are we going?' They weren't headed down the path to the bar. Wobbling, Beth fell against him.

'It's OK. I'm just taking you for some air.'

She wanted to get back to Vince, Vince and Corinna, didn't want to leave them alone, but it felt like too much effort to protest. So she let herself be led towards the beach.

Alison – now

Tom was absolutely going to kill her. She was a little ashamed of herself, truth be told. OK, so maybe the doctor hadn't meant strictly no getting out of bed at all, but she very likely had not meant 'visit a category-A prison' either. And yet here she was, holding out her arms for a pat-down like at airport security. She remembered back then, Tom asking so solicitously if the machines could harm the baby. Alison hadn't even thought of that. She kept kind of forgetting about the pregnancy, in a strange way. Like a bag she was lugging around with her. *Oh yeah, I brought this with me again.*

She reminded herself she was here for a reason. Her heart broke for Lucy Brady, the young girl left for dead on a playing field on a misty November night. If Vince Castries was to be believed, the man she was here to see had instigated that. Invited Lucy there, knowing she had a crush on him, the handsome captain of the football team, and passed her around his friends before strangling her.

Alison could imagine it all too well. The fluttering in Lucy's stomach as she put on a nice top under her coat, despite the cold, and layered up her lip gloss. Telling her parents she was going to a friend's house to watch *Buffy*, although her sister knew the truth. Maybe faltering when she saw Peter's team-mates were still there, but perhaps they'd leave soon. Handing around a pre-made bottle of vodka and Diet Coke, which had all their DNA on it when it came to the trial, maybe relaxing a bit as the alcohol hit her bloodstream. Laughing, waiting, hoping.

Then the moment of the turn, when she would have known what was happening to her, where this was going, but not been able to stop it. The muddy ground beneath her back. The air dying in her throat. And Ana Garcia had been strangled too, hadn't she? Was that a coincidence? Alison hardened her heart, though she also hated to see long-term prisoners, their learned helplessness, the usual lack of remorse, the waste of it all.

She knew the guard who'd come to collect her, a no-nonsense woman in her late thirties with an all-consuming love of *Strictly Come Dancing* that you'd never guess at from her severe appearance.

'Hiya, Mae.'

'Alright, Alison. Look at you! Ready to pop. Been away, have you? You're lovely and brown.'

'Yeah, Tenerife, one of those babymoon things.'

Mae wrinkled her nose. 'We went once. Didn't fancy it much. Too hot, and all Spanish food.'

She walked Alison in, unlocking and locking doors as they went. 'Surprised you want to see this one. Very old case, isn't it? He'd just turned eighteen when he did it.'

'I know. Possible link with something new.'

Though her head hurt, trying to put the pieces together. A fall, or perhaps a push, from a balcony in South London. The murder of a Spanish singer, and another murder over twenty years ago. What were the threads tying these things together? She could not grasp them, and she was aware that time was running out for her to solve it.

Mae had stopped walking and was looking at her with concern. 'You alright? Not going to have it here, are you?'

Alison panted, pausing for a moment to catch her breath. 'I'm only seven months gone, Mae. I'm just tired.'

The other woman chuckled. 'I thought that with my first. Come back to me when you're pregnant with two underfoot as well – that's tired.'

No way, thought Alison silently. She was increasingly thinking they'd be 'one and done', as the annoying mum-fluencers said.

Peter Johnson was waiting for her in an interview room. He had the puffy look of a man who'd grown up behind bars, and a wary watchfulness that set Alison's pulse racing even more than it was from the walk. She took a seat gladly. 'Hi, Peter. I'm DI Alison Hegarty.'

'We met before?' He watched her closely. 'I don't recognise you.'

'No, we haven't met. I'm investigating another case I think could be linked to yours.'

He leapt on that. 'Like, new evidence? Right, because my last appeal got turned down, and I've been in over twenty years, you know. That's more than the usual tariff for this kind of crime.' He'd got more time for the luring, the set-up, being the only one whose DNA was found on her. For being a few days over eighteen, unlike the other boys. 'You see, it was all wrong. I never even invited her! She just came. She was obsessed with me. So the sentence wasn't fair.' Ah, a man who'd had a long time to study the legal system. Not stupid. He'd been headed for Durham University before his conviction.

She held up a hand. 'I'm sorry, Peter, this is nothing to do with your case.'

His shoulders slumped. 'Then why . . . ?'

'I'm hoping you might be able to clear some things up for me.' She looked at him squarely across the table. 'What can you tell me about Vincent Castries?'

'Who?'

'The boy who gave evidence against you back then.'

Peter sat back, his face twisting in a scowl. 'That what he's calling himself now? His real name's Darren. Darren Charles. That's what we all knew him as. And I can tell you plenty.'

On her way back out to the car, Alison realised she should go home and rest. And she had fully intended to do that, until she received a message back from Alejandro in Tenerife. She read his email and immediately dialled the station number, getting through to Colette.

'DCI Milton.'

'Ma'am, I'd like to bring Joel Hardiman in for questioning.'

'Didn't you speak to him already?'

'I did. But he hasn't exactly been honest with us.'

Beth – then

‘We should get back,’ she kept saying, but somehow she and Joel were now sitting down on the beach, listening to the wash of the waves. The sand was scratching her skin, but the breeze was warm and pleasant.

‘It’s fine. What are you, joined at the hip?’

‘Well, hardly. He can’t get away from me fast enough these days.’ She’d been too honest. She was drunk. And where even was Vince? Why hadn’t he come after her, like Joel had?

Joel rested a hand on her leg, covered by her thin cotton dress. ‘I can see that, Beth. It’s not right, is it? He should respect you more.’

‘He should. But he doesn’t.’ Her voice was thick with tears and drink.

Joel was holding her hand now. His was rough and warm, and it was nice to be touched, so nice that she found herself leaning into his shoulder, and then his arm was around her. She said, ‘You guys seem so happy. You and Corinna. How do you do that?’

He laughed, and it sounded a little bitter. ‘Oh, Beth, you don’t know the half of it, trust me. Like what she’s up to right now.’

Beth pulled away. ‘What do you mean?’

‘Nothing. Just let it go. We can’t control what other people do.’

‘You mean – her and Vince . . .’ Surely not. Beth loved Vince, but slim, tiny, beautiful Corinna would hardly go for a man pushing forty with unstable bowels, given he wasn't rich, and she had this dreamboat in her bed. None of it made sense. She found herself scrabbling to her feet, sand under her palms.

'Beth, wait! You're in no condition to go wandering off.'

'I have to find Vince.'

'Trust me, he doesn't want to be found.'

'I don't care. Don't care!'

He was her husband, damn it. That should count for something, those vows they had made, even if he seemed not to remember these days. She set off back towards the bar, so drunk that her footsteps would not stay in a straight line, her sandals clattering on the path. She had only one thought in her head. Find Vince. Stop whatever might be happening.

Alison – now

'Why am I here?' said Joel, looking around him nervously. 'Am I under arrest?'

'Not yet. If you're arrested, you'll be cautioned.'

'Do I need a lawyer?'

'That's up to you. I just have a few questions to ask you.'

'But why am I here?'

She had asked him to come to the station, knowing how the forbidding atmosphere, the public-service blue and cream paint, worked on people's consciences. Even the totally blameless started to wonder if they'd committed a crime under these circumstances. And she didn't think Joel was blameless at all, especially after what Alejandro had told her.

'I just said: I have questions.' She spread out copies of the photos she'd found in their apartment. 'Do you recognise these?'

He leaned over to look, then paled. 'Ermmm. Yeah. Corinna took them.'

'And why? Why have you taken so many pictures of another couple, who you supposedly only met out there?'

'That's true. We did meet them there. But I don't know why she took them.' She waited. Joel sighed heavily. 'Look, Corinna's in a coma. We don't need any more aggro.'

'I'm aware of that, and I'm sorry, but I do need some answers.' No answer. 'Joel, I have reason to suspect you and Corinna are implicated in the murder of Ana Garcia de Vasquez out in Spain. You may not know this, but it is possible for you to be extradited there to answer questions. Not to mention a few other little allegations, such as credit-card fraud and skipping out on bills.' Alejandro had told her he suspected Joel and Corinna might be a pair of fraudsters he was looking for, who had left several luxury hotels without paying, after indulging in some credit-card skulduggery.

She stared at him. He was not a smart man, she knew, and she suspected not brave either. She tried: 'You'd really rather you or your girlfriend be charged with murder than tell me what's going on?' Another second of staring and Joel collapsed.

He heaved another sigh. 'She isn't,' said Joel, looking at the floor.

'Sorry?'

'She isn't my girlfriend, not really. Corinna. She – it's just something we do.'

Alison stared at him. Realisations were coalescing in her mind – ideas – clues. 'Explain.'

'It's just – this thing we do,' he said again. 'We – Corinna – we make friends with couples on holiday, then ask them to invest in my company.'

'And you persuade them to do this by taking pictures of them? The husbands, at least? With Corinna?'

'That's the general idea.' He was squirming under her gaze, just how she liked it. 'It's just a play.'

'A love scam is what it sounds like,' she said severely. 'That's a crime, you know.'

'We never did it in this country. And is it a crime, really? If people just – decide to invest?'

'If you forced them to by taking compromising pictures of them with your not-girlfriend, yeah it is. It's blackmail, or extortion. Definitely illegal in most countries.' She supposed it was part of their scam to get the photos developed in physical form, more dramatic maybe than displaying them on a phone.

'Oh. I didn't know.' He shrugged. 'They always seemed up for it, the blokes.'

Idiot. 'What I want to know is, why did you target Vince and Beth? They're broke, surely. He lost his job a while back.'

A strange look spread over Joel's face. 'Huh. Well, I guess that explains a lot, if Beth didn't know.'

'Didn't know what?'

He gave a surprised little laugh. 'Dude, Vince Castries is minted. Or he's going to be, anyway. He filed a patent for, like, some solar panel thing, some component, and the legal stuff is still going through. Some issue with his old job and who owned the copyright, but apparently it's gonna get sorted out soon and he'll be rolling in it.'

'What? And how do you know this, when his own wife doesn't?'

Poor Beth. Just completely in the dark about her entire life. And maybe responsible, Alison had to remind herself, for a woman being in a hospital bed hooked up to tubes. She had to check her sympathy.

'I dunno. Corinna found out about it. She keeps tabs on these things. You know, possible investors. They have a bit of cash, they can put it into my crypto fund, and everyone's happy.'

'Are you even qualified to run an investment fund?'

Another shrug. 'I've read books. Listened to podcasts.'

And the worst part was people actually seemed to believe him. 'So you and Corinna are what – business partners?'

'That's probably the best way to describe it. It's not like *nothing* goes on between us. I mean, I'm a bloke, and she's gorgeous. But most of it is just personas, for the likes online, and for the leads. They lap it up, poor bastards. I lurk about and take some videos, pics, then we show them what we've got, and nine times out of ten, they pay up.'

'How come no one has ever reported you for blackmail?' Or maybe they had. She'd ask Alejandro to dig up any reports of scams in Spain.

He gave that same little chuckle. 'Dude, they're usually in a blind panic. And I don't ask them for money. I act the outraged boyfriend, flex my muscles, threaten to tell the wife, punch them in the face, et cetera. I let them suggest investing in my company. It's so easy to play people; you'd really be amazed.'

'Stop calling me dude, will you? It's Detective Inspector.'

He eyed her. 'Gonna be "Mummy" soon, by the looks of it.'

God, she hated this man. Hated his tattoo sleeves and stupid haircut, short on the bottom and long on top, hated his voice and his manner and his entitlement. 'So tell me the truth about Beth and Vince. You just happened to be in the same resort as them? No, of course not. You followed them out there.'

'Yep. Again, very easy. Looked at the wife's Instagram, and booked into the same hotel, arrived the next day. Struck up a chat in the spa, met them in the bar that night. Got them super-drunk. She went off to bed, like we hoped she would, after I flirted a little bit too hard, fed her too many cocktails. Not that I had to encourage her! That woman can drink, know what I mean? Sometimes the wife falls for it too, with me, and we can do a double-con, both of them desperate to cover it up. That's always beautiful. Or, you know, she might be the one with the cash. We did an MP one time, extra leverage. A big CEO with a house husband. We can do all sorts. Corinna feels weird about women, though – I don't know, solidarity or something.' He seemed to remember where he was.

'Anyway, that's the truth. I don't know anything about the dead girl, swear.'

'I have CCTV of you talking to her in the bar. Her pianist said you were pestering her.'

'Pestering! Mate, do I look like I have to pester women? Yeah, I talked to her. That's a crime now too? I thought she could help us out, truth be told. Make a few euros for herself. Pretty girl, you know, plenty of attention from the husbands in the hotel. But she wasn't up for it.'

'And Vince? Did he go for your "play"?'

'Not really. I was surprised. I mean, he didn't seem all that keen on his missus. But Corinna said he wasn't interested at all, not even after her best moves. Think she was a bit miffed, to be honest.' He looked sad for a second. 'She might be OK, the doctors said. She could wake up any time.'

'Let's hope so.' Not least because Alison had some very pressing questions for her too. 'So tell me the truth, Joel. You gave Vince Castries an alibi – said he was with you all night, though the CCTV suggests otherwise. Was that true?'

He only hesitated for a second. 'No. I went after Beth, sat with her for a bit on the beach, then she ran off. Corinna was with Vince, but she said he just wanted to find Beth, so she gave up, went up to bed. She came up a while after me.' Alison had guessed as much, and it fitted with what she herself had seen, Joel and Corinna on the balcony at the same time she'd heard the scream. 'We had a few drinks on the balcony, went to bed. That's all.'

'So why did you lie? Why protect Vince?'

'I don't know, to be honest. Corinna said we should, since it would alibi us too, 'cos I'd talked to the girl a few times, plus we didn't want them looking too closely at our, eh, other activities.'

'Is that why you sought them out in London too?' She hadn't understood that bit either. The apartment was clearly as much of a facade as their relationship.

'Corinna said we needed to find out what they'd told the police. In case it looked bad for us, you know.'

Clearly, she ran the show. 'I'm going to ask you one more time: do you have any idea where Vince Castries is now? Did you help him get away?'

Joel looked genuinely confused. 'Why would I do that? No, mate, I've no idea where he's gone. Or why. Makes no sense, does it?'

Unless Vince was afraid of getting caught, for something much worse than Corinna's fall. Alison thought it all over, opening the manila file she had with her. 'One more thing, Joel – do you recognise this man at all? This is one of the pictures I found in your apartment, which looks to have been taken on the beach where Ana's body was found.'

Joel craned over to where her finger was hovering, the photograph of the crowd around Ana, the man who had caught Alison's eye. 'Him? No, never seen him before. Just some looky-loo, I guess.'

Alison was certainly going to check if they could be charged with any crimes in Spain or the UK. But the most pressing thing he'd told her was that Vince's alibi, the one that had set him free from Spanish custody, was not true after all. The events of that night were still a mystery, and no one had been proven innocent. Not Vince. And not Beth either.

Beth – then

She woke up with a start. Where was she? What was going on? She was lying on something hard – a plastic sun lounger, with no cushion on it. Her mouth felt dry and tacky. It was dark. The moon overhead, the whisper of the sea. Slowly, her memory returned. She was at the hotel. They'd got drunk with that couple, the young, hot ones, and Joel had waylaid her coming out of the loo, and had he actually been holding her hand on the beach? Shame swept over her. Yes, her marriage was in tatters and her husband was like a stranger. But she'd never been a cheater – she hated cheating, hated it more than anything – and she shouldn't have let her guard down like that. There hadn't been more, had there? No, she remembered running off, leaving Joel on the beach. But what had happened next? She'd been looking for Vince. She must have passed out here by the pool. She'd had so much to drink. More shame.

Have to find him. Have to find them. A nameless fear was growing in her, the things Joel had said – *Trust me, he doesn't want to be found* – the smirk on the face of the pretty younger woman. All her pain and fear and anger rising up in her like vomit. How could this be happening? It was like a nightmare, like one of those terrible dreams you have to sit through as if strapped into your seat for a horror film, but it was real. This was actually going on now, as she lay here. How could he? He knew they could see into Joel and Corinna's room from theirs – would he really have gone there with her? Maybe he just didn't care. Or maybe he was sending a message – *This is how little I think of you.*

She heaved her legs off the lounger, noticing that she still had her sandals on. She didn't know where her bag was, with her phone and room key.

Somehow orientating herself, Beth made her way towards the pool bar. There was the towel hut, locked up and deserted. The pool still glowed like a jewel, but no one was to be seen. She reached the bar, knocking her hip on a chair and yelping. The place was deserted, the chairs upturned on to the tables. Vince was not here. Or Corinna. What time had she gone off to the loo – not quite one, she thought? Time seemed to have shrunk and dilated at the same time, her nap more like being wiped out with anaesthetic than sleep. But at least she could see her bag still there, on the table where she'd left it. She took out her phone, but there were no messages. No calls from her husband, worried that she had gone to the loo and not come back. With another man on her heels. God, it was after two in the morning. She had been passed out for over an hour.

Beth turned back towards the main block of the hotel, to their room. That seemed the most likely place to find Vince – and the thought occurred dimly that she could see into Corinna and Joel's room from there too. It didn't seem possible. Not Vince and Corinna. It made no sense. But where were they, then? And why had Joel said those things? Where was he now?

There! That was her, wasn't it? Corinna. In between the two buildings was a pathway lined with shrubs, lit dimly by security lamps. In a pool of darkness, Beth saw the glow of a cigarette, remembered Corinna sucking on her vape pen. Perhaps she'd come out to sneak a real smoke. A smell of perfume. A flash of red dress as whoever it was crossed their legs, gracefully. There she was. Beth was not going to stand for this. She heard the slap of her own sandals as she moved forward, into the dark.

Alison – now

'So how's the conference?' She settled back against the pillows with her phone propped up, doing her best to look like a woman who'd been in bed all day. Tom was pixellated on the screen as he moved around his hotel room, unpacking. The only person she'd ever known to leave a room looking neater than when he'd checked in.

'Oh, you know. Hours of droning on about cybercrime and the danger of AI.'

'Well, that's a new crime, at least.' She was always fascinated by how quickly humans could monetise, and criminalise, any new technology.

Tom talked for a while about how older people were falling for scams that cloned their kids' voices or their phone screens. It was easily done, and soon there would be no need for Joel and Corinna's brand of honeytrap, as the whole thing could easily be faked. Tom did sound interested in the topic, despite himself. She uh-hummed along. 'And the hotel – there's a pool?'

'Yeah, I had a swim. Not quite as fancy as Tenerife.'

'It's Beth they have in custody, you know. Colette said I can do the interview, once we're ready.'

Nigel had insisted they keep Beth in for the night, running the clock down as they looked for more evidence on whether to charge her with something, assault or GBH, or even attempted murder, which would be Alison's remit. He had officers searching Beth and Vince's flat right now. They'd need authorisation to keep her in for much longer.

He sighed. 'No use in telling you to relax. I know that by now. But please, Ali, take it easy? I'll be back the day after tomorrow, and I don't want to find you in hospital.'

'I'm fine! Feeling absolutely grand.' Not entirely true, but a bit of tiredness was to be expected. It had been a much longer day than she'd planned, but she'd found she just could not let the mystery drop.

'Corinna still with us?'

'Yeah. They seem to think she might wake up, even. She was lucky.'

'No sign of the husband, Vince?'

'Nope. They think he made a run for it while the paramedics were in. And his alibi for Spain was bollocks; Joel admitted as much. No sign of activity on Vince's bank account, and we're getting the phone records, but there's not a trace of him so far.' The man had just vanished. Alison had traced his mother in Reading already, but she claimed not to have seen him in over twenty years.

It made her think even less of Vince Castries than she already did, that he had disappeared now. His wife had stood by him out in Spain, helped to free him from custody, and he wasn't here to do the same for her. 'Also, I – eh – read the transcripts of the interviews on the Lucy Brady case. The ringleader, Peter Johnson, he always claimed he actually hadn't asked her to meet him that night. She seemed to think he'd left her a note, but he said it wasn't him. That someone else lured her down there.'

A small evasion, since she knew what Tom would think about her visiting a prison at the moment. Peter Johnson had said plenty about Vince, who he felt was a traitor who'd lied to save his own skin. Peter's story was that Lucy had wanted him, turned up without warning and thrown herself at him, that it was all consensual and he'd left her alive that night. Maybe one of the other boys had killed her, or some other mysterious passer-by. The same story he'd told at eighteen, which no one had believed.

Tom said, 'Well, that all seems suss. What happened to the other boys involved? They should be out by now.'

Peter Johnson had not known about his fellow convicts, wasn't in touch with anyone, he said.

'I need to look into that. I'll be careful, before you say it.'

'So why's Beth been arrested, if Vince is the one who ran after the fall?'

'Joel says she lost her temper, that he heard her scream. But he didn't see what happened, apparently. So unless Vince turns up or Corinna comes round, there's not much else to get from the situation.' And by tomorrow they would have to charge Beth or let her go. That reminded her. 'So, guess what, I ran them all through PNC and had a ping on Beth. She was arrested ten years ago for assault. Charges dropped in the end, but it shows a capacity for violence, doesn't it?'

Tom was sceptical. 'She looks like she wouldn't say boo to a goose. You're thinking she was mixed up in it, out in Spain? I thought you thought she was the poor battered woman.'

'Maybe. I don't know. You can be both, can't you? Victims do snap sometimes.' There was even a term for it – reactive abuse. Alison had been paying attention at her coercive control seminars. 'I think it's pretty unlikely, though. I'm wondering if someone hurt her in the past and she eventually defended herself. An old boyfriend or something. There's often a pattern to these things.' She couldn't shake the idea that Beth had been mistreated, that she was scared of her husband. She'd had a bruise, she'd been crying, she had lied at first and said she was with him when he found the body. Vince was the one involved in a murder in the past, who had changed his name and was paying out a mysterious sum to someone, who had lost his job and not told his wife. Whose alibi for the more recent murder was false. 'Plenty to follow up, anyway.'

'Which you'll get your DCs to do?' he said. 'Please, Al.'

'Eh. Yeah. I will.'

'And you've remembered the fall is your case, not the murder in Spain?'

'Of course.' But they were connected, somehow. She was sure of it.

After she said goodnight to Tom and promised once again to relax, she gave her email a final check. It was a grudging update from Nigel, who said he had found 'something of interest' in the search of Beth and Vince's flat, which was being sent to Forensics. Alison fired off a response asking for whatever it was to be checked against the forensics report on Ana Garcia. They wouldn't like doing it – it was extra expense, and they weren't keen on working with results they hadn't produced themselves, but if there was a DNA link between Ana and Beth or Vince, it might confirm some of the dark suspicions forming in her mind. Or dispel them.

She took out her notebook and ran over what she knew so far.

Beth Jones – long-ago arrest for assault, which she had never mentioned during all the time Alison was trying to help her. Bruise on wrist after the night of the murder. Very upset. Lied at first about Vince being with her all night. Very drunk that night.

Vince Castries – linked to a dead girl more than twenty years ago, gave evidence against his friends. Peter Johnson claimed Vince had been there for longer than he said, had only run home when Lucy started to scream. That Vince wouldn't have told anyone what happened if the police hadn't come knocking. Certainly he hadn't told anyone about the attack that night, as he let himself into his mother's house and went straight for a shower, then to bed. Hadn't tried to save her. And Vince had also been the one to find Ana's body in Tenerife, conveniently putting his DNA on her. And no one could account for his whereabouts that night – his supposed alibi had now fallen apart.

Corinna Cooper – in hospital unconscious, the only one who could truly say if she'd fallen, given that she had a habit of sitting on the edge of balconies, or if Beth had pushed her. Had pursued Vince and Beth out to Tenerife.

Joel – claimed they were doing low-level love scams to try and fund his ridiculous 'start-up', and that he and Corinna weren't even really a couple but put it on for show. That she'd been the one to suggest targeting Vince Castries in Tenerife, and seeking them out in London too.

That was what Alison didn't understand. Vince wasn't rich – his bank accounts were almost empty. Joel claimed he was about to come into some money, but was that enough of a draw to go all the way to Tenerife? She needed to find out the real reason he'd left his job. She also didn't really understand why Joel and Corinna had lied about Vince's alibi. It didn't make sense – was it just to cover up their own scams? Would they rather a killer went free than being caught in some minor blackmail, which would be hard to prove without any victims willing to come forward? She supposed she'd known people go to great lengths to cover up less.

And then poor Ana, the beautiful singer with the big dreams. Vince had been watching her in the bar, but that proved nothing, and so had Joel. Both Eduardo and Maria Theresa said a man had been hassling her. There were chunks of that evening, both couples extremely drunk, that were unaccounted for or didn't make sense. Beth had been alone for some of it, when she supposedly had gone off to bed. And since Vince's alibi from Joel and Corinna was a lie, all three of them had also possibly been on their own at times. Any of them could have interacted with Ana.

Glowing with the satisfaction of a mystery to solve, Alison turned off the light. She was thinking of Beth Jones, likely trying to sleep in a police cell, and of her husband, who was God knows where.

Beth – then

Waking up with a face sticky from sweat, Beth realised she was lying across the bed fully clothed, the curtains unpulled, letting in blazing sunshine. She was in her hotel room, at least. Her skin felt shrivelled, and she had all her make-up on. God, she had been drunk. Those mojitos . . . then sangria, then shots . . . and Vince, Vince had—

Where was Vince? She looked around the small room in an almost comical pantomime. Obviously he was not there. The door to the sliver of bathroom was open so she could see he wasn't in there either. The T-shirt he slept in was still folded up on the chair. He hadn't come home that night.

She grasped for the memory, slippery as a fish, and saw in her mind a red dress. Had she seen Corinna somewhere – challenged her? Beth realised that her wrist ached, and a terrible fear settled over her. What had happened last night? She remembered a scream. Was it her, or Corinna?

Where was Vince? Why hadn't he come looking for her? Did he really care so little? And where was Corinna? And how had Beth got up to bed? She groped for her phone and couldn't find it in its usual spot. The clock on the night-stand, which had so annoyed Vince with its red blinking, told her it was only 7 a.m. They could well still be out drinking. Beth sat up, her head still swimming and her eyes gritty. She went to the balcony, and saw Joel and Corinna's room had its blinds open, but no sign of anyone inside. Were they all still out?

Jittery with dread, she showered, brushed her teeth, and threw on floaty clothes to protect against the sun and hide her raw face and mind. As she got dressed, she sent several texts to Vince that were not read or answered. It was early still, so she couldn't have slept for long. She had a vague memory of seeing the red glow of sunset last night. The moon on the sea. Joel's voice in her ear. *Mind the step there, babe.* She looked down – there was a spreading bruise on her ankle as well as her wrist. She must have tripped. God, this was humiliating. She was normally more in control of her drinking, and famously had not been sick since one too many WKDs back in 2003. Vomit-free since '03, she liked to proclaim. Was that still true? She did feel depleted, her body crying out for electrolytes. Breakfast would be starting soon. But where was Vince? Maybe he'd got up early, gone for some air or a swim . . . but no. It was obvious he hadn't come back.

She tried to think when she'd last seen him, but the memories were so hazy. At dinner, or on the beach? She had a vague memory of going back to the bar, finding her bag – there it was now, abandoned on the floor of the room – but no one was there. She looked at her phone again – the messages still hadn't turned blue. Had Vince lost his phone? That was when she felt the first surge of alarm. None of this was like him – not answering messages, not telling her where he was, staying out all night drinking, even. Where was he?

Outside was so bright it hurt her eyes, even in sunglasses. She made her way to the beach, feeling the heat from the sun through her flip-flops, shielding her face against the glare. The place was largely deserted, except for staff putting up umbrellas and loungers, the guests still sleeping off cocktail hangovers. On the beach, the swish of the waves seemed louder than ever, and a few families from the hotel next door had already set up camp for the day. There he was! A man was sitting at the edge of the water. She recognised the slump of his shoulders, and that was the shirt he'd been wearing the night before, the one with the pineapple pattern, though he'd got some kind of dark stain on it all around the waist. Water, perhaps?

Beth called, 'There you are. Where have you been?'

She allowed her fear to give way to annoyance for a moment. How dare he stay out all night? How dare he not check up on her? He'd have to apologise profusely, and then maybe at least he could stop being so angry at her for whatever she had done, and they could enjoy the holiday.

Vince was sitting on the sand, facing away from her towards the sea. He was trembling – she went to put a hand on his shoulder, and he flinched away.

'Love? Are you OK?' This time her annoyance was replaced with sympathy, and then fear again.

His voice was different. Hoarse, terrified. 'She's dead,' he said, and gave a long moan that chilled her despite the rising heat of the day. 'She's dead. I'm sorry, but she's dead.'

Alison – now

She was doing her best not to touch any surface with her clothes or skin, and had refused the cup of tea offered after spotting dog hairs inside the fridge. She didn't have a dog, of course, but would this be her once she had the baby? The harried woman had a toddler pulling at her jeans, whining about raisins, a small baby leaking milk on to her T-shirt, and a barky Jack Russell who'd been shut in the kitchen but was making himself heard.

'Sorry, sorry!' she shouted. 'It's a madhouse here. Well, you'll find out soon enough.'

Jemma Maxwell was two years younger than Beth Jones, Alison knew, and they had become good friends when they worked together as newly qualified teachers thirteen years before, prior to Beth leaving the profession entirely. Jemma now lived in South Croydon, abutting Alison's patch, so Alison had come to see her after the revelation that poor, sad Beth Jones had once been arrested over a violent crime, and that Jemma was the victim. Tiredness tugged at her, like a hook dragging her insides, and she knew she had overdone it, and that she shouldn't even really be here.

'That's OK. I'm just here to ask about . . .'

'Beth, I know.' Jemma transferred the baby to her other shoulder, wincing as her hair got caught in a little fist. 'What's she done now?'

That was an interesting statement, Alison noted. 'Why don't you tell me what happened between the two of you?'

'Well, she assaulted me. Beat me up.'

Jemma had made a complaint against Beth for GBH and wounding with intent, but the CPS had not agreed, and the case had eventually been dropped. So Beth didn't have a criminal record as such. Nevertheless, she had been arrested, and there had been some kind of incident, and Alison wanted to know about it.

'Can you tell me why?'

Jemma sighed. 'She thought I stole her boyfriend. But they'd broken up already, or they were breaking up, at least.'

'And you two were friends?'

'We were. But she didn't take it well. Look, I know it wasn't ideal, but Alex and I fell in love. I mean, it was meant to be.'

She indicated a wedding photo on the wall, a slimmer Jemma with a stodgy-looking man that Alison couldn't imagine two women fighting over. So Jemma was now married to the object of that tiff, and Beth had been left to deal with Vince Castries. It seemed unfair.

'What did she do to you?'

'God, it was so unprofessional. What if a parent had been there and seen? We were on a work night out in the pub, and she came screaming over to me, saying he'd broken it off with her and she knew it was because of me, that we'd been messing around, and how dare I. She said I'd broken the girl code or something stupid like that. Then she clouted me right across the face. Scratched me, even. I dropped my glass and it smashed on my foot; I needed a stitch. I actually still have a scar.'

'And what happened after? You called the police?'

'Well, yeah, but you didn't do anything. Apparently, having it on CCTV isn't enough. She had to leave the school, at least – don't think she's even teaching now.'

Alison did not have a huge amount of sympathy for this woman, but she had to admit it was relevant information. That Beth Jones, when provoked, would go to battle to keep the man she loved. She had been left once before, and drawn blood in retaliation. What might she have done when she thought her husband of eight years was betraying her? The evidence was mounting up. Corinna in hospital, another woman dead out in Spain.

Gavin the DC came in from the garden, rosy-cheeked from playing football with Jemma's oldest, who was seven. 'Anything I can do, ma'am?' She'd only brought him along to appease Colette, and to do any legwork required.

'Why don't you take a statement from Jemma here? I just need to check something.' She went outside through open French doors, into a patch of artificial lawn with a swing set and a small boy looking at her curiously.

'I think your mummy wants you inside.'

'You look massive,' said the child.

'Thanks.'

'Are you going to have a baby?' He continued to stare.

'That's the general idea. Now go on, run along.' She didn't want him to overhear the call she had to make now.

Alejandro picked up on the third ring. 'Aleeson. You have something new?'

'Still looking into it, but it's likely we'll have to charge Beth Jones soon. Probably assault. Don't think we can make attempted murder stick.' Which meant that it also was not really her case. 'What about your end?' She'd already told him Vince's alibi was false.

'There is something I have to show you, Aleeson. We finally finish going through all the security cameras from the hotel. Stay on with me, but I will send you a file.'

Something popped up in her WhatsApp, and she clicked, the video file downloading slowly. It was another CCTV feed, from a hotel corridor.

'This is the fourth floor in the B building.' B building was where Joel and Corinna's room had been, though Alison seemed to recall they were on a different floor, fifth or sixth. Nothing happened for a while, and then someone came along, stumbling a bit, cannoning off the wall at one point.

Alison listened to his breath as she watched. 'What time is this?'

'You can see. 2.40 a.m.'

Two hours after Beth Jones had gone to bed and supposedly passed out – so what was she doing on this video, wandering around the hotel, in a building she wasn't staying in? Two minutes after Alison had heard a woman scream.

'Have you got any film of the others going up to bed?'

'Vincent, he never goes up, he is out somewhere all night. Joel, he goes up around 1.30, and Corinna, she is not long after this, about 2 a.m.'

'Separately?'

'Separately.'

That confirmed what Joel had said. And then, almost two hours after Joel had lost sight of her and she was supposedly passed out, Beth was staggering around the place.

As so often happened in a case, the facts as Alison knew them fell apart and rearranged themselves in her head. Not Vince lying. Beth. Beth lying, telling Alison different versions of that night. Beth saying he didn't come back to the room, that she hadn't been with him after all when he found the body. Beth, who knew her husband was watching a woman sing in the bar night after night, a pretty young woman. Beth crying and distraught. Beth with a bruise on her wrist which Alison had assumed was from Vince, but which could have been from someone else grabbing her, pushing her off. Beth with a history of violent behaviour when betrayed. A woman's scream, then Beth in the area minutes later, drunk and out of control.

Beth.

Beth – then

'Vince.' She shook his shoulder again, but he hardly seemed to realise she was there. 'Vince, come on. We have to do something.'

They were sitting on the beach and there was a dead body floating in the surf, and her husband's clothes were soaked with seawater and maybe worse, and he kept saying, 'I'm sorry, she's dead.' He could not look more suspicious if he tried.

She had gathered that he'd gone into the sea to try and rescue whoever it was, which explained why he was all wet, but she didn't understand anything else. Her brain went into damage control mode.

'Look, what happened? You found them like this? Where were you coming from?'

He was in the same clothes as the night before, so clearly had not been back to their room. Had he been with Corinna all night? Oh God, was that who was in the water? Beth waded in a few steps, could only make out dark hair plastered over a white face, and some kind of red dress. It was a woman. But not Corinna. Someone taller, younger, not blonde. It was that singer, wasn't it? Ana. The singer from the bar.

A memory struck her. She had seen Ana last night, hadn't she? They'd spoken at some point. She remembered a cigarette glow, and seeing the red dress, thinking it was Corinna, realising it wasn't. And then what? A dim memory of a woman's scream. Beth's wrist ached and she touched it reflexively. Her next memory was of wandering the hallways in search of Vince, trying to find Joel and Corinna's room. The sound of voices and music. Had she found them? Shit, why couldn't she remember? Why did they drink so much? Why was Ana dead – had she fallen into the water somehow?

Why did Beth have a memory of her screaming?

'Vince,' she tried again. 'What happened?'

He started to cry. 'She's dead.'

'I can see that she's dead, but – did you just find her like this? In the sea?'

He seemed to be nodding, his head down between his legs as if he were going to be sick. Beth was overwhelmed by it. The months of cold-shouldering, the holiday from hell, last night, which had been awful, and now she had found him with an actual dead body, the poor beautiful singer he'd been going to the bar to watch.

'Please tell me! What happened? Did you do this?' She hissed the last part, hardly believing she was even thinking these words.

Did you do this – or did I?

'No, no. She's dead. I'm sorry.'

'No, you didn't do this?'

Of course he didn't. He was still her Vince, wasn't he? Not capable of something like this. But Beth herself? Another memory. The face of a different woman, smug and mocking, and Beth lunging at her, tearing into her skin, the sound of breaking glass, another scream. Jemma. Something she tried to never think about.

Her mind was racing. She heard voices, and saw a mother and young boy approach from another hotel, and behind her a hotel employee was starting to put out loungers. Any second now they would see what Beth had seen, her husband soaking wet with a dead woman in the sea.

'Pull yourself together, will you!' She dragged him to his feet and dusted sand off him. Resisted the urge to wipe the tears from his face. 'Now just stick to the story. We came down early for breakfast and we found her. Together. OK? You've been with me all along.'

Would anyone notice he hadn't changed his clothes since last night, or that he was wet with seawater? And what about Joel and Corinna – where were they? Would they say Beth had gone back early to the room, or that she had been running around the hotel, alone and drunk? No matter. She had to at least try to salvage this.

Beth stood up and started waving her arms at the hotel employee. '*Hola!* Please, there's a woman – *hay una chica!*' She didn't know the Spanish for *She's dead*, and some part of her was still hoping maybe Ana wasn't, that she could be magically revived by CPR like on TV, though Beth didn't know how to do it.

People were running now. She groped for Vince's hand and squeezed it tight, though it was cold and floppy as if he were the one dead. *What did you do?* No matter. She'd made her choice, picked her story, and she would stick to it. They would get out of this.

Him

It had been almost two weeks now, and he felt himself able to breathe again. He was much nicer to her than usual, asking her each morning what she had planned for the day, and offering to cook dinner several times. It was pathetic how happy this made her, even though he was going to buy it all from the deli and throw the packaging out before she saw it.

Two weeks since the return from Spain, and all was quiet. Had she suspected anything, he wondered, about their abrupt departure? She had given him some strange looks the day after, when he'd insisted on leaving. They'd lose the money, she'd said, and the new flights would cost too. He'd guilt-tripped her to cover it up. *Could you really stay on and have fun while some poor woman is dead?*

He'd seen how that cowed her, how her shoulders sagged. No, she supposed he was right. She was sorry she'd been so insensitive. So they'd flown home early, and he had waited every day for a knock on the door. Someone would have seen him with the woman, either on that night or the others he had gone to the bar to watch her, tried to talk to her. But police were stupid the world over, and the British ones weren't going to talk to the Spanish ones. They were hardly going to cross-reference every guest at the hotel with anyone who might once have been in the vicinity of another murder. There had been hundreds of guests in that hotel. They wouldn't have the time or resources to investigate every single one.

All the same, the last two weeks had been spicy. He felt himself on red alert every time the doorbell went or he saw a police car in the street. Every morning he woke up and scanned his phone in case there'd been a message overnight. The hotel asking him to come back for an interview, perhaps. Or he'd finally push her too far, and she would call the police herself, tell them how he had vanished that night, and come back with his clothes wet and sandy, and made her leave the next day.

But now time had gone by, and he felt himself relax. So much so that his mind started to wander. That was four times now that he'd been on the scene when young women had turned up dead, and yet no one suspected him, or they did but then passed him over for someone else, someone more obvious. Maybe that meant he was invincible, somehow.

Maybe that meant he could do it again.

Alison – now

She would miss this too. The buzz of knowing a breakthrough was near, that a picture was coming together, the spring in her step that almost counteracted the weight of the baby she was lugging about.

Today Colette was wearing a purple trouser suit, as if channelling Hillary Clinton, and walking on her mini-treadmill as she reviewed Alison's findings. 'You think you can make a blackmail charge stick with these scammers?'

'I don't know. If I can dig up some victims, maybe, but there weren't any direct complaints against them here or in Spain.'

That was assuming Joel and Corinna even used the same names all the time. Blackmail was notorious for never being reported, its victims willing to do anything to keep their secrets. It was why it worked so well.

'Hmm, it seems a bit tenuous, Alison. What about your fall – still no direct witness to any form of push?'

'One's unconscious, one's missing, one didn't see anything. And Beth says she can't remember, it was all a blur.'

Convenient, though in Alison's experience that often was true of the moment a violent crime took place. Perpetrators spoke of a rush to the head, a feeling of being taken over, of losing control. Beth would likely get off without an attempted murder charge, unless they could prove intent.

'Still no sign of Castries?'

'No sign.' It was strange. He was not a man who appeared to have friends, or even close family, so where could he be?

Colette continued to click through her iPad. 'So Jones has a previous arrest for assault, charges dropped. And she'd reason to believe the fall victim was involved with her husband?'

That bit didn't make any sense to Alison, beautiful Corinna with grumpy, balding Vince, but then Beth would not have known that the other couple's attentions were intended as a love scam. Though that didn't sit right with Alison either. Why go all the way to Tenerife to target a man whose windfall had not even come through yet, and might never?

'I think she imagined as much, yes, whether it was true or not. I think – it's possible she's responsible for both incidents. Corinna Cooper's fall, and also the case out in Spain.'

Colette looked surprised. 'What would she have against some Spanish woman she'd never met?'

'Same reason, maybe. Jealousy. The husband had been going to the bar at night to watch Ana sing. And Beth did have some injuries out there, consistent with a struggle of some kind.' Not to mention the lies she'd told Alison about her whereabouts that night, and being caught on CCTV roaming round the hotel long after she was supposed to be in bed. 'There's one more thing. The victim was wearing a long red dress that night, quite similar to the one Corinna Cooper had on. It's possible that Beth mixed her up with Ana that night, given she was drunk off her face. Attacked the wrong person.' But then how had Ana ended up in the sea? Beth would not have been strong enough to drag her there, surely.

Unless she'd had help.

Colette said, 'I hate to say it, but I think we have to give this fall over to Borough. Nigel can ask to keep her in longer, if he wants. Unless the victim wakes up and talks, we don't have enough to even charge, I don't think. If she dies, well, we'll think again. But the doctors are hopeful?'

'She's hanging on, yeah.'

'I think the case is off your desk, Alison. Which you'd imagine would be a good thing!'

Alison sighed. She knew she should be pleased to wrap up her work before she went off, but the mystery of it tugged at her. The idea of never knowing what had happened in Tenerife would haunt her. 'OK.'

An email pinged on the tablet as she turned to go. Colette read it and looked up sharply, without pausing her pace. She was walking in her stockinged feet, her Jimmy Choo heels sitting under the desk. 'Did you ask Forensics to check something against your Spanish victim?'

'Well, yes – I think there's a link, like I said.'

Colette pressed pause and her treadmill slowed its roll. 'I can't even be annoyed at you about the budget, because you thought right. Forensics recovered some blood from an item in Beth Jones's wardrobe in London, and it matches with the DNA of your dead woman.'

'It's Ana's blood?'

'It seems to be.'

Alison couldn't believe such obvious proof had simply landed in her lap. If Beth was guilty, why would she have held on to something that contained such damning evidence? And Ana had been strangled, anyway – there was no blood at the scene to get on clothing. 'What was the item? Nigel never said.' And that was annoying too, needless secrecy designed to keep her out of the loop.

'Shoes,' said Colette, stooping to put her own back on. 'A pair of high-heeled shoes. Ana's mother has confirmed they belonged to her.'

Beth – then

The hotel felt deserted at this hour, the corridors empty and cold on her bare skin, a sullen hush hanging over everything, with not a breath of wind. She had an unpleasant flashback to the night before, groping her way along a corridor, totally drunk and disorientated. When had that been? When she was going back to her own room? She could barely remember, and was struggling to work out now which was Joel and Corinna's room.

About an hour had passed since Vince had been taken away by the police, along with Ana's body, and Beth was going out of her mind. She hadn't been allowed to go with him. Why had they taken him – just because he'd touched the body, or because he'd been the one to find her? His DNA would be on her, from where he'd tried to save her, and maybe because he was black they were more likely to suspect him. Surely that would not be enough for a murder charge, if indeed Ana had been murdered and not drowned. Had the hotel employee or the mother with the kid given statements, said Vince had been acting strangely, crying and saying *She's dead,* over and over?

With no idea what to do and not speaking any Spanish, Beth had gone in search of the only other people who might know what had happened the night before. The story she had presented to the police, and the English detective, Alison – late night, very drunk, finding the body together – was a good one, an alibi that relied on the small child hopefully not telling anyone the man had been on his own when the woman arrived. The problem was, it wasn't true. Not true at all.

This was the room, yes. The door was open and a cleaner's cart stood outside, but no one was in sight. She could hear voices just round the corner, speaking in Spanish, so presumably the cleaner had just popped out. Beth slid inside, feeling itchy with guilt.

Joel and Corinna had gone, that was the first thing she noticed. Checked out. No clothes or suitcases remained, just a ransacked room left for someone else to clean up. Jesus, what a mess. There were wet towels on the floor, the toilet looked to be unflushed, dirty glasses and empty bottles of beer and wine everywhere. Cigarettes crushed out in a dish on the night-stand, sandy footprints everywhere, and on the balcony, more mess.

Had they really just gone? Without even saying goodbye? Beth was sure they'd said they were staying for the week. She looked around the space, the wicker chairs and table, the burnt-out tealight with several butts in it that didn't look like tobacco. Under the table were two tiny plastic baggies. Beth was not particularly streetwise, but even she could recognise a cocaine holder. Both empty. Had Vince done this with them – was that why he was so out of it this morning? Maybe they'd test him at the station, and discover he'd been breaking the law. Although, if they thought he had killed the singer, then illegal drugs were probably the least of her worries.

Something else caught her eyes, half-hidden by the plants on the balcony. A pair of women's shoes, high, sparkly, impractical. The kind of thing no one would wear on a beach holiday, surely. They didn't seem like Corinna's – Beth had only ever seen her in jewelled Havaianas, or barefoot and dusted with sand, her toe ring glinting on her brown feet. But she did recognise these, she thought. A sudden memory. Darkness, a woman's voice, these shoes flashing in low light. A scream. Her mind shrank in on itself at that, and her hands began to tremble. Her memory was full of black holes. The shoes had some staining in the heels and soles, a pale brown.

'*Señora?* The cleaner was in the doorway with a mop bucket in her hand. A black woman, looking tired and hot.

'Oh – sorry. *Perdone.*' She thought about saying she had the wrong room, but didn't know how to.

What would happen to the shoes if she left them there? They might get thrown out, and vital evidence lost. Or be used as evidence against Vince, if he had also been here last night. Without thinking, she scooped them up with her fingers through the straps, as if they were her own, and walked out with as much confidence as she could muster. She told herself she was just making sure they were safe.

Their own room had been cleaned and smelled of bleach, the air conditioning way too cold as always, causing a chill when it was nearly forty degrees outside. She thought of melting ice caps with despair. So much waste in a place like this. The plastic straws, the plates of food too big to finish, the groaning buffet thrown out each day, the jet skis and air conditioners and patios to warm the air when it wasn't quite hot enough to be outside. What hope was there for anyone? Even lives were expendable here, thrown away and wasted, a beautiful and talented young woman with everything to live for.

Beth sat on the edge of her bed, made up taut and tight as if she and Vince had never slept in there. Maybe the night before last was the last time they would ever share a bed, and she hadn't even known it. The shoes stood in the middle of the floor, cheap and uncomfortable things a young woman could pull off, but which Beth would never wear, settling for trainers or Birkenstocks.

Tears pricked at her eyes, for Ana, but also selfishly for herself. Their make-or-break holiday had broken them. Vince was in jail, and even if he got out, how could she ever ask him about what had really happened that night? Why those shoes were on the balcony, and if he had been there too, with Corinna. She was afraid that the answers might be too much to bear. Because she also could not remember what she had done last night, except for odd flashes that didn't make sense, the bruises on her wrist and ankle, and that terrible feeling in her chest, guilt and sadness, and overwhelming, paralysing fear.

Alison – now

The recorder was playing up again. Alison glared at Nigel until he picked up the machine and tapped it off the table, whereupon it issued the familiar beep that showed it was recording. She gave her name and Nigel's – she was not thrilled he was there, but it was better than losing the case entirely to CID. The evidence about the shoes had allowed them to hold Beth longer on suspicion of attempted murder, though she'd have her work cut out to connect the Spanish death to Corinna's fall.

Beth sat opposite, shivering in a grey hoody her sister had brought her. Apparently the sister was quite the character – Carmel had some choice words to say about her – which was quite unlike the shaking mess of a woman opposite. Even the solicitor she'd engaged, Veronica, was a drippy woman with a persistent sniffle who Alison had always found irritating.

She began with her medium-nice tone, the one she started off with when things weren't open and shut. To lull them in.

'So, Beth. You understand you are under arrest for the attempted murder of Corinna Cooper on September seventeenth of this year. I have also been authorised by the Spanish police to ask you some questions in connection with the murder of Ana Garcia de Vasquez there, on September third of this year. Depending on your answers, you may be extradited to Spain and face further charges there.' Clearly, Alejandro had been working for a while to get her the authorisation, as it had come through much faster than expected. And that meant Beth was really in a whole lot of trouble, in both countries.

Beth gave a sob. 'I don't know what happened. I just don't. I don't remember Corinna falling, any of it. It's like I just – blacked out for a minute.'

'But you were angry at her?'

'I was – yes. They were up to something. They don't even live in that flat, did you know that? They basically – hunted us down for some reason. Wormed into our lives, and I don't know why. And she had this picture—' She stopped talking abruptly, blanching. Alison gave a sigh that she managed to keep inward.

'What picture was this?'

'She had a picture of – something to do with Vince's past. When he was at school.'

'To save time, Beth, I'm going to let you know that we're very well aware of Vince's past involvement in the murder of Lucy Brady, back in 2002.'

'You know more than me then,' she muttered, picking at her cuticles.

'You weren't aware of it?'

'I found out a few days ago. That he had a different name back then, even. I didn't know any of that. And he's been paying out money every month to someone – and getting texts from unknown numbers. I don't understand what's going on with him, but I think they're involved somehow. Joel and Corinna. Or Corinna, at least.'

Beside Alison, Nigel was frantically writing down all this information. Alison had not expected Beth to spurt like a hydrant, but she nodded as if she'd already known all this. She would get someone on Vince Castries's bank account asap – they were already monitoring it in case he showed up somewhere. 'So what was this picture?'

'It was of Vince's football team, the ones who went to prison. The same one was at Vince's mum's house. So why did Corinna have it too? It's so weird.'

'Where's this picture now?'

'I don't know. I had it in my hand when I – went out to the balcony.'

It certainly wasn't there now. Alison recalled the shards of broken glass that could have come from a shattered photo frame. 'And how are Joel and Corinna connected to that case?' Could Joel be one of the other boys? He was too young, surely – thirty-two, according to his passport – but that could be fake as well.

'I've no idea.'

'And to be clear, Beth, have you any idea where Vince is right now?'

'No. None. He left, I guess, when they were – when the paramedics came, and the police.' Her voice was bitter, as well it might be. He'd left her alone to face all this. 'I can't think where he'd even go. He doesn't speak to his family, or have many friends.'

'That's all you have for us?' Nigel injected a sneer into his voice and Alison struggled to not roll her eyes. She'd never found 'bad cop' got you very far – she normally went for 'disappointed cop with zero patience left', which was even more true than usual now. She'd had to push her chair back from the table to accommodate her bump.

Beth wrung her hands together. 'I'm sorry, that's all I know about how Corinna – fell. I figured out she had some connection to that old case, Lucy's murder, and I realised they must have been playing us all along, and I just . . .'

'What?'

Beth glanced to her lawyer, who was also silently scribbling. 'I don't remember.'

'And what about Tenerife? Have you remembered any more about that?'

'I told you everything I know. I woke up in the hotel room, and Vince was gone, so I went to find him and he was on the beach and she was – in the water.'

'Which you lied about at first, when we talked.'

'I – yes. I wasn't under caution, we were just talking. I was trying to help him. I knew he wouldn't have done a thing like that.'

'And now that you know about Lucy Brady, has that changed?'

Beth said nothing, but her eyes filled with tears again. 'He's a good man,' she said, unconvincingly.

'What if I told you we had CCTV evidence of you in the hotel that night, awake much later than you said – after 2 a.m. – in Joel and Corinna's building?'

Beth froze. 'I – I don't remember.'

'You don't recall getting up again – did you even go to your room that first time, when you left the bar?'

'I don't know. I just can't remember. There's just – bits.'

'You must have been pretty drunk to have blacked out like that.'

'I was. Joel was – feeding me booze.' She looked hopeful for a second. 'Maybe he spiked me. That could be true, right?'

'It could.' There was no way prove it, however, after so much time, and by all accounts Beth had needed no help to be that drunk.

At a nod from Alison, Nigel slid a picture over the table. In a pompous tone he said, 'For the recording, I am showing Ms Jones a photograph of evidence I recovered from her home late last night. Do you recognise these items, Beth?'

Impossibly high, and encrusted in rhinestones, they didn't seem like the kind of shoe Beth would ever wear. Plus, they weren't her size.

Beth picked up the picture. 'Yes, I recognise them. They're Corinna's.'

Interesting choice of story. Alison said, 'These shoes have traces of Ana Garcia's blood on them, Beth. You can see it in the brown staining there, on the heels.'

'Oh. Well . . .' Several looks crossed Beth's face as she tried to work this out. 'Maybe they're Ana's, then. But I don't understand how they could be . . .' She trailed off.

'Beth, I'm going to suggest you tell us how you got these shoes. You understand it's very damning evidence, you having items in your possession with a murder victim's blood on them. Coupled with the CCTV evidence and your history of lying. You must see it's not looking good.'

Beth was biting her lip hard now. 'OK. I can tell you how I got these at least, yes.'

Beth – then

She couldn't believe Joel and Corinna had just left. Was it possible they'd gone before the uproar, before the body was found? But it wasn't long after 7 a.m. when she saw Vince sitting on the already-hot sand of the beach. Surely they wouldn't have been up and out by then, after a night of heavy drinking and more. So why they did they leave in such a hurry? They'd not even taken all their things. A little glimmer of light was opening up in the dark cell of Beth's mind. That was suspicious behaviour, right? Fleeing the scene of a crime? So maybe they knew something about what had happened last night, the terrible blanks in her memory like patches of fathomless water. But how was she going to find them?

She sat by the pool, feeling strange that she was fully dressed. She could hardly put on her swimsuit when her husband was in jail. The rest of the guests had adapted rapidly to the murder, reading their books and even drinking their cocktails, served by the same staff, with smooth, emotionless faces. How many of them were mourning their colleague Ana right now, and still had to make a tray of pina coladas for the noisy hen do? The only concession to the death was an increase in the number of discreetly uniformed security guards and the lack of pounding music round the pool.

Corinna had definitely said they were here for the week, hadn't she? So they had checked out early. Was there somewhere else they'd expressed an interest in, or would they have flown straight home already? Maybe that was risky – the police could find out who had been on a flight, but they wouldn't be able to check every single hotel on the island. *Think, Beth, think.*

Corinna's voice, that annoying mid-Atlantic whine. *I've heard that La Caleta is meant to be super-chill. Just like really relaxing and spiritual.* Beth grabbed her phone and looked up the place – it was in the north of the island, a small beach area studded with hotels. Could they have gone there? Of course, there was a chance that whatever they knew was not something Beth or Vince would want coming to light. And with that thought she swam over another dark abyss.

What was she going to do? They had arrested Vince. He'd been put into a police car after the body – after Ana – was taken away, and Beth had been left on the beach, asking desperate questions to uncomprehending officers. They clearly thought Vince had killed Ana, since he was the one found with the body. And Beth could not remember what she'd done that night herself. More disturbing memories surfaced – a red dress, the smell of cigarette smoke, the slap of flip-flops on concrete. She turned her phone over in her hands, but she didn't know who to message. She was desperate to talk to Joel and Corinna, but didn't have their numbers. Where could they have gone in such chaos? Was it possible they hadn't heard about the death?

Death. Or was it a murder? Ana could have drowned, Beth supposed. But why had they taken Vince in? Was it just as a precaution? She didn't even know if she should contact a lawyer, or how to go about that in Spain, or where to find one that spoke English. Or was there a consul or ambassador she could ask for help? She seemed to remember reading something about how they could give you information but not help you get out of prison. Spain had seemed so familiar, such a safe holiday destination, but now it felt as alien as the surface of the moon. Who could she ask for help? There was no way she could sit here doing nothing – she had to go to the station herself.

Alison – now

'Can't wait to get home. I hate conference hotels.' On the screen of her phone, Tom was sitting on the edge of his bed, taking off his shoes.

'What is it tonight?' Alison had assumed a blameless position in bed, giving the impression of someone who had not put in a full day of work at the station.

'Team dinner, then karaoke.'

'Oh, no. I am sorry.' He hated karaoke even more than saunas.

He heaved a great sigh. 'You feeling OK?'

'Mm, not too bad.' In truth she was exhausted, her lower back aching, sleep threatening to engulf her any minute, but her mind would not stop whirring. Beth Jones had told them a lot, but insisted she did not remember pushing Corinna off the balcony, or not. They had permission to hold her for another night while they awaited a decision to charge. The bloodstained shoes Beth had also explained away, though Alison felt the story of finding them in Corinna's room was shaky in the extreme. Joel had been questioned too and claimed not to have known the shoes were in their room, which, having lived with a man for years, Alison actually could believe. She'd sent all the information to Alejandro anyway, so it was possible Beth could still be extradited to Spain to answer questions, though that would take a while.

'So what's the latest with the case?' Tom said. 'I know you won't have let it drop.'

'I'm – mulling a few things over. Consulting.' She updated him on what she'd found out so far. Beth's history of violence, the bloodied shoes, the absence of conscious witnesses to the fall, Beth's various explanations. 'Colette thinks it's still not enough to charge.'

'Sounds well dodgy, though. Any more on the other couple?'

'Joel's very forthcoming with the info now I've explained that blackmail actually is a crime. He says they don't have a fixed address, just move around all the time, keep some stuff at his mum's garage in Birmingham. And says he's no idea about the photo Beth claims was there, the one with Vince's football team in it. He doesn't remember seeing it, apparently.'

'So it's all bollocks, their lifestyle?'

'Largely, yeah. A giant fraud, but sadly not one I can nick them for. He did say Corinna had changed her name.'

'Not Cooper?'

'Not Corinna either. But, helpfully, he didn't know what her actual one was. He says they met when they were both working on the cruise ships, then she got fired for hooking up with guests and extorting them for money.'

'Nice people. How old is she, did you find that out?'

'Apparently she's thirty-five. The hospital has her DOB. Why, what are you thinking?'

Tom spoke slowly. 'Probably nothing. But they definitely went out to Tenerife to target Beth and Vince, right? They said just for money, but that seems off, given he's not got any. I was thinking – that girl, Lucy, the one who died. I'm pretty sure she had a sister. Younger.'

'Oh, yes – the one who knew she was going to meet Peter Johnson that night? You think *Corinna* could be the sister?' It was a leap so big Alison had not even considered it. 'And she, what, stalked Vince out there, wanting revenge?'

'I dunno. Worth seeing if she has any links to the old case, though, no? Since she had that photo, allegedly.'

'I suppose. I need to find out who Vince has been paying out the money to as well. I've got his bank on it, should know tomorrow.'

'What about that other picture you found, the one Corinna and Joel took?'

'Oh, of the man on the beach? I'm drawing a blank on him, though I'm sure I saw him somewhere about. Joel knows nothing, I'm pretty sure.'

'Well, send it to me! That is what I do, remember. Recognise people.'

'Oh, OK. I didn't think you'd be interested.'

She WhatsApped him the photo and watched him stare at the screen, that familiar furrowed-brow expression that meant he was running through his mental Rolodex of every person he had ever met.

'He was at the hotel for sure. I remember seeing him at breakfast, I think. But not doing anything dodge. Just a guest. If you ask the hotel, they might recognise him.'

Alison's phone dinged then, and a message popped up from Gavin. *Boss! Corinna Cooper showing signs of waking up!!*

It was after nine already, and Alison was in her pyjamas. All the same, she knew she was going to that hospital. She lied, 'Sorry, love. It's my mum. Better call her back. Enjoy dinner.'

She hung up and pulled on some clothes. She hadn't moved as fast in months.

Beth – then

The air in the Spanish police station was stifling, smelling of BO and floor bleach. An electric fan did little to cool the waiting room, only flicking the sweat off her face. Vince had been in the cells for hours now and she had no idea what was going on, and so, at her wits' end and with no sign of Alison at the hotel, she had come to the station herself. It was a world away from the cool, perfume-scented hotel. Opposite her was a man clutching a bloody rag to his forehead, and a woman with a tear-stained, glum face, her tight and skimpy clothes marking her out as a sex worker. Or perhaps a very drunk tourist; it was hard to be sure.

Beth got up, holding the bundle of clothes she had brought for Vince, and went to the desk. Behind it was a disinterested woman in an epauletted shirt, doing something at a very old computer.

'*Hola?* Erm, my husband is here, yes?'

'*Sí?*'

'Vincent Castries?'

The woman said something in Spanish that Beth didn't understand.

'How long are you going to keep him? *Cuánto tiempo?*'

The woman picked up a phone and Beth distinctly heard her say the word *negro*. Wasn't that Spanish for black – was it also racist here? Her stomach sank. With all this anti-migrant and anti-tourist sentiment, what were the chances they might pin this whole thing on Vince?

'*Señora?*' A man had appeared beside her, short but handsome, in a shirt with rolled-up sleeves. 'You are Mrs Castries?'

'Eh, no, I mean I am his wife, but it's Jones, Beth Jones.'

'OK, Mrs Jones. I can give you some information, if you would like to come with me. My name is Alejandro Costa and I am the lead detective on this case.'

She followed him down a smelly, windowless corridor which echoed with faraway voices and occasional shouts, presumably from the cells. Was she being arrested too? Did they have to inform you if so, or was that just on American TV? He gestured to a seat in an equally depressing and bare room. Was Vince within these walls? If only she could see him, talk to him.

'*Señora.* We have your husband here in custody. In this country, we can keep him here for seventy-two hours while we investigate.'

She gasped. 'But – why? Wasn't it just an accident? She drowned?'

He fixed her with a dark gaze. In the tiny room, she could smell his sweat and aftershave. 'Why do you think this?'

'Well, she was in the sea.'

'We can't rule out a murder at this stage. So please, *señora*, tell me what you know. We are just asking questions at this point. But it will help your husband if you are honest.'

Beth wasn't entirely sure that was the case. She tried to remember what she'd said at the scene, automatically protecting Vince. 'Eh, well – we woke up early, kind of hungover, if I'm honest, and we went down to the beach and she was there.'

'Both of you went there together?'

That was a lie. She was lying to the police. 'Well . . .'

He jumped on that. '*Señora*, you must tell me the truth. Was your husband with you all night? I will be able to check this on the CCTV, you know.'

She swallowed. 'No. I woke up by myself, back in the room. I don't remember getting there.'

'You don't?'

The shame caught on her tongue. 'I was – I had a lot to drink. So I don't know where Vince was. He might have been there, got up early.' She knew this wasn't true, though.

'And you spent the evening with another couple – Ms Cooper and Mr Hardiman?'

She hadn't known their surnames before. 'Joel and Corinna, yeah. We had some drinks. Then I – I went to bed.' Also not entirely true, but she couldn't remember what she'd done between leaving the bar and waking up in bed. Only flashes. She tried, 'I think they left already. Their room was empty today.'

He frowned. 'It was?'

'I think so.' Surely he'd find all this out eventually. She was just nudging him along.

The detective made some notes. 'Did you recognise the woman who died?'

Would she tell the truth? Beth quailed. 'I thought maybe it was – the singer. From the bar.'

He nodded. 'She has just been identified by her mother. Ana Garcia de Vasquez is her name. Did you speak to her last night?'

Her mind was racing, trying to figure out what he knew, what she could remember, what Vince might have told them. In that moment, Beth realised she was going to lie again. 'No. I never spoke to her.'

The worst thing was, she didn't even know who she was lying to protect. Vince, or herself.

Alison – now

Corinna seemed to be one of those rare people who could look good in a sack, or while waking up from a serious neurological episode. She was pale and wan, her hair still greasy, but she managed to look delicate and pretty, the shadows round her eyes a flattering violet.

'How are you feeling?' asked Alison, trying to be gracious, plonking herself down on the hard plastic chair again. No sign of Joel.

'Awful. Like I got hit by a truck.' Her voice was hoarse from the tubes, but she sounded coherent.

'You're lucky to be alive, let alone talking.'

'I know. I suppose I'm just good at falling, from riding as a kid, maybe.'

Riding – did that mean she wasn't Lucy's sister after all? The Brady family didn't sound like they'd been the kind to go in for horses, but you never knew.

'So, Corinna, I need to take your statement about what happened.' *Did she push you?*, in other words.

Corinna shook her head. 'I don't remember it happening. All I remember is Beth coming out of our bedroom, where she'd been snooping around, and she was absolutely furious about something, she was shouting, and then I remember she was just kind of coming at me . . . but that's it. I don't know how I fell, or what she did. And

Joel didn't see either. We were out on the balcony, and he couldn't hear over the fan and the music.'

Convenient.

'You have a habit of sitting on the edge of balconies, I believe.'

'I suppose. But it's always been fine.'

'That's the thing about risky behaviour, it always is fine until it isn't. Do you think you could have fallen, if you were startled?'

'Maybe. I don't know.'

'And you don't know what it was Beth was angry about?'

'No.' She shook her head again.

'Well then, maybe you can explain why you rented that flat, and why you engineered bumping into Beth outside the supermarket.'

Corinna paused, as if caught out. 'We just – needed a place to stay.'

'While your house was being renovated, right? Except you don't have a house, do you? Neither of you owns any property in the UK.'

She licked her dry lips. 'Well – no. I suppose we don't.'

'So why did you lie?'

'I don't know.'

Alison sighed. 'Look, you're not well, and I'm pregnant, and my patience is thinner than it's ever been, and to be honest, it's never been much. So why don't you just tell me the truth? I know you went to Tenerife to track down Vince and Beth, and that you've been watching them, and you moved into the area to keep tabs on them. Joel already told me everything. Including about your little scams.'

'Not in the UK,' she said quickly. Clearly, the two of them had this excuse ready to go. 'Anyway, it's not illegal.'

'Blackmail certainly is illegal.'

'It's not blackmail. Jesus. No one forces them to do stuff, do they? It's not like we fake it like some scammers do, those deep-fake

AI people. These targets actually do shit, and we just gently remind them of how they can make amends, by investing in a perfectly legitimate company. It's not my fault men are always all over me.'

Alison sighed. 'Fine. So what's the connection to Vince and Beth? They don't have any money. They're broke, in fact.'

'He's due to get a big payout.'

'Come on, Corinna. To go all the way out there after them, you must have had better reasons than a possible payday. What were they?'

She avoided Alison's eyes. 'I – he's on the verge of something. He invented this little component, in his old job, and they tried to sue him to keep it, but he's winning the case. It could make him millions.'

Was that true? Alison needed to check that also, along with dozens of other loose ends. She was going to run out of time, not to mention that she had several other cases to clear before she could no longer stand up.

'It's why he quit his job.' Corinna sounded plausible. 'They were arguing over who owned the patent.'

'And you know this how?'

She shrugged. 'It's my job to keep up with who's about to get rich. Look for investors. I've been following the case; it's in the public domain, if you know where to find it.'

That sounded flimsy as hell. Was it possible this woman knew all about Vince's business, while his wife had no idea? Sadly, Alison knew it was very possible that a partner could know nothing at all about their significant other's life. But still, she couldn't shake the feeling Corinna was lying. 'Beth says you had a picture in the flat. A framed one, of Vince as a teenager, and his football team.'

Corinna looked carefully blank.

'The boys were involved in the murder of Lucy Brady – do you know who that is?'

She could almost see the wheels turning in the woman's pretty head as she debated how much to admit. 'She was killed. Vince was mixed up in it, as a kid.'

'Right. So why did you have a picture of those boys in your flat?'

She shrugged. 'Just more leverage over Vince. Beth didn't know about it, obviously. He'd changed his name.'

'And how were you able to find this out?'

She smiled. 'You can find out almost anything if you look in the right place. Electoral rolls, council records, Companies House.'

It was true, actually. Alison just didn't buy any of it. There were too many missing links. 'So you personally have no connection to Lucy Brady.'

'Of course not. I just – thought it was interesting, that's all. About Vince's past.'

'OK, and what happened that night, when the woman died in Tenerife?'

'Do I need a lawyer for this?'

She sighed again. 'No, Corinna. You've just woken up from a major head injury. If you needed a lawyer you'd be down at the station and under caution. Though I don't rule that out.'

'Well, we were drinking with Vince and Beth that night. Beth had too much and kind of wandered off, we assumed to bed, but I guess we didn't know for sure. Joel tried to go after her, since she was so pissed, but she wouldn't let him. I stayed with Vince for a bit.'

'And you what, seduced him?'

Corinna rolled her eyes. 'No. He was also out of it, and he seemed, I don't know – kind of broken. Not exactly in a sexy mood.'

'So nothing to blackmail him with.'

A cat-like smile played around her lips. 'You'd be surprised. If someone's that drunk, they don't remember what they did. A few smart angles and you're in business. But no, I didn't touch him. We just drank and smoked—' She halted.

'I don't care if you did some weed in another country. Go on.'

'Well, he wandered off too. Went to look for Beth, I suppose. I don't know what time, I guess around two. I went up to the room, Joel was already there, we sat on the balcony. We don't know what he did after that, or Beth.'

'Why did you check out so early?'

She shrugged. 'The plan had failed. No point sticking around. And also, it got weird. There was something bad between those two that we didn't like.'

'It wasn't that you knew a woman had died and wanted to flee the scene?' Alison was severe.

'No.'

That was also a lie, she was sure, but how to prove it?

'Beth is claiming she found some shoes in your room after you left, which have Ana Garcia's blood on them. Any comment on that?'

Corinna weighed this up for a moment, as if assessing whether or not Alison had any proof the shoes were ever in her possession. She sat up straighter. 'OK. I'm going to tell you the truth, though I don't actually have to if I'm not under arrest. Because Ana seemed really nice, and I'm sorry she's dead, I really am. I lent her my shoes.'

'What?'

'She came out towards the pool, and everyone had gone off, Vince too. I was just sitting there vaping, since Joel doesn't like it in the room, and she was limping because her shoes were cutting her feet. You know how it is when you've got some really uncomfortable new ones. She'd lost her car keys so she needed to walk home. I just said, here take mine. I had some flip-flops on. We were the same size, four. Thirty-seven in Europe. I said we could swap back the next day, but then, well, she died.'

Alison regarded her, looking for the lie. Corinna looked back, no trace of shiftiness in her aquamarine eyes. 'So what, you took her shoes back to your room and forget about them?'

'I guess I wore them to walk back to the room, left them on the balcony, and didn't take them with me the next day when we went. Why would I? They weren't mine, and we weren't exactly thinking about shoes, you know. We just wanted to go.'

'Did you see Ana with anyone that night – a man, maybe?'

Corinna thought about it. 'You know what, maybe? I saw her walk off, and I think maybe there was a man waiting for her, in that dark bit just before the lobby, you know with the fountain and the plants.' Could this be the man the security guard had seen Ana with heading to the beach – not Vince, not Joel, but another man altogether?

'Would you recognise him again – it wasn't Vince?'

'No, no one I knew. Not sure I remember much about him. I didn't think it mattered.'

'So why did you lie about being with Vince that night, if you weren't?'

She shrugged. 'We just – I guess we felt sorry for him. And, you know, an alibi for him was one for us too. I guess we were a bit worried. It did look kind of dodgy, what we were doing. Following them out there, taking those pictures. Me having talked to Ana, for a minute even, and Joel had talked to her in the bar a few times. I think he liked her, but she wasn't interested, of course. I forgot about the shoes.'

It looked dodgy because it was illegal, but the story did kind of hold water. 'And where were you the rest of the night?'

'We went to bed, of course. Like normal people. Sat on the balcony for a bit, had some more drinks.' And Alison knew that was true because she'd seen them herself. And heard them.

Whereas Vince Castries had gone where? Not back to his own room and his wife. Those hours of his time remained unaccounted for. Beth's too.

'This is some yarn you're telling me, Corinna. Had you ever heard of Vince Castries, or come across him in any capacity, before you learned about his patent?'

'No, I'd never heard of Vince. And it may be a yarn, but it's what happened.'

Alison had no way to prove otherwise. So far, there was no hard evidence against Joel and Corinna. She couldn't even prove the shoes had been in their room – it was only Beth's word that said so. Meanwhile there was ample evidence stacking up against Vince and Beth.

'Are we done?' said Corinna. 'I need to rest, the doctor said.' Clearly, a three-storey fall had done nothing to dent her sense of entitlement.

'For now,' said Alison. 'But I'll be back.'

This parting shot would have had more impact if it hadn't taken her quite so long to get up out of the chair.

Beth – then

She had asked the desk sergeant again how long Vince might be kept in, and got an answer she didn't follow, but which seemed to have a general air of how long is a piece of string. It felt wrong to leave him there, but she couldn't think what else to do. She could hardly admit to anyone back home that he'd been arrested, or that she'd found him with a woman's dead body. Beth said, 'I'll be back soon,' but she could tell the officer, or whatever she was, had not understood or cared.

She pushed open the doors of the police station and went back on to the scorching street, feeling the heat hit her right away. Being the afternoon, most of the shops were closed and shuttered up, but here and there homeless people sat in the shadows, some with signs in Spanish. She'd read that hundreds of migrants were turning up here every day, and recalled what she'd heard the officer say about Vince when he was arrested. *Negro*. It meant 'black' in Spanish, she knew, but the word made her stomach contract. She could never understand what he went through as a mixed-race man, or how he had to navigate the world differently.

Back in the square, she hailed a cab and told the driver the name of their hotel. She felt damp all over, as if sponges were pressing on her skin. As they drove, she was biting at a hangnail, worrying over how to enlist Alison's help, how to find Joel and Corinna, how to clear Vince's name. And underneath it all a far worse fear – should she even be trying to clear it? There were a lot of things she didn't know about her husband, and, after all, the night did have several large black spots for both of them. She remembered him sitting on the beach in some kind of trance, saying over and over, *I'm sorry, she's dead.* What was he sorry for? Was it just shock, or something even worse?

And worse again. Why couldn't she remember the night before? And why did what she could recall not make sense?

It was only when she got back to the hotel, and was making her way wearily to her room, that the memory came back, so shocking it made her gasp. She hadn't gone straight to bed that night! She had fallen asleep first on a lounger, then woken up and become obsessed with finding Vince, convinced that he was in Joel and Corinna's room. She remembered getting off the lounger, shoving her feet into her flip-flops. Thinking that she wasn't going to put up with this anymore. She was going up there right now, to tell him he was her husband, and that if he wouldn't come with her right away, it was over. And if Corinna got in her way in the meantime, well, that was just tough.

The memory took shape. She was running down a hotel corridor just like this one, her own flip-flops loud in her ears, and she caught sight of herself in the lift mirror. Red-faced, crying, with sangria spilled down her dress like blood. The hotel deserted at that time of night, all the holidaymakers gone to bed, stupefied with drink and sun. Outside, the pool glowing turquoise with its underwater lighting, and the palm trees swaying in the warm breeze. Her thoughts were crazed. She had to figure out which room Corinna and Joel were in. Beth and Vince were on the fourth floor, so they must be the same. She pressed the button for the lift, then got out and realised she'd got muddled and gone up a floor too high, as they didn't have a ground floor in Europe. Then she somehow got lost on her way back to the lift, found the stairs instead, which were bare stone. Her feet clattered. What if it was too late by the time she got there? What if – something had already happened, that they couldn't come back from?

There was the fourth floor at last. Which room would it be? Then she found a window and looked for their own balcony, her swimsuit drying on it alongside Vince's trunks. She counted back laboriously. It must be this one. Room 743. Voices could be heard inside, and music. Beth rapped firmly on the door.

And after that? Nothing. Nothing at all. But once again she touched a hand to her left wrist, feeling the bruise there, tender and pulpy like rotten fruit. What had happened that night? It was all just blanks and terror.

Now, alone in a different but identical corridor, she leaned against the wall as her legs gave way beneath her. She was the one who'd been roaming around the hotel alone that night, drunk and full of rage. Her own behaviour was just as suspicious as Vince's, if not more so.

Then it came to her. The English detective, Alison. The one who kept interfering and watching Beth at the pool. Who seemed to somehow see the unhappiness she was doing her best to conceal, and maybe even knew something about Vince that Beth herself didn't. That was who Beth had to talk to.

Alison – now

She'd been on hold now to the Spanish hotel for fifteen minutes, and was slowly losing the will to live with the smooth jazz on-hold music and inability of anyone to understand what she was asking for. She'd dutifully sent all her information to Alejandro, who had confirmed that Corinna was wearing the high-heeled shoes on the CCTV footage of her going back to her room. Her story seemed to check out. He also confirmed that Beth Jones had reappeared in the bar long after she'd supposedly gone to bed, after 2 a.m. Finding it shut, she had retrieved her handbag from one of the tables and staggered off towards Joel and Corinna's room. Not long after there was the scream. Then the CCTV of her in their building. Then, a little while later again, she had gone to her own room, so drunk she was slumping against the wall of the lift. It wasn't looking good for Beth.

Alison had also passed on her hunch about the strange man in the photo, but Alejandro was understandably sceptical about it. After all, between the two couples, he already had plenty of viable suspects without pinning it on a random man with an odd expression on his face. Did that even mean anything or was he a total red herring?

Still no sign of Vince Castries, and no suggestions from his wife, who remained in police custody. They had also tracked down his mother and sister, who said they hadn't seen him in years, but confirmed that Beth had been to visit a few days previously, and learned all about Vince's past involvement in the murder of Lucy Brady. Alison knew that Beth would have to be released soon, if they weren't going to charge her for pushing Corinna. The Spanish case would have to be let go. And yet Alison could not bring herself to do that, not yet.

Finally, the line picked up. '*Hola, Hotel Los Colibris?*' A husky female voice she recognised.

'Maria Theresa, is that you?'

'*Sí?*'

'It's Alison! The detective. You know, the very pregnant lady.'

'Ah yes, how are you, *señora*?'

Even fatter and slower was the answer, but she said, 'Oh fine, fine. Listen, since you've been so extremely helpful so far, I'm wondering if there's something else you might be able to assist me with . . .'

A few minutes later she had WhatsApped the mystery man's picture to the receptionist, who was going to show it around the building and see if anyone recognised him or could match his name to a booking record, and in turn had received a giant spreadsheet with all the guests staying at the time of the murder.

Next, she did a search around Lucy Brady, discovering that Tom was correct – some newspaper articles from the time mentioned a sister, who'd given evidence against Peter Johnson, knowing that Lucy had gone to meet him that night. If Lucy was nearly seventeen when she died, a sister could be around Corinna's age now, assuming Corinna was in fact thirty-five, as Joel had told the hospital. But why would she have followed Vince out to Tenerife, after all these years? Maybe because Beth had Instagrammed extensively about what hotel they were staying in, giving their exact location. One of the many reasons Alison didn't post online, or own an Apple

Watch, or log run times on apps. Back in the day, stalkers actually had to work for it – now you were just handing it all to them on a plate. Assuming all this was true, would Corinna have gone so far as to frame Vince for murder? It seemed far-fetched even for the thrillers Alison had tried to read on holiday.

She groaned as she scrolled through the spreadsheet of guest names from the hotel. Supposedly, they had all been 'interviewed', but she knew in practice the police would not have had the resources to look into every single one in depth. The man in the picture was very likely to not even be British. There were a lot of German tourists staying in the hotel, and as it was she was really pushing her luck involving herself in a Spanish case that might have no connection at all to the one she was currently investigating. He might not even have stayed in the hotel. Could have been from another one, or an Airbnb, or maybe he was even a local.

'Need help, boss?' Gavin was helpfully at her elbow. The smell of his Lynx Africa almost knocked her sideways. He reminded her of how Tom had been when they met, a little cocky, or at least pretending to be, hiding the fact that underneath he was a boring, dependable dad-in-waiting. And soon Tom really would be a dad. As always, the thought curdled her into terror.

'Yes, actually. I'm going to send you a list of guests from a hotel in Spain – I want to know if anything flags on them. Focus on the British ones for now.'

Gavin's keen smile paled as he looked over her shoulder at the dense list of names. 'What am I looking for?'

'Anything. Convictions, suspicious behaviour, checking out early, that kind of thing. You'll know if you see it.' His vision of police work had likely involved dangerous undercover work, or chasing down suspects on crowded streets, not ploughing through Excel, but this was where most answers came from, and he would learn. 'By the way, did the results on Vince Castries's bank account come through yet?'

'Oh, yeah! Here's who the money's been going out to.' He passed her over a piece of paper. The surname on the account seemed familiar. Alison's hunch was growing even stronger, needling at her. She needed to pay someone a visit.

'No recent activity?' He'd been wise enough not to use his phone or bank cards since he had absconded, but surely he would have to soon. Unless of course something had happened to him as well.

'Nothing. But we did get the phone records, at last.'

'Oh, good. Show me?'

He passed her the file and she pored over it. Nothing sent or received for several days, which made sense when his wife was also in custody and hardly anyone else had his number. But there were a number of texts sent to him over the previous two weeks, from an unknown number. 'Can you try to find out who that's registered to? I'm going out now. I have to check something.'

'Alright, boss.'

He should by rights call her *ma'am*, but she didn't correct him. It seemed only yesterday that she herself was this keen and fresh-faced, hoping her own DI would notice her efforts. Could she do this job with an infant? She thought of the harassed look on the face of Jemma Maxwell, the beans caked to her jeans. With a groan, she stood up again, bracing herself on the desk. This was more activity than the doctor had allowed, she knew. At least she could sit down in the car.

'She was so pretty, wasn't she? And good at school, and she had a lovely singing voice too, though she was too shy to let people hear it. I should have got her lessons.'

Julie Brady had lost her daughter over twenty years ago, but it was clear she still loved to talk about her. They were sitting in an overly chintzed living room full of pictures of the dead girl, stopped forever at sixteen.

'Very pretty,' Alison agreed, putting down her glass of water. At least being heavily pregnant made people more likely to invite you in when you went round to call on them unannounced and asked to talk about the murder of their daughter years before. By rights she should not be here alone, but she didn't want some clumsy or over-enthusiastic DC causing upset feelings. 'I'm so sorry for what happened, Julie.'

Julie's smile faded and she busied herself putting away the old leatherbound album. 'Three of them hardly did any time, you know. Five years! What kind of punishment is that for killing my Lucy?'

Alison had already acquainted herself with the fates of the Football Four, as they had been called in the media for a time. Two of the three not convicted of murder – Jeffrey Campbell and Ali Shah, who were both seventeen at the time and not linked to Lucy's body by DNA evidence – had served five years. Shah, who had dual nationality, had moved to Pakistan. Campbell was now living quietly in Bracknell, working in a warehouse, and had begged Alison not to tell his girlfriend, with whom he had an eight-year-old son, what he had done. Alison had no reason to do so, though she couldn't avoid the bitter irony that he'd got to live his life with barely a blip, while Lucy would never have a job, a partner, or a baby either.

The third boy, John Fleming, had also served five years but later gone back inside for GBH, attacking a man outside a nightclub with a broken bottle. He had died in a prison brawl a few years back.

Alison said, 'I know it must be hard, dredging it up after all this time. I'm actually here about your other daughter, though.'

Julie looked puzzled. 'My other daughter? What do you mean?'

'Well, when did you last see her?'

The woman looked utterly baffled. 'Karen's in Australia. Got married out there. We miss them, of course, but they're happy.'

She indicated a framed picture on the mantelpiece, a blonde woman with too much sun damage on her face, standing on a beach with a block-like man and two blond kids. Manifestly not Corinna. God, Alison hated it when her hunches were wrong. She had driven all the way to Reading on this whim, still desperately trying to tie up her loose ends.

'I'm sorry, Julie, I'm mistaken about something, clearly.' But still, she was here, so she'd take a shot. 'Is there any chance you recognise this woman?' She held out a printed picture from Corinna's Insta, taken at the hotel in Tenerife. Sitting dangerously once again on the balcony, the sunset orange behind her mane of hair. Thankfully Alison had found some cached images, since the accounts were now offline.

Julie stared at it diligently. 'She does look familiar, you know.'

'Yes?' Aha. She'd known she was right. Or at least, on the right track, if completely wrong about Corinna's true identity.

Julie was doing her best to think it over. 'Um – now, I could be wrong about this, but I think she might have been in our Karen's class. What was her name? Deana, Davina, something like that, I think. Rhymes with Corinna, almost, come to think of it.'

Alison took back the print-out. 'That's so helpful, thank you. You don't know if she had anything to do with – with Lucy's case?'

'Oh, yes. She was at the court for the verdict.' Julie's face turned pale with sorrow at the memory. 'I remember she shouted to me

– "I'm sorry", something like that. I couldn't really take it in, you know, I was that overwhelmed.'

Alison's heart was quickening as it always did when a breakthrough was near. OK, her hunch wasn't exactly on target, but it was something all the same. Despite her claims, Corinna did have a connection to Lucy Brady after all, and that was why she'd followed Vince out to Tenerife. And that meant she was lying about something bigger than a flimsy love scam. 'Who is she, then?'

'She's his sister. That boy.' Alison was about to ask which boy, but then Julie said: 'She's Peter Johnson's sister. That's who she is.'

Beth – then

Alison, the English detective, had patches of sunburn on her shoulders that looked like she was wearing a cut-out top, and the white sunglasses marks of a grumpy panda, but right now she seemed like the wisest person in the world, because she was actually trying to help.

'So you believe me?' Beth was almost tearful in her gratitude. 'That he didn't do it?'

It was the next day, and she'd waited in the bar area until she saw Alison coming down for breakfast. So jittery she could hardly hold a glass, Beth had already sunk two cocktails out of sheer nerves, and had barely slept for five minutes in a row, thinking of Vince stuck in a jail cell.

She had told Alison a highly edited version of her own story. Admitted that she was not, after all, with Vince when he found Ana's dead body, but omitted the disturbing memories coming back to her of that night, her own bruises, her memory of shouting at someone in a red dress, the shoes she had taken from Corinna's room, which were now hidden in her own suitcase as she tried to figure out what to do with them. The sound of a scream. Herself in the lift mirror, red staining her clothes, hours after she was supposed to be in bed. That had just been spilled sangria. Right?

Alison scratched at a mosquito bite on her arm. 'I've seen this happen before, unfortunately. A British tourist in the wrong place at the wrong time, and what with language barriers and maybe, shall we say, different investigative priorities, they get into hot water. Make sure you keep in touch with the consul and document everything.'

'You think I can get him out?' The clock was ticking, she knew. Vince would not cope much longer in that windowless police station. He had been right on the edge for months, and this would surely push him over. She wished she had been allowed to see him.

'They can hold him for seventy-two hours here. There's a good chance he'll be released after that, unless they find other evidence. I can't do much officially.'

'So you don't think he did it.'

'I can't say for sure, Beth. But there doesn't seem to be enough evidence to hold him.'

'Thank you. Oh, thank you.'

'The problem is, since your initial story wasn't true, and he wasn't with you all night, he's going to need some kind of alibi. That other couple you were drinking with, where are they? They checked out already, apparently.'

'I know. I don't have their number, but they said they were staying the week, so it seems a bit weird they would just go.'

Alison frowned at that. 'No one should have been allowed to leave, with a crime like this. We'll have to track them down.'

Good. Corinna and Joel checking out early, the morning after someone had been murdered, that was good for Vince, and for her. Anyone else looking suspicious was helpful.

'They mentioned going to La Caleta, up north? So that could be a good place to start. I did tell the detective at the station as well.'

'I'll speak to him again. Though he's not massively keen on me sticking my oar in.'

'Thank you so much for your help. I'm sorry to spoil your holiday.'

Alison rolled her eyes. 'Truth be told, I'd rather be working. Is that awful? It's so boring, isn't it, this kind of holiday? Just sitting about in the sun? I can't even drink.'

Beth had not been bored. More entirely terrified, but she nodded anyway. She drained her drink, looking out over the crowded beach, the pulse of dance music rising from the pool. Why had they come here? She hadn't understood that when you go on holiday, you just take your problems with you. Things between her and Vince were worse than ever, both of them lying, both of them suspecting the other, Vince in jail, her remembering all kinds of disturbing things about the night Ana died. And now a woman was dead, and it might all be Beth's fault. She just had to hope she could get Vince out and they could flee the country, and that Joel and Corinna hadn't already had the same thought and left Spain altogether.

Alison was looking at her, she realised. 'What?'

'Beth. I just need to know that you've been honest with me. If there's anything else you remember that you haven't said.'

Beth quailed under the gaze of the detective. There was so much. The shoes, which were still in her hotel room. The scream. The red dress, the smoke. Her bruised wrist and ankle. Her fear, her terrible, terrible shame. The memory of looking for Joel and Corinna's room, knocking on the door. Waking up on the sun lounger. Not knowing how she had got to bed.

'No,' she said. 'That's everything.'

Him

'Well, say something.' He tried to keep the irritation from his voice.

She looked down at the brochure. 'I'm just surprised. I mean, we only just got back from a holiday.'

'And I felt bad that you didn't get to relax, so I booked this as a surprise. I thought you'd be pleased.'

And why wasn't she? Most women would be happy that their husband had organised a surprise trip to an all-inclusive resort in Mexico, but here she was, looking like a wet weekend, not meeting his eyes.

'Yes, yes, of course I am. It's lovely, darling. I just – I don't know if I can go next week, is all. It's very short notice.'

'Why can't we do something spontaneous for once? We both ended up working the week of Tenerife, so I claimed back the days, and I spoke to your office and did the same for you.'

He'd charmed the HR woman into agreeing to it, left her thinking *what an amazing husband* and *I wish mine would do that for me*. It was so easy to manipulate them. Too easy.

His wife reached out and brushed the cover of the brochure, blue seas and pools and images of smiling couples clinking cocktails. 'It's lovely,' she said again. Her voice was pinched.

'Maybe you can tell your face that then,' he said peevishly. He snatched it away. 'It's not cancellable, but I suppose we can just lose the money if you'd rather.'

'No! No, darling, of course not! I'm just in shock.'

'Why aren't you happy? Isn't this a nice thing?'

He was frustrated. Just when he thought he had worked out how people ticked, something like this would happen. She was malfunctioning more and more recently. Not responding to his kind gestures like cooking dinner (or pretending to), or complimenting her outfit, or even booking a holiday.

'It's just – you know, what happened last time. It was scary. That girl dying.'

'I know it was very sad, but it was nothing to do with us.'

There was a tiny pause there, no more than a second, but in that moment all the fear he had been keeping at bay rushed in like a tsunami. She knew. She *knew*. Or suspected, at least. But would she say? Knock down the house of cards their entire life was built on?

'Right?' he risked, looking her in the eye.

She looked away first. 'Of course not. How exciting, a surprise trip. I must get my legs waxed. When do we go?'

'Saturday,' he said. Just a few days from now. And in Mexico, as well as sun and sand and margaritas, there would be women. Backpackers, migrant workers, locals. Women vanished all the time in Mexico. It was very sad, the epidemic of violence. So many dead women that no one would notice one more.

Alison – now

Corinna had made a shocking recovery. She even appeared to be wearing make-up, and her hair was nicely brushed. She was wearing a grey tracksuit and scrolling through her phone, sitting on top of the covers on the hospital bed. 'Oh, it's you. I'm getting out soon, they said. Can't wait to be away from the UK, to be honest. All this rain. It's why I moved in the first place.'

She seemed very confident of being allowed to leave the country, for someone who had confessed to fraud and blackmail.

'I'm glad you're feeling better, Corinna.'

'Yes, well, I'm lucky to be alive. But then I've always been resilient.'

'You are lucky, actually. And when you've recovered a little more I'll be wanting you to come down the station with me and make a formal statement about your connection to Peter Johnson, and why it was you stalked Vince Castries all the way to Tenerife. Why you've been texting him threatening messages for months now, from a different number. That was you, wasn't it?' Though the phone was unregistered, it had been purchased at a shop near Corinna and Joel's current address. Alison was sure she changed the number often.

Corinna had been putting on sticky pink lip gloss with the use of a little compact mirror. For a moment, her mouth froze in an o, like a boiled sweet. Then she rallied. 'I didn't stalk him. It's a free country, isn't it?'

'But you are Peter Johnson's sister, aren't you? Davina, not Corinna? Not something you felt the need to tell me previously.'

'Well, I wasn't under caution or arrest when we talked, you said so yourself. And yeah, I am his sister, so? It's not illegal to change your name either. Especially when everyone thinks your brother murdered someone. Corinna was my aunt's name, and I was married for a bit in America, so that's the surname.' Apparently she had moved around a lot, adopting a new accent and changing herself bit by bit until she was almost unrecognisable as a teenage girl from Reading.

'It's certainly illegal to harass someone over text, Corinna.' Alison couldn't adjust to calling her by the new name.

'Oh. Is it?'

'Very much so.'

'Well. You can't prove that, or you'd have arrested me or something.' She folded her arms. Unfortunately she was right.

'So what's your game? You don't think Peter did it?' Alison sank down again into the uncomfortable chair, the hospital smell tickling her nostrils. Soon she'd be in hospital herself.

'Of course not. He's my brother. He wouldn't have done something like that.'

'Well, what happened that night, then? In your opinion.' Corinna would have been nearly fifteen then. Old enough to notice things.

Corinna sighed and put down her lip gloss, folded her arms petulantly. 'It was Vince, wasn't it? He lied. Sent all those boys to prison, got away with it himself. Peter told me Vince had always liked Lucy Brady, used to stare at her across the classroom and really freak her out. Of course, she only had eyes for Peter, but it was hardly his fault, what happened.'

Alison tried to take this in. 'You're saying Vince killed Lucy himself, and framed all the other boys for it?'

'Well, I don't know who killed her, do I? They were there, the others, I think. But not Pete. He wouldn't do a thing like that.'

'Where was he, then? Your mother gave evidence that he didn't come home until late, and that he put his clothes straight in the wash.' Plus there was clear DNA proof that he'd had sex with Lucy.

'Of course he did, he was playing football – there was mud! He just – I don't know. He said he didn't really remember. They'd been drinking. Probably he smoked something. But Pete didn't hurt her, I know that, and he definitely didn't invite her that night, that was lies. And somehow he ends up with the longest sentence of them all! It's so unfair. Just because Vince – or Darren, that's his real name – was jealous of him. And look, the other boys got out of prison already, and Peter's still in there. It's not fair.'

This was partly because of his violent behaviour as an inmate, Alison knew, but refrained from commenting. 'And the DNA tying him to Lucy's body?'

Corinna wrinkled up her pretty nose. 'I don't know about that. It's easy to fake, isn't it? To plant.'

'Not really.'

'Well, it's not a crime to have sex. Probably she threw herself at him. I remember her, you know. We did netball together, and she was always running after Pete – so embarrassing. I was in the same year as Lucy's sister, right pain she was too.'

'Are you prepared to make a statement about anything you know around Peter's arrest, and the night of Lucy's murder?'

'I did! Loads of times. The police, your lot, they just never listened.' Her voice was bitter. 'And my dad left, and Mum just gave up, lay on the sofa drinking vodka and blaming herself for not making up something for the police. She was so stupid. She didn't even know why they were asking those questions, when she dropped Peter in it. Drank herself to death, eventually. So, can you get the case reopened?'

With DNA evidence and no alibi, plus the testimonies of the other boys, who had all painted Peter as the ringleader, it was highly unlikely. But Alison had more pressing purposes right now. 'I'm sorry you had to go through that, Corinna. But it doesn't explain why you went to Tenerife.'

She sighed. 'I'd been looking for Darren for years to get him to withdraw his statement. Tell the truth at last, and at least let Peter get out of prison before he's forty. Have some kind of life. He'd changed his name, you know. Took me ages to find him, but I did.'

'How did you?'

'He was at a wedding last year, someone she was friends with, Beth, but a guy I went to school with was there too. Think he's the bride's cousin or something. Anyway, we keep in touch a bit. He likes me.' At this she gave a coy smile. 'He ran into Darren at this wedding, realised he'd changed his name, and found out Beth's name too, where he worked even. Beth's a real yapper when she's drunk; you may have noticed. So then I started following her online and it was all on her Insta, everything they did. I called up his work and pretended to be a journalist, found out that he'd logged his patent, got his phone number. It's easy to get people's information. You just need a good cover story.'

Alison took this in. 'But why did you go to Tenerife – why not confront him in London?'

She sighed in frustration. 'I didn't know how to find him. He quit his job and Beth never posted exactly where they lived. It was annoying. Then when she mentioned the hotel they were staying at, I knew I'd be able to get talking to him there. Get him drunk. Make him do the right thing.'

'But you didn't get the chance out there?'

'Well, no. He didn't go for it that night, and then – Ana was dead and we had to get out of there.'

But Corinna/Davina hadn't given up. Instead she had tracked him down in London, infiltrated his life. No wonder Beth had been so angry, to find they were stalked like this. And she likely suspected Vince had cheated on her too, with this younger, beautiful woman. Alison did feel sorry for her, even if she might have pushed Corinna off a roof.

'Let me see if I have this right. You saw where they were staying on Beth's Instagram, followed them out to Tenerife without Joel's knowledge . . . ?'

'Yeah, he didn't know about any of this,' she said quickly.

'Just about the scamming.' Alison was severe.

Corinna rolled her eyes. 'That's what you care about? It's dumb, but it does bring in cash, though bless him, his stupid fund is never going to go anywhere. Joel hasn't a clue. He doesn't even know my real name.'

'So you went out there after Vince, then followed him back to London when that didn't work. Pretended to be their friends.'

'Well, Peter's still inside, isn't he? I just wanted to apply some pressure. Get Darren – Vince, whatever – to tell the truth, finally. Literally none of that is even a crime.'

'Blackmail is very much a crime, Corinna, but we'll come to that. Does Vince know who you are now?'

'He didn't. I – hadn't found the right time to tell him.'

Alison understood. She had still been hoping to compromise Vince in some way, and blackmail him. 'And how does all this lead to the death of a woman in Spain?'

'I . . .' Her shoulders sagged for a moment. 'Honestly, I have no idea. I only spoke to Ana once or twice. I felt sorry for her, getting all that gross attention from men. Even Joel kept hanging about her, like he had a chance, and every night in the bar there were all these sleazy dudes drooling over her instead of spending time with their wives. I don't know what happened to her after we talked that night and swapped our shoes. I really don't. I went to bed and she was having a cigarette, then she said she'd walk home. That's all.'

'Did you see Beth Jones at all after she left the bar?'

'Beth? No. Wasn't she in bed?'

'She didn't knock on your room door?'

Corinna shrugged. 'Not that I heard. We had the music pretty loud, though.'

Alison looked at the selfish, beautiful woman in the bed, her glamour undimmed by the bandage she wore around her head. She had lost her entire family after the events of one muddy November night, and had been trying to free her brother, even if he didn't deserve it. Those five boys, one of them dead already, were the only people who knew what had really happened that night, and the true fate of Lucy Brady. Everything else corroborated the verdict that Peter Johnson had killed her, with collusion from the other three. But she could see why Corinna didn't want that to be true. Did she believe this woman, who had lied so much?

Actually, she did. She would send the information to Alejandro, but she knew it was unlikely extradition would be granted for credit-card fraud or blackmail, especially when no one had actually made a complaint about their activities. It was likely no charges would be brought against Joel and Corinna, and that, once again, no solution to Ana's murder would present itself.

Her phone buzzed and she fished it from her coat. Gavin.

Boss, big news! Vincent Castries is back. And he wants to hand himself in.

Beth – then

'Watch the step there.'

'I'm not an invalid, Beth!' But he was walking like one, after two days in jail, shuffling to the reception of the station in the clothes she had brought for him. Beth wanted to get out of there as soon as possible. Part of her didn't believe the police had let Vince go, and would not rest easy until they were on a plane to London and it had actually left the tarmac.

It was over. That was what the police had said. Beth had spent the past two days in a nightmare, contacting lawyers and consuls, desperate to talk to someone back home, her sister, or work friend Janice, but also not wanting anyone to know what had happened. Eventually, Joel and Corinna had been tracked down to a hotel in the north of the island, where they claimed to have gone to 'find a bit of chill'. Beth didn't understand it, but maybe they just were the kind of people who'd spontaneously walk away from a week's hotel booking. They had given Vince an alibi, said he was with them all night until the early morning hours, before wandering off towards the beach on his way back to Beth. That they'd all been in Joel and Corinna's room together until then, drinking and smoking. Except Beth knew Vince never touched weed and didn't drink much, and she knew Joel had been with her, at least for a while. What happened after she'd knocked on the door of their room?

Surely Vince would have heard her calling, if he'd been in there. So why was everyone lying? Even Beth herself, she had lied. She hadn't told anyone about finding the shoes in Corinna's room. Or about her own memories of waking up on the lounger, then trying to get to Joel and Corinna's room in the hope of finding Vince. Or about the flashes she was getting of a red dress and smoke. Corinna had been wearing a red dress, and was a vaper. But if she'd been the one to give Beth the bruise on her wrist, she obviously hadn't told the police about it.

Beth looked at Vince now, fussing with the buttons of the shirt she'd brought. How strange it was that you could live beside a man every day for eight years, and marry him, and love him, and wash his pants and clean his hair out of the sink, but find one day he was a total stranger. They had reached the door out of the cell area now, and the guard looked them over without much interest. A key clanged in the clunky lock, and Beth's breath caught in her throat. They walked through. He was free. Vince looked haunted. Like he hadn't slept or eaten in days, his hair curling without its usual pomade.

They waited in reception for him to sign his release forms, every second agony. Beth kept glancing through the glass of the front door, to the hot street beyond. They were almost free and away. So close. The sergeant was on the phone, and waved to them for a moment. Beth moved forward, her hand groping for his, but he pulled away, and she felt the silence between them, thick with questions. *What happened? Did you do it? What the hell is going on?*

In a low voice, she said, 'Vince – do you remember where you were that night?' She shouldn't be asking here, she knew. But she couldn't wait.

'Bits of it. I drank so much.'

They both had. 'You were with Joel and Corinna? In their room?'

He looked carefully away. 'I guess so.'

'And then what? I didn't see you until the beach, and that was, what, seven in the morning?' Hours had gone by, where anything could have happened.

Vince looked up at her, and she saw the pain etched around his dark eyes. It struck her that they had not looked directly at each other for a long time. 'I don't remember a lot of it. I just saw her in the sea as I passed, and I thought she might be drowning, so I went in after her. Isn't that what anyone would do?'

'But – why were you even on the beach? It wasn't – well, it's not how you would go from their room to ours. Is it?' Even now she felt afraid to ask him questions, timid. Because she might not like the answers. Because she did not know how to respond to questions about her own activities.

He didn't answer for a long time, as the desk officer finally got off the phone and passed him a clipboard. Beth waited while he fussed for a few minutes, signing the forms and taking back a clear plastic bag with his phone and watch and clothes from that night. She recognised the shirt that had been soaked with seawater, neatly folded.

He turned towards the door, and paused there, about to push it open to the blinding heat of the street. Then, he spoke. 'Look, Beth. Neither of us really knows what happened that night. We were both so drunk. I'm lucky to even be out of here. So let's just go. Let's go home, just forget this ever happened. You've got a cab waiting?'

'Y-yes.' Their bags were in the boot, the flight was booked for just over two hours' time, and they were leaving Tenerife. They'd been told they could go home, though they might be recalled if anything else came up, and were required to notify the police here if they changed their address or contact details. Beth knew it didn't matter. Once they were back in the UK it would take something huge to extradite them back here. She had looked it up. As soon the plane took off, they were safe. So why didn't she feel better?

Outside, she could see people eyeing them from pools of shade in front of the shuttered shops, see the graffiti on the walls. *Tourists Go Home.* Well, she was going to. Vince climbed into the cab, his face still shuttered and blank. The relief of getting him out of prison settled back into her old worries. She still didn't know why he'd been acting strangely for months now, or where he'd been that night. What he had done, what she had done either. It seemed they were not going to talk about it. A pact of silence, each protecting the other and themselves, so that the truth of what went on, what happened to Ana, might never be known. Silence that would drive them even further apart.

Beth was still standing on the street, as if frozen, as much as she wanted to leave. What were they heading home to? How could anything ever be the same again? From the front, the driver said something in Spanish, indicating a crowd gathering further down the street, with placards and the echo of a loudspeaker. More anti-tourism protests. Beth quickly got into the car beside Vince and did up her seat belt, and they sped off to the airport, and freedom.

Alison – now

Gavin was bubbling. 'That's good news, isn't it, boss? He wants to confess to both, the push and the thing in Spain too.'

Alison wasn't so sure. She wasn't actually a fan of the spontaneous confession, having learned over the years that three-quarters of them were usually fake. Sometimes crackpots, sometimes the altruistic trying to shield someone else, sometimes misguided guilt. In this case, she didn't know. There was definitely something dodgy about Vince Castries, she just wasn't sure what. 'Yeah. We'll see.'

'What you waiting for, boss? He's in interview room two. Can I sit in?'

God, he was so keen. She remembered being like that, before cynicism set in, before she could predict ninety per cent of what suspects and witnesses were going to say before they said it, before she knew how many cases were just never going to get solved, how many weeping victims would be left alone to deal with their pain.

'What? Oh. No. Has to be Nigel, sorry.'

Gavin drooped, then rallied. 'Still, it'll be good to get it solved. Good for our stats, and then you can stop worrying about this Spain murder before you go off on your break.'

'It's hardly going to be a break, Gavin.' But he was sweet. Somehow, she knew that whatever Vince had to say would not in fact stop her worrying, because she was already sure that what he was going to tell her would not be the truth either. 'Any word on those hotel guests yet?'

He indicated the computer in front of him, a big, boxy model that pre-dated Alison. 'Still working through it.'

'Alright. Let me know if anything comes up.'

There was Vince Castries, viewed for the third time in his life under the fluorescent lights of a police station interview room. This one was not quite so bakingly hot as the one in Spain, and it did have a window, set high up in the wall. But the bleak look on his face was the same. He appeared to have not slept for several days, and his clothes were rumpled and stained. Alison manoeuvred herself to sit, reflecting on how being twice her normal size had really affected her patented sweeping-in move. Nigel, who had egg on his breath from his lunchtime sandwiches, was eyeing her dubiously. She reached to switch on the recorder and did the preliminary introductions and caution, trying to assert the upper hand. No solicitor, which made sense if Vince was throwing himself on the pyre.

'So, Vince, where have you been all this time?'

He shrugged. 'I had to – think about some things. Look, I did something when I was younger, and it's eaten away at me ever since.'

'This is about Lucy Brady?'

She caught Nigel from the corner of her eye, keeping her tone as light and neutral as possible. If this went well, they could have three cases solved by the end of the interview.

Vince blinked for a moment, perhaps surprised she knew about it, then rallied. 'Yeah. Lucy.'

'You knew her?'

'A bit. She liked Peter. Peter Johnson, from my football team.'

'And you liked her?'

Vince stared down at his hands on the table. The skin was rough and dry, and he nodded. 'Here's the bit I want to confess to. It was me who asked her to come to the field that night.'

'Oh?' So Peter had been right to say he'd never lured her there at all.

'I said – I told her Peter would be there, and that he wanted her to come. That he'd told me to ask her. It was stupid. But I thought if she came down and we talked, she might see that I was a good guy. Peter – he wasn't. He used to say awful things about girls. He didn't care about her, but I did.'

'So what happened? She turned up, and then what?'

'It all went wrong. It all just – went wrong.'

'Tell me, Vince.'

Her voice was low, understanding. Giving the impression she understood him and cared about him. Alison could do that even for the biggest scum of the earth, but in this case she actually did. Something about Vince made her pity him, and worry for him, even though he was implicated in the deaths of two women. She was rooting for him, despite herself. *Come on, Vince, don't disappoint me.*

'The other boys didn't leave. I thought they'd head off home straight away after practice, since it was really dark and cold, but then she turned up early, and they hadn't left, and she'd brought vodka and Coke, like mixed up in the bottle, so we all started drinking.'

'You too?' His DNA had not been found on the bottle, unlike the other four. Another reason he'd got off while they had gone to prison.

'No. I didn't like drinking, and I was annoyed. I wanted them to go. But Lucy, she only wanted to talk to him. Peter. She was sitting beside him, like leaning against him.'

'So what happened then?'

He let out a full-body sigh. 'What I told the police, it was true. I was cross, I went home. They were all still there, the four of them and her. I didn't hurt her.'

'So the only thing you didn't admit was that you invited her there, not Peter.' Alison felt Nigel gently tut beside her. It was hardly the great reveal they'd been building to. It might reduce Peter Johnson's sentence by a few years, but that was it. If Corinna was hoping that Vince would miraculously take the blame for the murder, she'd be disappointed.

'Yeah. But if I hadn't, she'd still be alive. You see? It was my fault. I started it. I got her to come there, and she wasn't safe.' There were tears in his voice. 'It was my fault she died.'

'Vince – just inviting her there wasn't a crime. Misleading, maybe, but not a crime. You didn't engage in any assault on Lucy? She was fit and well when you left?'

'She was drunk, but she seemed happy. I thought her and Peter would get together.' Instead, she had ended up dead. And Vince had been blaming himself the whole time.

'Did you know Corinna was Peter's sister?'

He nodded. 'Not at first, of course. She was just a kid when I knew him, and her name was different, so I didn't recognise her. But there's a resemblance, yeah. I saw it right away, then I thought I was mistaken, but I knew for sure the night she – fell.'

'When Beth found the photograph, the one of the football team?'

'That's right. Corinna was going to use it to convince me, I suppose. Make me feel guilty. I grabbed it when I ran. I didn't want to – I didn't want to complicate things.'

'So why did you run, Vince? I don't understand.'

'I was afraid, and I – I had to think. So I went back to the woods, near where it happened. Where she died. Lucy.' And now he had come back, ready to confess.

'When you came in you told the officers it was you who pushed Corinna.'

'Yes. I did it. I pushed her.'

Alison stared at him. He didn't quite meet her eyes. 'Why would you push her?'

'Well, she basically stalked me! She followed us out to Tenerife, and I'd just worked that out, that it was her sending me those texts, threatening me, and she was trying to blackmail me, even. It was horrible.'

'So you thought you'd push her off a balcony.' But it was Beth who had found the photograph, and lost her temper. Who had stormed out to the balcony.

'I – wasn't thinking. It wasn't deliberate. I was trying to protect Beth – she was upset, I thought they might – fight. That Beth might get hurt. I don't know.'

Alison couldn't prove this either way, if Corinna and Beth insisted they didn't recall what had happened. 'And who is it you've been paying the money to?' She was fairly sure she knew the answer to this one too but wanted him to confirm it.

'One of the other guys. John. He died in prison, and his family – they didn't do so well after. He always said he never touched Lucy.' The other three boys had all maintained this. That only Peter had been with her. But Vince's word had sent them all to prison anyway. 'His sister has a kid, so I send money to them. I try to help. Make amends, if I can.' He looked bashful for a moment. 'I might be coming into some cash, you know.'

'I've heard. So Corinna – Davina, whatever her name is – is mistaken. Likely it was Peter who killed Lucy after all, perhaps or perhaps not aided by the other boys.' Peter had maintained the sex was consensual, that he'd left her there and some other mysterious assailant had come along and killed her, despite only his DNA and clothes fibres being on her. His argument seemed pretty tenuous.

'That's what I think. He wasn't good. I wasn't surprised he hurt her. That's why I – why I felt so bad. I knew what might happen to her, and I still went off and left her there. So it was my fault.'

Somehow this tortured confession was just making Vince Castries seem like the good guy. Alison sighed in exasperation. 'Alright. So now tell me about Spain. Tell me about Ana.'

Vince looked up, his brown eyes sad and hollow. 'Well. I think maybe that was my fault too.'

Beth – now

She was under arrest. In a police cell. Somehow, she found that it was easier to bear this than when Vince had been arrested in Spain. She had resigned herself to it. They were going to charge her with pushing Corinna, attempted murder, or murder if she died – and Beth could not believe she'd survived at all.

It felt like she had been in a long time – three nights, if you included the one when she'd been brought here, very late, after Corinna fell and she was arrested and searched and swabbed and her clothes taken. That meant it was bad, she knew. They'd kept her in longer than the normal limit, so they must have a strong case. And after all, maybe she was guilty. She didn't remember exactly what had happened on the balcony, drunk and blind with rage, nor did she remember being in Tenerife that night, what had happened after she'd gone looking for Vince. But she did know she was capable of it.

Alison was most likely aware by now of Beth's previous arrest, for clawing at Jemma's face that time. She was so deeply ashamed of that she had buried it deep, never told Vince, even. Left her teaching job, tried to start over, though she would never forget the feel of the woman's skin under her nails, the look of shock on Jemma's face, the way she had screamed. A friendship lost, a career destroyed, and all over a man who clipped his toenails in front of the TV. What a mess.

The door opened then, and Alison came in, looking red and very pregnant. She sat down opposite Beth and stared at her with an exasperated expression.

'Is this . . . ?'

'It's not an interview. You'll know if it's an interview. I've just been conducting one with your husband.'

'Oh.' So Vince had turned up. She had been worried, she realised, at his disappearance, his silence. Not that he had left her forever. More that he might have – done something to himself. 'Is he alright?' she asked, hearing the hope in her own voice.

'Physically, yes. Mentally, I'm not so sure. He's just confessed to involvement in at least three crimes.'

Beth didn't understand. 'You mean he . . . ?'

'Something to do with Lucy Brady, which I think actually is true, though not a crime. He also says it was him who pushed Corinna.'

Oh God. 'No. No, it wasn't! That's not true. He wasn't even near her. He was standing on the other side of the balcony.'

She remembered that at least, as the fog of rage and fear lifted. Charging out there, Corinna perched on the edge with her stupid vape pen, Vince on the other side, leaning with his elbows on the balcony wall. She remembered a moment of relief that they were several metres apart, clearly not touching. But after that – it was just Corinna's surprised face, then the stomach-twisting moment she vanished backwards over the balcony. Did Beth push her? That's what she didn't know.

'It definitely wasn't Vince, whatever he said. It was – look, I really don't know if it was me or if she just fell. But it wasn't him. It was me who was angry. That she'd stalked us, and that she was – she wouldn't leave Vince alone. I didn't understand it.'

So why would he say it was him who'd pushed Corinna? She didn't understand that either.

Alison went on, 'On top of that, he says he killed Ana Garcia after all. That the alibi Joel and Corinna gave was false – well, they said the same, so I'm pretty sure that's true. He says he held Ana under the water until she drowned. Won't say why. It just "came over him", he claims.'

Nothing made sense. Was this even real? Was she here, in a police station? Was Vince in the next room, saying all these mad things? That he had killed a woman? Never in her darkest moments, when it was clear he was lying about something, had Beth believed it.

Then Alison said, 'The thing is, I know he's lying about that, because Ana wasn't drowned. She was strangled.'

'Oh.'

'So. I have a husband and wife, both of them lying about different things. Somehow managing to shield the other one with their made-up stories. Almost like they're protecting each other.'

Was that why? Was Vince lying for her? To protect her?

He thought *she* had killed Ana?

Alison sat back, fanning her face. 'I'll be honest with you, Beth, my patience right now is as thin as Kate Moss in the nineties. And I'm not known for it at the best of times. The Spanish case is not my jurisdiction, and despite your husband's babbling I've yet to be convinced there's a crime to be answered for in Corinna's fall. I'm running out of time to get things squared away. So I want you to actually tell me the truth, for once. We'll get in your lawyer and her hankies and some warm-body officer and you're going to tell me what you actually remember, OK?'

Beth raised her eyes to the other woman's frank, penetrating gaze. 'I don't remember everything.'

'But you did see Ana that night.'

'I think so. At first I thought maybe it was Corinna – they both had red dresses on. But she doesn't smoke, she vapes.'

'Alright.' Alison heaved herself up again. 'Give me time to set up a proper interview, and then you're going to tell me everything, because frankly I've had it up to here with you and your husband, not to mention pretty-boy Joel and his lying not-girlfriend. If I never see any of you again, it'll be too soon.'

Alison – now

Colette looked faintly impressed as she glanced over Alison's paperwork, re-applying her Chanel lipstick. 'So they were both lying, to try and protect the other.'

'If we can believe them. Kind of sweet, I suppose? In a way?'

'Maybe. So there's no way to prove this Corinna case?'

'Well, Vince now says she just fell after all, got a shock when Beth came storming out with the picture. I don't think there's any sense in pursuing it. Even Corinna admits she can't remember Beth pushing her.'

'And the Spanish case?'

'Someone definitely murdered that poor woman. But I don't think it was any of those four idiots, though they all had contact with her that night. I'll send what I know to the detective there, and he can make a call. But I highly doubt he'll want to question Beth again.'

So Ana might join the long list of women left for dead, in bushes or ditches or in the foundations of houses, sometimes never even found, their killers walking free until new evidence surfaced, or until they did it again. They might never be caught at all, dying warm and safe in their beds of old age. It drove Alison crazy.

'So. You're done, Alison.' Colette handed back the file.

'What?'

'I'm signing you off, from today.'

'But . . .'

'No buts. I'm not going to be responsible for you going into early labour in the station tea room. You've pushed yourself too far.'

Alison opened her mouth to complain, then shut it. She knew Colette was right. Her behaviour the last few days had been highly irresponsible, given the shock she'd had in Spain, and if Tom were not away she would never be risking it. The Spanish case might just have to remain unsolved. She was at least satisfied in her own mind that neither couple here had been responsible for it. They were all covering up other, smaller lies, other secrets, and now they would have to make their peace with those alone. No crimes had been committed, except for moral ones.

Her mind returned to the photograph from the beach, the strange man smiling at the dead body. Maybe it was a red herring, a trick of unfortunate timing. How could they ever hope to trace him? She said, 'OK, I'll get off home then.'

'Ask that keen young DC to drive you home. Tom can collect your car when he's back.'

She sighed. 'Fine.' Colette was right. She'd pushed herself far too far. 'Well, will you keep me in the loop of my cases?'

'No, DI Hegarty, I won't.'

'Oh.'

'I'm giving all your cases to Miriam.'

DS Bashiri. At least she was competent. 'Fine. I'll get my coat.'

Colette stopped her with a quick hand on the arm. 'Oh, and Alison . . . good luck. You can do this, OK? It's not going to be easy, but any number of idiots manage it, and you're far from an idiot. So don't panic. You'll be a great mother. Or, just as rubbish as the rest of us, at least.'

A ridiculous lump had come to her throat. 'Thank you, Colette. I appreciate that.'

She was crossing to her desk to grab her coat when Gavin popped up. 'I think I got something, boss. Maybe.'

She wasn't really listening, thinking she might not be back here for a full year, so she'd better make sure she cleared out her desk drawers and didn't leave behind any perishable food. 'Hmm?'

'That list of guests. One couple did check out early, when they'd paid for the whole week.'

'Yeah, we know about them.'

'Not Joel and Corinna. Another couple.' He squinted at his screen. 'David and Penelope Farnham. They actually live not too far, outside Sevenoaks. I got on to that receptionist you know, and she said she thought he was the man in the picture. David Farnham. Remembered him arguing to get a refund as they were leaving early. Upset about the murder, apparently, and didn't want to stay.'

Alison was so tired. Now she had allowed herself to stop and feel it, it was dragging her down, exhausting. She could send Gavin, or a team of PCs, to check this lead out. Leaving the hotel early was hardly incriminating – she was kind of surprised more people hadn't, after a murder had taken place on their doorstep – and she was also surprised more people hadn't asked for their money back, a nasty death ruining their nice all-inclusive experience. 'Just that?'

'Well, I ran him through the computer and he had an arrest, years back.'

'What for?' She was putting on her coat, ready to leave.

'Flashed a young woman. Indecent exposure, charges dropped.'

Alison sighed. She calculated the driving time to Sevenoaks – barely half an hour in the middle of the day. 'Alright. Let's pay them a quick visit to cross them off, and then you can take me home. I think we'll have to drop this, sadly, once I go off. But you've done some good work, Gavin. Well done.'

She could see he was disappointed it hadn't led to more, but this was the job most of the time. Trawling through data looking for one tiny detail that might be meaningful, cases that never got solved, dead ends, difficult calls to make when you couldn't do everything due to time and budget cuts. Often, there was no resolution, no ingenious breakthrough. Just hard work and victims left to piece their lives together as best they could.

As they headed out to the car park, she cast one last affectionate glance at the dingy, coffee-stained office with its depressing fluorescent lights. God, she was going to miss it.

Beth – now

Getting out of custody was a low-key affair. She signed some papers, and was given back her handbag and phone and the clothes she had worn to Joel and Corinna's what felt like lifetimes ago.

Vince was waiting in reception, his own clothes looking rumpled and slept-in, his eyes sunk with exhaustion. They were both free, unless something drastic happened. There would be no charges pressed over Corinna's fall, and she would make a full recovery. She was already making inspirational TikToks about it, no doubt. In time, Beth might be able to forgive herself. It had been her fault, even if she hadn't pushed Corinna. As for poor Ana, it might be that no one would ever know what happened. Beth was sure now she had seen her while looking for Vince that night – the red dress, the smell of smoke, the scream, the bruises – but could she really have strangled a woman with her bare hands? And how would she have dragged the body to the beach? Alison seemed convinced neither Beth nor Vince had done it, but then who had?

It was finally time to tell each other what they knew.

She walked up to Vince, unsure of what was happening now or if they were even going home together. If home existed now. 'Can we go and get a coffee?' she asked.

There was nowhere nice near the police station, so they went into a greasy spoon, where the coffee was Nescafé and the sandwiches only three pounds. She was starving, but knew that the sick anxiety in her stomach would not let her eat. The waitress took their order, and when she left Vince finally spoke.

'I'm sorry that you got drawn into this, Beth. None of it was your fault.'

'Are you going to explain? I mean – all of it. Before the holiday, during, and these last few days. What's been going on? Why did you confess to those crimes?'

He looked down at his hands, and she saw how dry and sore they were, and her heart ached for him. 'When I was younger, I sent people to prison that I cared about, just to save myself. I can't let that happen again. Especially not to someone I love.'

Beth did not understand, and then, finally, she did. The way he had withdrawn even further from her after the holiday, the way he wouldn't fight his arrest in Spain, the way he had disappeared and then handed himself in, confessed to pushing Corinna and also killing Ana. 'You thought I did it. That I hurt Ana.'

'I thought she was Corinna at first, in the water – the dress, you know. And I thought maybe you'd made the same mistake that night. And I knew you weren't happy.'

There it was. He had finally broached the subject that had been swelling between them for months now, like some terrible mushroom about to burst and release its spores.

She said, '*You* weren't happy. I was only unhappy because of that. I thought you were going to leave me.'

He looked up in surprise. 'Beth, no! I would never do that. I was just in a bad place. After John died in prison, I knew it was my fault he was in there in the first place, and all the guilt came back, about Lucy and her family and all of that. I was getting these threatening messages off Corinna, though I didn't know it then. Telling me I'd lied back then and I should be ashamed of myself. And you know, I had lied, about something at least.' Peter

Johnson's sentence would be reviewed now that Vince had told the truth about who had invited Lucy there that night, but Alison said he was unlikely to get out anytime soon. She'd also said there was a possibility of other charges for Vince – perjury, obstruction of justice – but it was so long ago and Vince so young she doubted anything would come of it.

'So you didn't like Ana. That's not why you kept getting out of bed?'

'No, no. I just couldn't sleep, and there were people in the bar, at least. Company. I was – losing my mind a bit. Plus I was lying to you about work, and I hated doing that. We had never lied to each other.'

'Alison told me about the patent. Why didn't you say?'

Vince had apparently invented some component that helped make solar panels more efficient, and been locked in a legal battle with his old workplace over the ownership. When he left each morning for the past four months, he'd been going to a co-working space to build his own business, which he had recently sold to one of the largest energy companies.

'I couldn't. I'd signed an NDA.'

Dimly, it registered that they could be rich soon. Or he could. There might be no *we* to speak of now.

'So you weren't leaving me.'

'It was nothing to do with you. I was – deep in my own head. All that guilt, about why did I get to have a great career, and a loving wife, when the other boys had nothing. I'm so, so sorry I couldn't see how bad things were. I thought if I at least took the blame for anything you might have done, I could make it up to you. Stupid, I know.'

The relief was instant, despite the circumstances. He still loved her. Then the pain returned, because how could they ever come back from all of this?

'I didn't push Corinna, did I?' she said.

'No. She fell. I just – thought if anyone was getting charged, it might as well be me.'

'And it wasn't me who hurt Ana. I have some gaps in my memory, but I don't think I could do that.'

'It wasn't me either. I – actually wasn't as drunk as I made out. I spent most of the time looking for you, and then I did sleep on a lounger for a bit, like I said. But I never saw her, or at least not – not alive. I woke up there, on the beach, once it started getting hot. It was horrible. My eyes were so dry and I had this overwhelming sense of – like, dread, I suppose.'

Beth understood – she had felt the same when she woke up in their room, which she also didn't remember getting back to.

Now he said, 'And what about you? What do you remember?'

'Me? Well, I fell asleep too, I think, for a bit. Then I couldn't find you, so I went to the room, passed out.' Not that she could recall that. But she had found herself stretched out over the bed, fully clothed. 'I thought you were somewhere with Corinna. I think I was looking for you. I think – I think I did see her, Ana, and I even talked to her. I just wish I could remember.'

'We were in the bar for a while, Corinna and I. After you left.'

'I just went to the loo.'

'You didn't come back for ages, they were shutting the place up. You were with Joel, I thought.'

She had suspected him, and he had suspected her.

'So this is all just wrong place, wrong time?' Not him. Not her. But Ana was still dead. 'So then – who was it?'

He shook his head. 'I hope this detective friend of yours can figure it out, and soon. Because whoever it was, they'll do it again.'

She shook her head. 'I wish I knew for sure if it was me. I don't think I could have done that, strangled her, got her body down there. But, Vince – I've done this kind of thing before.

Hurt someone. Not badly, but I did lose it one time, and I hurt somebody. I'm capable of it.'

He sighed deeply, playing with a packet of sugar on the table. 'Beth – that's the other reason I've been withdrawn all this time. I don't know how to talk to you about this, but I have to try.'

Her stomach turned to slush again. She knew what he was going to say. Deep down, she knew.

'Beth,' he said, hesitantly. 'We need to talk about what's been going on with you.'

Him

Two weeks had gone by since their return from Spain. The tan faded, the clothes all washed and repacked ready for Mexico, and he was thinking it was fine, just like last time and the time before, and even before. Sometimes, he even let himself replay it, at least the parts he remembered. More of the night had returned. How he had found her looking around the bushes in the courtyard of the hotel, the shady part where the cameras conveniently did not reach. She'd lost her keys, she said, so he helped her search, not finding anything. He'd offered to call her a cab, but first maybe he could talk to her about her career? He'd heard her singing – well, she knew that, he had tried to talk to her in the bar several times, but she'd always been distracted – and he worked in the industry, he booked acts for a venue in London. He wanted to take a picture of her, to send to the owner. Maybe down on the beach, in the moonlight. Have a few drinks, talk. And who knew, perhaps they'd find her keys too.

It always amazed him how easily women believed what they wanted to hear.

He hadn't meant to hurt her. Just talk, enjoy her company. It was her fault for walking away from him – he'd been offering her a great opportunity! Well, OK, he hadn't, but she didn't know that, and in the moment neither did he. He honestly believed what he was telling her. Such was the power of delusion.

She had been walking away from him, rejecting him, and he'd felt the familiar rage build in him. How dare she? Who did she think she was? Just some cheap nightclub singer. Then that other woman had appeared, walking towards the accommodation block, the petite one he'd seen about the place with her muscle-head boyfriend. She was also beautiful, though a little annoying and loud. Ana had said something like, *Oh look, there's my friend, I'd better go,* which he knew was a lie to get away from him, and that made him even more angry. He had waited and watched as she exchanged shoes with the second woman, which had baffled him – why? Maybe they were actually friends? Then she'd sat and smoked, looking at her phone for a while, perhaps trying to get a cab. He'd kept watching as a third woman appeared, one he'd also seen around the hotel, frumpy and sad. She was horribly drunk, and even accosted Ana for some reason, drawing a scream from the singer. The scream had alarmed him, and he'd fled from his watching spot in the shadows. He had waited in the car park, slipping round the back of the hotel to avoid cameras again. About ten minutes later, Ana had appeared wearing flip-flops instead of the high jewelled shoes she'd had on before, which was a disappointment. She was setting off with purpose across the car park, as if she was going to walk home, when he caught up to her. *Come with me*, he'd said. *I've found your keys.*

He hadn't meant to hurt her. Just to talk. Why did women never want to talk anymore?

All had been quiet since, and he had started to breathe again. Tomorrow they'd be on a plane to Cancún.

But then, it happened. The moment he had dreaded for years, woken up sweating from nightmares about, pictured in the dead of night while she slept beside him, oblivious. They were just sitting down to dinner when he heard the buzz of a radio, and the doorbell went.

She said, 'Who on earth could that be?'

But he knew. He could see the outlines through the bubbled glass of the door, a woman and a man. Something about their clothes, the firmness of the knock, told him these weren't Jehovah's Witnesses or election campaigners. It was them.

A few minutes remained of his normal life. They had found him at last, and he knew that it would all crumble now. All the things she had been able to explain away, she would at last understand what her intuition had been trying to tell her. The police would put together the parts of the puzzle he had done his best to scatter. This was it. He pushed away his plate of pasta, already cold and sticking together. Wondered briefly if he would ever eat a home-cooked meal again.

'I think it's the police, David!' she said, alarm rising in her voice. How stupid she was. Of course it was the police. This moment was always going to come. It was just that he hadn't known the exact day.

Alison – now

Impatient, she leaned again on the bell of the semi-detached house in a nondescript street in a nondescript suburb. 'Remind me of the names?'

'Farnham. David and Penelope.'

Someone was coming to the door now, a worried-looking woman in her mid-forties perhaps, dressed in Boden florals and with slippers on her feet. Alison could hear the six o'clock news and smell food – she had interrupted dinner.

She explained who she was, and let Gavin say he was 'DC Gavin Grady', since it seemed to still give him pleasure.

'Could we come in for a moment? It shouldn't take long.'

'We're just having dinner.'

'I know. I promise it's just some routine questions.'

They were shown into a pristine living room. No family photos – they didn't appear to have children, or many close relatives at all. Alison spotted a brochure for Los Colibris sitting on top of a neat stack of magazines.

'So you're just back from Tenerife,' she said, nodding to it as she sank on to an overstuffed leather sofa. Gavin sat on the other end, while Penelope remained hovering, wringing her hands together.

The place smelled of furniture polish and some underlying damp note – shuttered up, stale. Two suitcases sat in the hall – had they not unpacked yet from Tenerife? Surely they weren't going away again so soon.

'That's right.'

'I'm looking into any local connections to the murder that occurred while you were there. You're aware of that?'

'Of course. We didn't want to stay on after it happened. Poor woman. We saw her sing a few nights, she was very good.'

That did explain why they'd left early. Kind of.

'Is your husband here?'

She called his name. 'David!'

He appeared in the doorway, a nondescript man going bald at the temples, in a button-up shirt and slacks, with no tie. Nice-enough looking. Forgettable. It was definitely the man from the picture.

Penelope said, 'It's the police. They have some questions about Tenerife.' Her voice was strained and high.

'What about it?' He was frowning.

Gavin spoke up. 'We noticed you checked out early, when you weren't due to leave for another few days.'

'That's right. Who'd want to stay when something so awful had happened?'

He did a good impression of someone empathetic, caring. But then there was the past arrest. Alison didn't want to mention it now in case the wife didn't know, so she turned to the woman and said, 'Could I trouble you for a glass of water? I need to make sure I drink enough at the moment, as you can see.'

'Of course! I'm so sorry, would you like a tea or something?'

It would keep the wife away for a while longer. 'Yes, please. Gavin, will you go and help, please?' He did so with alacrity. On the way home she might tutor him on the many nuances of accepting refreshments in the home of a witness or suspect, and how you could turn this to your advantage.

Alison was left alone with David Farnham, who was still frowning. He seemed calm, but she could sense something – the tick of his heartbeat, the rising sweat on his brow.

'Was there something else?'

'Maybe. Can you look at this picture for me?' She passed him a print-out of the one from Corinna and Joel's flat. 'Is that you?'

'Hmm, yes, it is. Where did you get this?'

'It's just a picture from the scene of the crime. You were on hand when the body was found?'

'I saw the commotion and went down to take a look. Poor girl.' He passed it back. She could hardly say *Why have you got a strange expression on your face in this picture*? Expressions and hunches were not evidence.

'We ran all the hotel guests through our records, Mr Farnham, and we did find a past arrest for you.'

He froze. He was standing a few metres from her, and turned now to look out the window. 'What does that have to do with this?' His voice was quiet.

'I don't know. I wanted to know your whereabouts on the night of the murder, if you had seen Ana around the hotel.'

'Should I not be under caution, if you're going to ask me questions?'

A man who knew the law. That always raised alarm bells for Alison, and she had them now, a faint ripple of the hairs on the back of her neck. She would have stood and moved between him and the door, just to be safe, but it was harder to get up now. She kept her voice easy. 'Not unless I have reason to suspect you. These are just questions.'

'Well, no, I never spoke to her.'

'OK.' Alison passed him another print-out. 'Is that you, in the lobby bar?'

It was an image from the CCTV, sent over by Alejandro, one of thousands captured during those days before Ana died. It showed David Farnham, quite clearly talking to Ana by the piano. It might have been Alison's projection, but the woman's body language looked tense, as if she were trying to get away.

He paused. 'I suppose it is, yes. I must have forgotten.'

From next door, she could hear the murmur of voices, a cupboard opening and closing. Alison struggled to her feet, running over in her head how to handle this. This was not nothing. She could arrest him now, but would he come quietly? Did she have powers of arrest for a crime committed overseas? 'Mr Farnham—'

It happened so fast. She took a step towards him, and he whipped his hand from his pocket, and turned to her, and she felt like she had been punched. *Who would punch a pregnant woman?*, she thought, outraged, but then she looked down and saw blood on her hand and coming through her white shirt, and what looked like a pocket knife sticking out of her. And David Farnham was shoving her to the ground and running from the house.

Beth

One month later

'Well?' said Vince, turning to her in the empty room. 'What do you think?'

'It's lovely.' She walked across the bare floor, footsteps echoing with no furniture, to examine the moulding on the Edwardian fireplace. 'But – it's kind of big, isn't it? I mean, if it's just for . . .'

There was the question that sat between them, unbudgeable as an elephant. Was this elegant three-bed terrace for Vince alone, or would Beth live there too? They had spent the past month apart, Vince staying with his mother and getting to know her again, while Beth attempted to get her drinking under control and sort her life out. It had been a bitter pill to swallow, when he outlined to her just how much she had been putting away those last few months. How she'd started on the cocktails after breakfast in Tenerife, and been sozzled by dinner each night. Wine after work every day, leaving evenings with friends barely able to stand. He had tried to avoid going to the bars or restaurants at the hotel, but she'd insisted. It was why he'd encouraged the friendship with Corinna and Joel, he said. Not only did they understand the horror of what had happened in Tenerife, and offer alibis, but as wellness pedlars he thought they might be a good influence on Beth. And most of their old friends had stopped inviting them places, after Beth had passed out or picked a drunken fight one too many times.

She'd not even realised, and that was her greatest shame. Boozing had led her to attack Jemma all those years ago, and she had let it creep back up again. It was just so accessible now. Gin in a can on the train, a glass of prosecco at the hairdresser's, wine with dinner, a cocktail in the pub after work. Making excuses. She was stressed. She was worried about Vince. Everyone else was doing it. She could see now how Tanya, and even Janice, had tried to divert her from pubs and bars of late. It was also why Vince had left that wedding early the year before. Not just because he'd been recognised, but because Beth was so drunk she'd fallen over.

She was ashamed, and broken, and that made her want to drink more. But she was trying. She hadn't had a drink at all since that terrible night at Joel and Corinna's. Nothing like being involved in two serious crimes to give you a wake-up call.

Vince looked at her now, twirling the estate agent's brochure in his hands. He could buy this place for cash, now that that the sale of his patent had gone through. He'd be set for life. And her?

'We've been through a lot,' he said gently. 'I've been awful, I know.'

'And me. I'm sorry. I couldn't even see it.'

'I – Beth, I'm not a good person. I lied back then, and the other boys maybe got more time as a result, and John died, for God's sake. That's on me.'

'It's not on you, Vince. Someone killed Lucy. It wasn't you.'

Peter had appealed on the basis of the new evidence, but his conviction and sentence had been upheld.

'It could have been me. I mean, I could have stayed like they did, gone along with it, if I wasn't pissed off. And it was me who invited her there in the first place.'

Unintended consequences. She had been thinking about that a lot recently. Now they knew that another man entirely had been responsible for Ana's murder – and at least two other women who'd died in holiday spots, and even his teenage cousin when he was just seventeen, which he'd said at the time was an accident – she could at least rest easy that it wasn't her who'd hurt the singer. Or Vince. Or Joel or Corinna. But had the fateful convergence of the four of them caused it anyway? Put Ana in that man's way? Did Beth accosting her, mistaking her for Corinna, as she now remembered she had done, send Ana back into his path as she headed to the car park? Did Corinna lending Ana the flip-flops encourage her to walk home alone? Or Joel talking to her in the bar or Vince getting out of bed at night to watch her, unable to sleep and looking for distraction? If the four of them had gone to bed on time, like normal people, would Ana be alive today, singing her songs, smiling her beautiful smile, dreaming of bigger things? There was no way to know.

Vince spoke haltingly. 'I know it's been hard, and there's a lot of water under the bridge – a lot. But I'd like to try, at least. To see if we can live here. Together. Just to see.'

Death was forever and no coming back from it. It meant there was no hope, no future, no redemption. Ana was gone, her life snuffed out, and nothing could ever make up for that. But Beth was still alive, and so was Vince, and that meant there was always hope. No matter how small, it was there.

Alison

One month later

'Looks good on you,' she observed, as Tom pulled the blue plastic cap over his largely bald head. 'Not sure it's entirely needed when you've hardly got any hair.'

'Oi. You're talking big for a woman in compression socks and a gown that shows your bum.'

She laughed, and then sobered instantly. 'Oh God. Is it going to be OK?'

He gripped her hand. 'It's going to be OK.'

'But it's early.'

'Only two weeks. That's nothing.'

They had been advised to go for a Caesarean now, rather than waiting for her due date. The extra complication of a minor stab wound to the abdomen had added to the already risky nature of the pregnancy, given her previous collapse in Tenerife. Luckily, Tom was an understanding man, and on his hasty return from his conference had not chided her for going to the house of a suspected killer and getting stabbed in the process.

Alison found that annoying. Only *technically* stabbed, she would say. Really, he'd hardly scratched her before running out the door, to be tackled by Gavin before he even made it out of the driveway. Gavin felt absolutely terrible for what had happened, and had already sent a hideous yellow teddy as a gift for the baby – 'Because that works for a boy or a girl, yeah?'

She knew there was no one to blame but her own cavalier attitude, and of course the murderous nature of David Farnham, a beige man in every sense, who worked as an accountant and had killed at least three other women besides Ana. A hitchhiker in Australia while he and Penelope had been on their honeymoon in the same town, and a local woman found strangled on the beach in Thailand when they'd visited there. Even his fifteen-year-old cousin, found dead at her parents' home, apparently fallen from a treehouse in the garden, while only David was home. Killing was one way to spend a holiday, she supposed, since you could always fly home before you got caught. Penelope had broken down and told them everything, the dark suspicions she had carried for years. One death on your holiday was sad. Two was worrying. But three? She had been terrified, but not known what to do. She was more scared of him than the police.

That case wrapped up, Alison was at last ready to have her baby, and soon she would know if it was a boy or a girl. If it would like her or not, if she would love it right away or struggle with post-natal depression. If she would hate being at home for months, miss the job desperately, or if she'd love it and never think about the strip lighting and parade of lowlifes she saw every day, not to mention many of her colleagues who she'd cross a road to avoid. The future was unknown, and she could not even imagine how she might feel when she found herself a mother in just a few hours.

A thought occurred, and she was already reaching for her phone before she realised.

Tom tutted. 'It's in the car, remember? You wanted to be "fully present".'

'I know, I just remembered I have to tell Miriam something about a case, and . . .'

'Ali.' He shook her hand gently. 'Let it go. It's time, OK? You have to stop.'

And so, having surrendered her clothes and underwear and phone and jewellery and dignity, Alison lay back on the bed and got ready to do just that.

BOOK CLUB QUESTIONS

1. Vince and Beth are on a 'make or break' holiday in Tenerife. Do you think this kind of trip ever helps a failing relationship?

2. Beth finds herself going through her husband's possessions and is ashamed of her actions. Would you ever do this, or have you ever?

3. Is Alison wrong to meddle so much in the Spanish murder case? How much of her interest is to do with her impending maternity leave?

4. Have you ever made 'holiday friends', and if so how did it turn out?

5. The book also touches on issues of over-tourism, migration, and climate change. Do any of these influence your own travel and holiday plans?

6. Beth's dark secret is that she has a well-hidden drinking problem. How would you deal with this in a friend or loved one?

7. What did you think of the true killer being someone we hadn't really met before in the book? Is this a twist or a cheat?

8. The book features four couples in total – Beth and Vince, Joel and Corinna, Alison and Tom, and David and Penelope. What are the main issues facing each couple?

9. Beth and Vince are keeping a lot of secrets from each other. Is this ever acceptable in a relationship?

10. How much responsibility do you think Vince bears for the death of Lucy years before? Did any of the characters contribute to Ana's death, besides her killer?

ABOUT THE AUTHOR

Photo © 2023 Philippa Gedge

Born in Northern Ireland, Claire published her first novel in 2012, and has followed it up with many others in the crime fiction genre and also in women's fiction (writing as Eva Woods). Writing thrillers for Thomas & Mercer, she has sold over a million books and has had several number-one bestsellers. She ran the UK's first MA in crime writing for five years, and regularly teaches and talks about writing. Her first non-fiction project, the true-crime book *The Vanishing Triangle*, was released in 2022. She also writes scripts and has several original projects in development for TV, as well as having had four radio dramas broadcast. Several of her novels are also in development as television series. She lives in London and would love to hear from readers via the methods below!

Website and email via: www.clairemcgowan.co.uk
X: @inkstainsclaire
Instagram: @clairemcgowanwriter
TikTok: @clairemcgowanwriter
Facebook: www.facebook.com/ClaireMcGowanAuthor

Follow the Author on Amazon

If you enjoyed this book, follow Claire McGowan on Amazon to be notified when the author releases a new book!
To do this, please follow these instructions:

Desktop:

1) Search for the author's name on Amazon or in the Amazon App.
2) Click on the author's name to arrive on their Amazon page.
3) Click the 'Follow' button.

Mobile and Tablet:

1) Search for the author's name on Amazon or in the Amazon App.
2) Click on one of the author's books.
3) Click on the author's name to arrive on their Amazon page.
4) Click the 'Follow' button.

Kindle eReader and Kindle App:

If you enjoyed this book on a Kindle eReader or in the Kindle App, you will find the author 'Follow' button after the last page.